A STOLEN KISS

"I knew you would not disappoint me, Bastet."

"Julian."

"It is I."

Sabinah knew she should explain at once that she was not Bastet, but he took her face between his hands and touched his cheek to hers. "A few weeks ago I saw you from a distance, but I dared not approach you. I saw at that time you had grown even more beautiful."

"Julian, you must not—"

His mouth swept down on hers, and he pulled her closer to his body. Sabinah felt her heart thundering, and her knees went weak. The kiss was tender, long and drugging, and she was caught up in the wonder of it. It did not matter that Julian thought he was kissing Bastet; it only mattered that she would have this moment to remember for the rest of her life.

Tonight she would steal a little happiness for herself.

Other *Leisure* books by Constance O'Banyon:

DAUGHTER OF EGYPT
SWORD OF ROME
LORD OF THE NILE
HAWK'S PURSUIT
HAWK'S PLEDGE
THE MOON AND THE STARS
HEART OF TEXAS
MOON RACER
THE AGREEMENT (Secret Fires)
RIDE THE WIND
SOMETHING BORROWED, SOMETHING
   BLUE (Anthology)
TYKOTA'S WOMAN
FIVE GOLD RINGS (Anthology)
SAN ANTONIO ROSE
TEXAS PROUD
CELEBRATIONS (Anthology)

Constance O'Banyon

Desert Prince

LEISURE BOOKS NEW YORK CITY

This one is for you, Billie Bennet. There are no sweeter memories than those shared with a dear friend. Our families braved snowstorms and snowblindness together.

And for you, Leslie—how the time flies. You should still be a teenager.

A LEISURE BOOK®

January 2009

Published by

Dorchester Publishing Co., Inc.
200 Madison Avenue
New York, NY 10016

ISBN 10: 0-8439-6007-8
ISBN 13: 978-0-8439-6007-5

The name "Leisure Books" and the stylized "L" with design are trademarks of Dorchester Publishing Co., Inc.

Printed in the United States of America.

10 9 8 7 6 5 4 3 2 1

Visit us on the web at www.dorchesterpub.com.

Author's Note

Being a lover of history, I find the most compelling and rewarding part of writing to be making the past come alive. I have always been fascinated by Egyptian and Roman history and have read every book I could find on the subjects, devouring them with a passion. While delving in extensive research on the history of Queen Cleopatra, I discovered so many different accounts of her life it boggled my mind, up to and including Shakespeare's celebrated version. In my four-book saga about the Tausrat family, I have interwoven their lives with Queen Cleopatra's, advancing the plot with events as they happened in her life. In doing so I tried not to play fast and loose with history, attempting instead to stay as close to the facts as they are known. Where there is little knowledge about certain events, or even many different accounts, I chose to tell my own version as it might have occurred.

Think about it: The world must have trembled and almost spun off its axis when Cleopatra, Julius Caesar, Marc Antony, and Octavian (Augustus Caesar) clashed. Seldom have we caught a glimpse through the thin veil of history where four such powerful personalities touched each other's lives. I have tried to do justice to each of them, but as a writer of fiction, I embellished, while keeping true to what is known of these extraordinary personalities.

Take a journey into the distant past. Hear the whisper of hot desert winds as they uncover great mysteries. Smell the exotic aroma of frankincense and myrrh. Listen to the sounds of hoofbeats clatter across stone streets. Hear the distant clashes of swords in battle. Glimpse marble palaces and towering obelisks in a world of wealth and glory that has never been equaled. Experience love, hate, betrayal, and extraordinary loyalty.

The past beckons. Walk with me through the ancient land of Egypt.

DESERT
PRINCE

𓅃 PROLOGUE

Alexandria, Egypt
Twelfth Sextilis, 30 BC

Looking resplendent in his ceremonial robe, with a white tiger skin draped over his long red mantle, Kheleel, the high priest of Isis, practically threw himself out of his litter, which was no easy task considering his stature and girth. Kheleel's size had always worked in his favor since he usually towered above those who sought his counsel; it also allowed him to intimidate those who doubted his powers.

The day was hot, and he dabbed a clean linen cloth beneath his kohl-lined eyes before swiping it across his shaved head. Kheleel's mission was a dire one, and he dared not hesitate or stop to catch his breath. Lumbering forward, he shoved aside a blind man in rags who held out his rusted cup, pleading for alms.

There was despair in the high priest's heart. He hurried down a graveled path that led through a magnificent courtyard with mosaic fountains guarded by twenty-four marble lions. He bypassed the palace and took the curved walkway toward a tall, imposing marble structure that was simple, but elegant in its beauty. The structure was surrounded by a terraced garden and a view that swept out to the aqua-colored Mediterranean Sea. The sweet aroma of hundreds of exotic scents stirred in the air.

Gasping to catch his breath, Kheleel was forced to halt and bend forward because his lungs felt as if they would burst from want of air. Then with determined urgency, he surged forward, his goal just ahead.

Queen Cleopatra's mausoleum.

The two Macedonian guards standing before the beaten-bronze doors three times their height quickly stepped aside to allow Kheleel to enter. Even in his urgency he was struck by the splendor of the high ceilings decorated with gold filigree. Along the walls were statues of long-dead Ptolemys, and the black marble floor was so highly polished he could see his reflection. He hurried past chairs of gold inlaid with precious stones and a colossal jeweled mosaic of the goddess Isis.

Gathering his courage, he walked steadily toward the woman who stood so regal, waiting for his approach.

Queen Cleopatra.

Cleopatra was not a tall woman, but she was imposing nonetheless. Her green gaze settled on him, and he saw great sorrow in the shimmering depths. She wore a filmy green robe that accentuated her slim body, and her hair was unbound, falling across her shoulders in an ebony mass. Although the queen was not considered a great beauty, no one realized it while in her presence. Her personality was magnetic, her voice as sweet as music. She was highly intelligent, speaking and writing seven languages. Her bloodline was pure Greek. Though her family had ruled Egypt since the death of the great Alexander, she was the only Ptolemy who had bothered to learn Egyptian, a fact that endeared her to her subjects.

At the queen's right hand, standing tall and erect with his muscled arms folded across his broad chest, was Cleopatra's trusted Sicilian guard, Apollodorus. To the queen's left stood her head handmaidens, Charmion, whose golden hair was bound about her lovely face, and Iras, a dark-skinned beauty with long black hair and honey-colored eyes.

Although her world was crumbling about her, Cleopatra appeared calm and serene, but the high priest expected nothing less from this noble queen.

"My good Kheleel," Cleopatra said, "I summoned you to enlist your aid. There is something of great import I must ask of you."

The high priest saw the empty alabaster sarcophagus that stood on a golden base, and its meaning struck him like a sharp blade. He bowed, casting his gaze to the floor because at the moment he could not meet the queen's eyes. "Anything, Great Majesty. Is there no hope?"

"None. Octavian will declare Egypt a Roman province, and there is nothing I can do to stop him. My doom was sealed the day the Roman Senate gave him complete power. As we speak, his armies are but a few hours from Alexandria. There is much to do, and I must act quickly."

"Lord Antony?"

In all the years the high priest had known the queen, he had never seen her cry, but the tears that now glittered in her green eyes brought tears to his own.

Her lips trembled, but she quickly compressed them. "As you already know, Antony rode out to meet Octavian. I have had no word from him. Whether he lives or not, he has no hope, for Octavian has the might of Rome at his back," she admitted in a trembling voice.

There was urgency in Kheleel's tone. "There is still

time for you to escape, Majesty. You must not remain
until the Romans arrive at our gates."

"Nay, I shall not run, good Kheleel—I shall not aban-
don my people except when death takes me."

He looked toward the empty sarcophagus, grief hitting him so hard he staggered. "Can you not strike a bar-
gain with Octavian, Majesty—abdicate in favor of your
son by Julius Caesar?"

"Have you not heard Octavian has proclaimed *himself*
Caesar's son? Think you he will allow my son by Caesar
to live? Nay, Caesarion is a threat to that cowardly im-
poster." Cleopatra's shoulders straightened. "Know this—
Octavian sent a courier with word that he would spare
my life if I would have Antony slain. Of course he
would spare me so he could later humiliate me and pa-
rade me in chains behind his chariot at his Triumph in
Rome." Her eyes glittered, and her fists tightened at her
sides. "There is not much I can do to thwart that man,
but I shall rob him of his fondest desire. His victory over
Egypt will not be complete without me."

Despite the hopelessness of the situation, Kheleel
admired his queen's bravery. "Must it end this way,
Majesty?"

"It must. Can I depend on you to help me?"

"Ask anything of me, and it shall be done, even unto
dying at your side."

The queen gave him an anguished smile. "Nay, my
trusted servant, you shall not die." She leaned closer,
her voice lowered. "Having celebrated sixteen seasons,
my son, Caesarion, is now of age. It will be difficult for
him to leave Egypt, but he must—never to return. Everything has been made ready for his escape, and you shall
be his escort on this most dangerous mission."

"Where can I take him that Octavian will not follow? Rome's reach is long, Majesty."

She handed him a sealed scroll. "This will reveal all. Keep my son hidden until the ship I have sent for arrives—it should dock by tomorrow morning. Then go directly to the harbor and look for a Bal Forean ship. You will know it by the figurehead of a hawk in flight. Trust no one. Not at the temple, not even onboard the ship. No one must know the identity of my son. Caesarion must forget who he is and be dead as far as the rest of the world knows."

"And your other children, what of them?"

She waved her hand dismissively. "Because they are not Caesar's children, they are no threat to Octavian. He will not dare harm them. Rome would never condone the murder of Antony's children."

Kheleel met her gaze. "Majesty, I beseech you to accompany us on this voyage."

There was impatience in her tone. "I have no time to argue this with you. I rely on you to escort my son to Bal Forea and place him in the care of Queen Thalia." She handed the high priest another scroll. "I have written instructions for the queen. Urge upon her the importance of raising my son as if he were her own. He must never challenge Octavian, nor think of Egypt as his home. I must know Caesar's son will live or else everything we had together will have been for naught."

Kheleel bowed to the woman who, to him, was Isis incarnate. "I will do as you bid."

"Before you leave, send your priests to purify my mausoleum. They must make it ready to receive me. Go now, my good and faithful friend. By my calculations, Octavian will arrive before sunset."

Once more Kheleel bowed. "May you fly with the spirits of the gods, Most Gracious Majesty," he said in a voice choked with emotion.

Cleopatra did something altogether unexpected; she took his hand. "There are few I would trust with this mission. I know you will not fail me." She suddenly dropped his hand and stood back. "Caesarion awaits you in the center room of the temple. Make haste!"

There was nothing for Kheleel to do but obey. He backed toward the door, then hurried down the corridor as tears flooded his eyes and rolled down his plump cheeks.

Without Cleopatra, Egypt was doomed.

Cleopatra stood for a long moment, wondering at what point in her life she had set her feet upon this path of destruction. Perhaps it had begun with the seeds of glory Caesar had planted in her mind, seeds that she, in turn, had enthusiastically replanted in Antony's mind.

Together they had had such dreams.

She sighed. With the might of Rome on the outskirts of Alexandria, it was too late for regrets. She was bereft. If Antony still lived, she must indeed be responsible for his death, but not to please Octavian.

Never that.

Charmion suddenly appeared. "Majesty," she said urgently, "Lord Antony has arrived."

Cleopatra's heart sang with joy. Her beloved was alive!

Then she met Apollodorus's understanding gaze—he knew as she did what must be done, and she saw pity reflected in her faithful servant's dark eyes. She swallowed twice, and she felt she could actually feel her heart break. But there was no other way. Turning to Charmion, she said, "Go to my husband at once. Do exactly as I have instructed."

The handmaiden bowed her head, unable to meet the queen's eyes. "I am to tell Lord Antony you are dead so he will take his own . . . life."

Cleopatra brought her hand to her heart. Hearing the words said aloud brought cruel reality crashing down around her. At this moment her beloved was near, and yet she could not go to him as her heart urged her to do. She had lived more fully with Antony than most people did in a lifetime. They had loved as few people ever had. She had borne him three children, and if the gods were willing, she would take his love with her into the next world.

Charmion took a step toward the door, then turned back to the queen. "What shall I do . . . afterward?" she asked sorrowfully.

"Have my guards hoist Antony's body into my burial chamber." Cleopatra looked doubtful. "Surely Octavian will not deny us the right to be entombed together. It is not much to ask in exchange for all the riches of Egypt."

Amber-colored clouds stretched across the sky, announcing sundown by the time Charmion returned to Cleopatra, her face streaked with tears. Going down to her knees, she raised a sad gaze to the queen. "The deed is done, Majesty. When I told Lord Antony you were dead, his grief was like nothing I have ever witnessed. He cried your name in agony until his torment was so great, he fell upon his own sword, saying he could not live in a world without you."

Cleopatra raised her face upward, biting her trembling lip. "Is he dead?"

"Nay. He still breathes, but faintly."

In that moment Cleopatra heard a grinding sound, and she knew her Macedonian guards were hoisting Antony up to the small opening in the tomb. With the help of Apollodorous and her two handmaidens, they pulled Antony inside.

Cleopatra sank to the floor, taking her beloved in her arms. "Antony, my Antony, the pain is all but over." She glanced out at the darkening sky. Night birds trilled their sweet song, and she felt the heat of the desert breeze on her face. It seemed a sundown like any other. Why did not the clouds weep and thunder crash across the sky? Great Antony was dying! Should not the ground tremble and dark clouds block out the sun?

Antony's gaze fastened on her face. "I thought . . . you dead . . . and was hurrying to join . . . you."

Grief cut through Cleopatra like the sharpness of a knife piercing her heart. She had grieved when Caesar had been assassinated, but Antony's death tore at her like thorns ripping her apart. To never hear his voice speak her name. To never lie in his arms and make love. She touched her mouth to his. "Soon, my beloved— soon we shall be together, and no one shall part us."

She raised tear-bright eyes to Iras, her voice no more than a whisper. "Help me dress, then bring me the basket of figs."

Iras reached out her hand to the queen, then let it fall to her side. "It will be as you say, Glorious Majesty."

Octavian glared at Vergilius, his newly appointed captain of the guard, and slammed his fist against the palm of his hand, his face contorted with fury. "Queen Cleopatra deceived me! She lulled me into believing she wanted to live, and all the while she intended to die by her own hand."

Agrippa, Octavian's second-in-command, glanced at the man who now held Egypt in his fist. His commander had pale hair and pale skin—too delicate to be called handsome, but striking in his own way. He was intelligent—had he not outfought and outfoxed the powerful general, Marc Antony?

"And yet," Agrippa observed, "you must admire the queen's courage. Imagine allowing a deadly cobra to bite her. Brave, extremely brave."

"I shall hear no praise of her!" Octavian said, his voice rising in fury. "Bring me the son she claims was fathered by Caesar."

"And the other three fathered by Antony?"

Octavian thought for a moment. "It must appear to the Egyptian people that I am merciful if I am to ingratiate myself with them. Have Antony's children sent to my sister, Octavia. Send word that she is to raise the offspring her husband begat upon that Egyptian harlot." Octavian felt pleased with himself. "Aye, the Egyptians shall think me compassionate, as well they should."

Apollodorus had been summoned by Octavian and appeared with a proud youth dressed in a white pleated kilt, gold bands on his upper arms, and the crown of Egypt atop his dark head.

Octavian walked around the young lad appraisingly. "You know who I am?" he asked Apollodorus.

The Sicilian stared at Octavian unblinkingly and said in a lazy voice, "You are a man of little importance who obtained greatness because your mother happened to be the niece of great Caesar."

Octavian's eyes blazed at the insult. "Careful, Sicilian. You tread the ground of treason."

Apollodorus crossed his arms over his broad chest, looking bored. "Under the rule of my queen, it was never treason to speak the truth in Egypt."

Octavian chose to ignore the second insult and circled the young prince once more. The boy stared back at him with an insolent glare, but Octavian's words were for the Sicilian. "And here I hoped we could be friends," he said in a mocking tone.

"I choose my friends with care and with a thought to their worthiness."

Again Octavian chose to ignore the taunt. "Does the lad speak Latin? Does he know he will soon join his mother in death?"

The only response he received from the boy was a contemptuous, haughty glare.

Octavian swung around to look at Apollodorus. "Tell him what I said. I want to see his face when you tell him of his death."

"He understood you. If he does not speak, it is because to him you are unworthy. He will *not* acknowledge the man responsible for his mother's death," Apollodorus replied in a hard tone.

Octavian glared at the man who had always stood at Cleopatra's side. "I could have your tongue torn out for your insolence."

"Then do it," the Sicilian challenged him.

Octavian shook his head. "I shall keep you in health in the event I later have need of you."

"Know this, Roman: I will not serve you in any way."

Octavian was growing angrier with each insult Apollodorus threw at him, but he would mask that anger for the moment. "Tell the prince he is to die." Octavian smirked, looking at Captain Vergilius, who ran his finger down the long blade of his sword. "I want to see him beg for his life."

Apollodorus placed his hand on the lad's arm and spoke in Egyptian. "Are you still prepared to die?"

The boy nodded and raised his chin bravely. "It will be my honor."

Apollodorus was proud of the young boy who faced death so fearlessly. Queen Cleopatra had already settled enormous wealth on the boy's family. But it was loyalty that made the young man die in place of his prince. "His Majesty understands your words."

Octavian snapped his fingers and motioned to Captain Vergilius. "Take this lad and see the deed done."

When Apollodorus moved to follow the boy, Octavian spoke, "Stay. I have questions to put to you."

Apollodorus glanced back at Octavian, not bothering to mask his contempt for the man.

"I have little doubt you would like to follow your queen in death," Octavian said. "Your loyalty to her is legend."

"Death has no sting for me. I would welcome it."

"Then answer my questions, and you are free to do as you wish with your life."

Apollodorus had already planned to follow his queen in death, so nothing Octavian said would matter to him.

"If you will tell me where I can locate Lord Ramtat, I shall reward you with more gold than you can spend in your lifetime."

Apollodorus became alert, his eyes narrowing, but he made no reply as he waited for the Roman to continue.

"Very well, if you cannot be tempted by gold, name your price, and I shall pay it."

Still Apollodorus said nothing.

Octavian was becoming frustrated and barely managed to hold on to his temper. "I understand Lord Ramtat's wife is half sister to Cleopatra—if that is so, it would make her eldest son—" He snapped his fingers. "What is the boy's name—I forget."

Apollodorus stiffened, dropping his gaze to hide his sudden concern for the Tausrat family. "I cannot say."

"Cannot or will not?"

"You may choose which."

"I want only the eldest boy, and perhaps the youngest son, and the mother as well. Lord Ramtat and his daughter have little to fear from me."

Apollodorus's brows knitted as he looked into Octavian's cunning eyes. "I would not help you even if I knew where Lord Ramtat is, which I do not."

It was the answer Octavian expected. This Sicilian could neither be bought nor bribed, but Octavian had other plans. "Bravely spoken. But know this—I shall have no pretenders coming forward to claim Egypt's throne. If I was told correctly, the eldest son was named after my uncle, the great Caesar. This namesake could misguidedly take it in his mind to stir up trouble since he is among the last of the Ptolemy bloodline. With the true prince dead, it is possible this young man could raise an army against me. Not that I fear an Egyptian army, but it would be an annoyance that I cannot afford at this time."

Apollodorus felt his throat tighten. He could not die as he had planned. Queen Cleopatra would expect him to protect her half sister and her family against Octavian's bloodlust. "The young lord is a prince in his own right. I would not look to harm him if I were you. His people, the Badari, are a fearsome tribe and number in the thousands. Your legions would be slaughtered if you came up against them in a desert battle."

Octavian glared at the man. "Go, go," he muttered. "I have no further use of you."

For a moment Octavian watched Apollodorus move across the chamber, and then he turned to Agrippa. "What would I not give for the loyalty that beats in the heart of that Sicilian. There is no deed he would not perform for his queen, even with her dead."

"There are many who are loyal to you," Agrippa bit out, affronted. "I, myself, can be counted among that number."

Octavian watched Apollodorus disappear out the door. "Not like him. He would happily have taken the cobra bite for Queen Cleopatra." He shrugged. "Keep him under constant watch. If he stays true, he will find the Tausrat family for us."

"But Lord Ramtat fought beside Caesar and is greatly respected in Rome. Surely you mean him no harm."

Octavian stroked his cleanly shaved chin. "I will not rest easy until everyone with Cleopatra's tainted blood has been slain." He smiled slightly, his mind moving on to other matters.

"Think of it, Agrippa—today, because of the bite of a deadly cobra, I have become master of the world!"

Apollodorus left the palace, his footsteps measured, knowing he was being watched. He stepped onto the wide stone road that meandered toward the sea. Pausing, he observed the sun making its descent for the day in blazing splashes of fiery red that spread across the western sky. To him it seemed as if the sun god, Ra, in all his glory, was paying tribute to a dead queen, who, though not always ruling wisely, had ruled with her heart.

🦅 CHAPTER ONE

Thick fog blanketed land and sea as Kheleel trudged forward, grateful for the mist that disguised their presence. Nervously, he glanced over his shoulder before he motioned young Caesarion to emerge from the litter. They were both garbed in bedouin attire, so it was unlikely anyone would recognize the young man as Cleopatra's son, the rightful king of Egypt.

To Kheleel's dismay, the unfamiliar long robe of Caesarion's disguise tangled around the boy's legs, causing him to stumble against a young girl, and almost taking the two of them to the ground. Unfortunately, the collision knocked Caesarion's kaffiyeh off his head, and it went flying through the air.

Kheleel quickly pulled Caesarion to him, horrified when the girl scooped up the fallen headdress and extended it to the boy with a surprised look. The high priest hurriedly grabbed it from her fingers and replaced it on the young king's head, rushing him toward the waiting ship.

With fear pounding in his heart, Kheleel glanced over his shoulder at the slim girl, noting her quizzical gaze. Surely she had not recognized Caesarion, he kept assuring himself. The poor young man was so overwhelmed by the death of his mother, and the Roman troops on every street in Alexandria, he had scarcely spoken three words all morning.

Looking weak and shaken, Caesarion leaned heavily against Kheleel. Feeling the young man's brow, the high priest realized he had a fever. In truth, he feared Caesarion was too ill for a sea voyage, but what else was he to do but obey the queen's orders?

"Take comfort, young one," he whispered, not daring to call Caesarion by his title. "All will be well."

He hoped.

Fourteen-year-old Sabinah, of the house of Jannah, had not been fooled by the bedouin clothing worn by Ptolemy Caesarion or the high priest of Isis.

She had recognized them both.

As she paused to watch them board a foreign ship, she leaned against a crumbling wall, her mind whirling. She, like everyone else in the city, had heard of the queen's death, and of Caesarion's execution.

But he was alive!

She slid to her knees, taking in deep breaths. She tried to understand what she had witnessed, but her mind was in a muddle. Was it possible someone else had died in Caesarion's place, and the high priest was smuggling him out of Egypt?

Sabinah slowly rose to her feet, taking in an unsteady breath. As the mist cleared a bit, she pushed her tumbled hair out of her face. Suddenly it occurred to her there was danger in possessing such knowledge. Glancing about, she saw no one watching her, but still she turned her footsteps away from the docks, then picked up her pace, walking quickly toward the marketplace, where she disappeared into the crowd.

She must tell no one what she had witnessed, especially not her stepmother or stepsister, for they were not to be trusted.

⩗ CHAPTER TWO

Egyptian desert

Apollodorus topped the sand dune and glanced down at the huge encampment in the distance. It had taken him an extra week to reach Lord Ramtat's camp because three Roman soldiers had been following him, making it necessary to lose them in the desert. Knowing Octavian, he had expected as much.

Apollodorus smiled grimly. The desert was an unforgiving place and struck hard at those who did not know its secrets. Octavian would never discover what had happened to his spies. But he would send more men, and still more. Sooner or later, one of them might discover the Badari encampment, and that was the real danger to the Tausrat family.

The Sicilian dreaded delivering his unhappy tidings. The family would be devastated to hear of the queen's death. When he rode into camp, tents emptied, and he was greeted with great affection by a multitude of smiling Badari. Dismounting, he went directly to the huge red leather tent that belonged to Lord Ramtat. The tribe numbered in the thousands, and although they were scattered across the vast desert, they could come together with astounding speed when summoned by their sheik. The Badari were famous for the horses they bred—the magnificent animals could outrun and outdistance any other breed—especially in the desert.

Lord Ramtat, himself, came out of his tent to greet Apollodorus. He was as tall as the Sicilian and wore his hair clipped short in the Roman fashion, a practical style for those in the desert. Ramtat's welcoming expression changed to one of doubt, and his forehead creased with concern when he read sadness in Apollodorus's eyes.

"Tell me quickly, is Queen Cleopatra safe?"

Apollodorus shook his head. "Let us go inside, and I shall tell you and the queen's sister at the same time."

Lady Danaë was slight and looked even smaller standing beside her tall husband. Tears glistened in her eyes, and it was clear she was trying hard to hold on to her composure. "My sister dead. How can that be? We had no idea she was in danger."

Ramtat looked bereft. "Why did she not send to me for help?"

"The queen knew her situation was hopeless, and she did not want you caught up in it," the Sicilian said.

Danaë sank slowly to her knees, sobbing. "All the light has gone out of Egypt—how dreary the world will seem without my beloved sister." She wiped her tears as her husband raised her to the shelter of his arms.

When Apollodorus looked into Lady Danaë's green eyes, he was staggered by her resemblance to her queenly half sister. There were differences, of course—the queen's face had been interesting, Lady Danaë's was beautiful. "Octavian did not want the queen's death—he wanted to take her to Rome as his conquest. Knowing the queen, you understand why she did what she did."

Ramtat comforted his wife. "Queen Cleopatra was Egypt in life, and still queen in death. When centuries pass, and we are all dust, she will be remembered."

A sudden horrifying thought hit Danaë, and she reached out to Apollodorus, her face pale, her hands trembling. "The children—what about them?"

"Fear not, Lady Danaë. The three that were fathered by Lord Antony were sent to Rome. They will come to no harm and will be raised by Octavian's sister."

Ramtat's lips tightened in anger. "They belong to Egypt, not Rome."

"What of Caesarion?" Danaë asked, fearing to hear of her oldest nephew's fate since Apollodorus had not mentioned him.

Apollodorus leaned in as if to share a secret. "As far as Octavian is concerned, Ptolemy Caesarion is dead, murdered by his orders." He went on hurriedly when he saw Danaë tremble. "Nay, dear lady, our king does not walk in the land of the dead."

"Tell me quickly," Danaë insisted.

Apollodorus explained how the high priest had smuggled Caesarion on board a ship headed for Bal Forea to be raised by Queen Thalia and her husband. He further elaborated on how a brave young lad had died in Caesarion's place.

Thalia was Ramtat's adopted sister, who could not be loved more if she had been born into the family. "What about Antony?" Ramtat asked stoically.

"Dead by his own hand. Octavian granted my queen's last wish and allowed him to be entombed with her. I like to think they will be together eternally."

Ramtat nodded slowly. "Caesarion will be well cared for by my sister Thalia. We can all be glad he is under her protection. She will guard his secret and keep him safe."

"After today, young Caesarion must never be spoken of again. What is said here cannot leave this tent," Apollodorus warned. He looked at Ramtat grimly. "There is yet more."

Ramtat motioned to a sofa and when they were all seated, Apollodorus spoke quietly. "Octavian's revenge reaches farther than you know." He met Danaë's gaze. "He has men searching for you, Lady Danaë, and your children, especially Julian. He wants to rid himself of everyone of the Ptolemy bloodline, except the three he will control in Rome." He hesitated for a moment. "Since Octavian believes Caesarion is dead, he turns his sights on Julian, seeing him as a threat to the stability of his rule in Egypt."

Ramtat shot to his feet. "Let that weasel attempt to take my wife and children," he said angrily. "There will never be a day my Badari could not take on a Roman legion."

Apollodorous shook his head wearily, burdened by the threat this family faced because of their ties to Queen Cleopatra. "It will not be a legion Octavian sends against you. It will be a continuous stream of men who will be dedicated to finding you. *He will not stop.* You know him well enough to understand that if he fails once, he will merely try again."

"He wants my children dead!" Danaë said in disbelief.

"And you," the Sicilian said pointedly. "I was followed when I left Alexandria. But fear not. The bones of those spies now bleach in the desert sun."

Ramtat drew in a deep breath. "My mother must be warned and brought here to safety. When Octavian learns of our villa in Alexandria, he will go after her for information."

Apollodorus nodded. "My thought exactly. Before I left Alexandria, I sent a messenger to warn Lady Larania, knowing if I went myself, I would be followed. She sent word to me that she would not be driven out of her home by a Roman upstart. Your mother is a most . . . courageous woman."

"I believe what you mean is my mother is a stubborn woman who will do what she pleases."

Apollodorus looked stern. "None of us should underestimate Octavian. Though he is cowardly and unpredictable, he has the might of Rome clenched in his fists. And he will use it against you, as he did my queen. Who would have thought she could be defeated?"

Ramtat nodded, glancing at his wife. "Though I believe Danaë and the children will be safe here in the desert, I am not willing to take that chance. I will make arrangements for us to sail to Bal Forea as soon as possible."

"I do not want to leave Egypt," Danaë told her husband. "My sister died bravely. Can I do any less?"

"The children?" her husband reminded her.

Danaë's face fell, and she nodded slowly. "Aye," she admitted. "They must be our first concern."

Apollodorus looked at Ramtat. "Herein lies the real danger: Octavian has commissioned a man with one task, and one task only—to locate your family. I have seen for myself that this man is as unscrupulous as he is relentless. He is the one who took the life of the young boy who died for Caesarion."

There was an edge to Ramtat's voice, and his gaze was like a razor, "Tell me his name."

"Captain Vergilius. I found out all I could about him before I left Alexandria. He came up through the ranks and is neither liked nor respected by his compatriots. Be that as it may, he is the man Octavian has appointed to find you."

Apollodorus watched a flare of anger darken Ramtat's eyes. The Sicilian knew his friend would rather fight than leave, but he was a man who would first consider the safety of his family.

Ramtat turned to his wife. "I need to get you and the children out of Egypt."

"I know," she said, clutching at his robe.

"I shall contact my sister Thalia, and have her send her swiftest ship."

No one took notice of Julian, who stood at the curtained area that led to the sleeping quarters. He clenched his fists, fighting back tears. His aunt, Queen Cleopatra, dead—his cousins taken out of Egypt. Hatred burned hot inside him for the man responsible for those deeds. When he could no longer hold back tears, he angrily brushed them from his eyes.

His bloodline was a proud one. From his father's side, he was a nobleman of Egypt, and a prince of the fierce desert Badari. From his mother's side, he had blood ties to Queen Cleopatra. He had been named for his father's friend, Julius Caesar, a fact that had always given him pride until now.

At that moment Apollodorus spotted Julian and motioned him forward. "Your son should be told everything," he suggested to Ramtat.

Lord Ramtat stood eye-to-eye with his sixteen-year-old son, who looked much as he, himself, had at the same age; the only difference was that Julian had his mother's remarkable eyes. Ramtat saw the angry glint that now burned in those green eyes. "I believe my son already knows."

Julian bowed his head in respect to the man who had not only fathered him, but was also the tribal lord of the Badari. "What will we do, Father?" he asked. "Do we ride to Alexandria and drive the Romans out?"

Apollodorus shook his head. "Young prince, there is a time and a season for everything. A man must never rush into retaliation—a wise man waits . . . bides his time, and strikes when the moment is right."

Julian's jaw tightened. "So we do nothing to avenge my aunt?"

"At the moment, that would be my suggestion," Apollodorus stated.

"What will *you* do?" Ramtat asked the Sicilian who had served his queen so long and faithfully. Ramtat could only imagine the anger that seethed inside Cleopatra's bodyguard.

"If you have no objections, I will accompany you to Bal Forea. It seems to me your son is in great need of patience, and perhaps I can teach him that, while I keep an eye on my queen's son as well."

Ramtat realized Apollodorus was doing what Queen Cleopatra would have expected of him. "I thank you. My hotheaded son is in dire need of your wise counsel. You have been a constant friend to us, and I would be honored if you would remain with us as long as you like."

Julian began pacing. "I care not for the notion of being driven from my home by the Romans. There is Mother's villa in Alexandria that is managed by Uriah. Few people know of its existence. Why could I not remain there with Uriah, or even here in the desert?"

Ramtat frowned. "Nay. I will not have your mother worried about you. You shall accompany us."

Apollodorus placed his hand on Julian's shoulder. "To leave when you cannot win is not a bad thing. You will one day return. Live and train for that day, my impatient one." Seeing the fire of rebellion in Julian's eyes, Apollodorus nodded. "As a prince of the desert, you must learn forbearance."

"Father—"

"It is decided, Julian. Speak no more of it."

Reluctantly, Julian nodded in agreement. It was not his father commanding him, but the high lord of the desert tribe, who must be obeyed by everyone, including his son.

In that moment there was a chattering of voices, and Julian's fourteen-year-old sister, Ayanna, and his young brother, Marcus, who had been named for Marc Antony, entered with their nurse trailing behind.

"Say nothing to frighten the young ones," Ramtat cautioned.

Julian watched his brother and sister joyfully greet Apollodorus, unaware just how much their world was about to change. But blood ran hot and angry through his body. One day he would return to Egypt and take his rightful place. Until that day he would learn everything Apollodorus had to teach him.

Ramtat drew in a deep breath and met Apollodorus's gaze. "My mother must be brought here to safety. She must be told that I command it of her."

"I will go to her with your orders," Apollodorus said, nodding. "I can sneak in and out of Alexandria without the Romans being the wiser." His eyes took on a wistful look. "As I once helped my queen sneak into Caesar's chambers when her brother's troops guarded the palace against her."

"I shall go with Apollodorus," Julian stated, all the while eyeing his father, expecting him to object.

It was Ramtat's inclination to refuse his son's request, but Julian was on the verge of becoming a man, and should not be held back. "You will be safe with our friend here. Do exactly as he tells you."

Julian had been expecting an argument. His eyes widened, and he took his father's offered hand. "I will do just as he instructs."

Ramtat noticed his wife stiffen, as if she might object. He held up his hand to silence her. "We must not stand in Julian's way. He will be safe with Apollodorus."

She nodded reluctantly.

"Have no fear, Mother. Like Apollodorus, I know well how to sneak in and out of Alexandria."

Danaë gripped both of Julian's arms, wishing she could hold on to him and keep him safe, as she had done when he was small. Now he towered over her, his expression pleading with her to not embarrass him with his hero, Apollodorus, looking on. So she dropped her hands and stepped back. "If there is trouble, you must seek out Uriah," was all she said.

Uriah had been Danaë's adopted father's slave, whom Danaë had freed and placed in charge of all her property when she received her inheritance. Not only was Uriah a dear friend, but he had also been her tutor, and a mentor to her children. Danaë's gaze went to the tall Sicilian. "Take care of him, Apollodorus," she said, her voice quivering.

He bowed to her. "With my life, Lady Danaë."

Julian stepped out of the tent and raised his face to the sun. Egypt was changing, but he would not change.

Hearing the cry of a bird overhead, he watched his falcon circle above him. His mother was an animal trainer, who had a special affinity with big cats and birds of prey. She had helped him train his own falcon, De-oro, who would kill on command. He watched De-oro circle wide and dive toward the ground, probably in pursuit of some small rodent.

Apollodorus appeared at his side. "We should leave now, young prince. There is need for haste."

"Allow me to cage De-oro, or she will attempt to follow me."

Ramtat stepped out of the tent, folding his arms over his broad chest. "Take our fastest horses and go the quickest way. I have great fear for my mother's safety."

The sun was well past its zenith when the two riders galloped away from the encampment.

Neither spoke—they knew what dangers awaited them when they reached Alexandria.

When the walls of the city were in sight, they dismounted and mingled with an Armenian caravan.

Leading their horses past the Roman guards, the two of them entered the city with no one being the wiser.

CHAPTER THREE

Alexandria, largest and most magnificent city of the world, was being stripped of her greatness. Egyptians were forced to watch as the Roman conquerors removed treasures from the temples and palaces of their dead queen to ship to Rome. Great stores of grain and foodstuffs were loaded onto ships to feed the insatiable armies of Rome. Those who opposed the invaders, and there were many at first, did not live to make another attempt.

As young Sabinah watched these atrocities, she feared for her people, who would have scant food to see them through until the next rainy season when the Nile would flood its banks, replenishing the farmlands. Though no doubt the Roman invaders would take that food, too.

Surprisingly, Sabinah's family, which had been destitute since her father's death four years before, had begun to prosper under Roman rule. Her lip curled in distaste as she thought of how her stepmother was ingratiating herself with the Roman officers by offering them the hospitality of her home. Roman men flocked to her stepmother's banquets since her villa was one of the few places in Egypt they found a welcome.

Lately Sabinah found herself being shunned by old friends and neighbors, even though she took no part in entertaining their enemies.

There had been a time when the Jannah family had been respected and moved in society above her father's station because Sabina's mother had been a friend of the Tausrats. After her father had married her stepmother, Trisella, Alexandrian society no longer accepted them, though the Tausrats continued to show them favor, and Julian often visited their home whenever he was in Alexandria. Sabinah knew in her heart he only came to see her stepsister.

Sabinah sighed. Bastet, with her stunning beauty, had of late turned her feminine skills to charming Romans. So far, Sabinah had managed to avoid the feasts the Romans attended.

"You should have remained at home. The mistress mentioned she wanted you to help her with her potions," Ma'dou chided Sabinah.

"Aye. She will be angry with me for leaving. But I do not care for the art of herbs and spices."

"It is not a bad thing to know. The mistress has many women coming to her for potions."

Sabinah shrugged, gazing up at the clouds that hung low across the sea, turning the oppressive heat into unbearable humidity. To escape Bastet's constant chattering about her conquests, and her stepmother's lessons on healing herbs, Sabinah had accompanied Ma'dou to the market. When the dour-faced cook smiled, her lips were so thin they gave the impression that she was frowning. Short and squatty, poor Ma'dou actually waddled when she walked.

Six Amalekite traders led their camels down the street

while a caravan of donkeys laden with papyrus stalks passed by. Three ragged children ran after Sabinah, hands open, begging for a coin. "Does it seem to you there are more urchins begging for alms than when Queen Cleopatra ruled Egypt?" she asked her companion.

"Aye. Rome has made paupers of us all," Ma'dou sniffed.

Sabinah reached into her sash, handing each child a copper. They quickly snatched the coins and darted away, disappearing from view. Sabinah was about to step onto the brick street, but paused in midstride as a column of Roman soldiers rode in her direction. She watched in horror as the Romans made no attempt to slow their pace even though old Fana, a deaf woman who sold garlic in a nearby stall, hobbled down the street, unmindful of the danger approaching her from behind. Someone called out a warning, but old Fana could not hear. Sabinah, who was too far away to help the woman, feared she would be crushed by flying hooves.

Just as it seemed there was no hope for the old woman, a bedouin tribesman leaped from the crowd, jerking her to safety. Old Fana pushed him away and adjusted her robe, angling her footsteps past the fishmonger's stall as if nothing out of the ordinary had occurred.

"Aiee, aiee," Ma'dou lamented, waving her plump hands in distress. "The Romans are a scourge upon this land."

"It seems my stepmother does not share your opinion," Sabinah stated with rancor as she watched the Roman column continue to advance in her direction.

"Hmmph, consorting with the enemy," Ma'dou said, her face paling before she glanced away quickly, as if she had said too much.

"You can always speak the truth to me," Sabinah told her, patting Ma'dou's hand. "As you well know, I share your sentiment. It is a bitter thing to encounter the enemy in my own home. My father would not have allowed it had he lived." Sabinah felt her face flush with anger. "Why do not the people rebel against them?" she asked, swirling around to the people in the stalls. "Why do you allow the Romans to treat you with such disrespect?"

A potter, seated at his workbench, dipped his fingers in water, then began forming clay into a rounded shape. He blinked at her, then looked away quickly. None of the others paid her the slightest heed—they were too frightened.

"If we all banded together, we could help each other," she said in a quieter voice, even though she knew it would be impossible for a group of merchants to have any effect on the Roman army.

"It might be possible, if they had your courage, little mistress." Ma'dou moved toward the fruit vendor, calling over her shoulder. "But you must not speak so, lest your words reach the wrong ears."

"It is a pity we all act like cowering animals when the Romans are about," she whispered.

Ma'dou shook her head. "Do not wander far. I want to get back home as soon as possible."

With a determined glare, Sabinah stepped into the roadway, refusing to give way to the Romans who approached her on horseback. Clamping her mouth in anger, she watched them draw nearer, too furious to be afraid, although the horsemen showed no sign of slowing their pace.

Sabinah was startled when a strong hand gripped her shoulder and yanked her out of the road. Turning to her rescuer in anger, she realized it was the same man who had saved the old deaf woman.

He wore the plain homespun robe of an Amalekite trader. Despite the heat, he also wore a hooded cape. "Have you no sense, foolish one? Romans do not stop for stubborn little girls."

She heard the anger in the man's voice, and it served to heighten her own fury. "I did not ask you to help me," she said, pushing his hand away from her arm. But when she would have stepped away from him, she caught sight of piercing green eyes.

He was no Amalekite.

She knew of no one but the prince of the Bardari who had that particular color of eyes.

Trembling, she could hardly catch her breath. "Lord Julian?"

Frowning, he quickly pulled the hood lower on his forehead. "Shh," he cautioned. "It is not safe to speak my name."

Sabinah's throat contracted as Julian stared at her. In the past he had often visited her home with the purpose of courting Bastet. For a time, her stepmother had hoped Julian would ask for her daughter's hand in marriage. Certainly Bastet, whose beauty made up for her lack of social standing, had used every feminine trick she could manage to ensnare him. Who could say whether she would have succeeded if the Romans had not invaded Egypt and placed a death sentence on anyone related to Queen Cleopatra?

Julian smiled. "Can it be my Little Sunshine?" he asked, using the pet name he had pinned on her years before. "How fares your family?"

It took her a moment to find her voice. "We fare well—better than some."

"I am glad to hear that."

Suddenly Sabinah's heart quickened with fear. "You should not be here. It is too dangerous for you to be seen."

"Unless you give me away, the Romans will not know who I am."

Her eyes widened, and she shook her head. "I would never betray you. Not if they inflicted a thousand cuts on my body."

Julian's lips settled into a smile. "I believe you, Sunshine."

She gripped the front of his robe in desperation. "Please, you must leave Alexandria at once. I have heard Octavian has put a high price on your head."

"I have no fear of him." There was a dangerous edge to his voice as his gaze moved over her face. "Have the Romans been a bother to you or your family?"

"Unfortunately they are regular visitors at our house," she said bitterly.

Julian had never cared much for Bastet's mother, and he was not surprised she was on friendly terms with the enemy. "Have a care, little one. Keep away from them if you can," he warned.

"I am not afraid of them!"

He smiled. "You are young and may not understand the dangers."

She was pleased that he cared about her safety. Why could she never think of anything clever to say to him? If only she had worn her new blue gown instead of the unadorned brown linen. "You are the one who faces danger," she said, glancing about to see if anyone was watching him with suspicion. It seemed everyone was staring at the retreating Romans and took no notice of the man they thought to be a foreign trader.

Julian laughed softly. "Fear not for me. Not everyone has your sharp eyes."

"It is easy for me to recognize you. I have known you all my life."

"It is fortunate for me that we met, Sunshine. I would ask a favor of you."

"Anything," she said with feeling.

"Deliver this message to Bastet for me. Say to her that I shall be just outside the garden walls of your house the fourth hour after sunset. Ask her if she will meet me there. But tell no one else."

Sabinah felt as if her heart had been crushed. All he wanted of her was to carry a message to Bastet. How could she tell him that Bastet was interested in one of the Roman officers? She was even afraid her stepsister might turn Julian over to the Romans for the reward. Before she could think of a way to warn him, Julian had turned away and was soon swallowed up in the crowded marketplace.

Ma'dou appeared at Sabinah's side. "Who was that?"

"Just someone asking directions," she answered, the lie coming easily to her lips. Now she had another secret to guard. No one must know that Ptolemy Caesarion had escaped death, or that Lord Julian Tausrat was in Alexandria.

"You should not speak to such a person. The mistress would not approve."

Sabinah still watched the spot where Julian had disappeared, wishing she was beautiful like Bastet, or even pretty, for that matter. Then perhaps Lord Julian would look at her the way he had always looked at her stepsister. "There is no reason to mention the incident to my stepmother, is there?"

"Nay. I will not."

Shortly after Sabinah's mother had died, her father had married Trisella, taking the woman's five-year-old daughter as his own. It was whispered that Trisella had once been a servant in the Jannah household. Whether that was true or not, Sabinah did not know because the servants were too frightened to speak of it.

Bastet easily caught the attention of every man who saw her; Sabinah was considered the plain one, a fact that her stepmother often pointed out to her. Unlike Bastet, who had beautiful ebony hair, Sabinah had inherited her dead mother's red hair, which was unmanageable and curled in a profusion of tangles about her thin face.

Sabinah sighed. Her legs were long and gangly, and she had the shape of a young lad. No amount of wishing would make her curvaceous like her stepsister. Her brown eyes were her best feature, and she did have long lashes, but that did not make her pretty.

Shaking her head, Sabinah silently walked beside Ma'dou, her thoughts on Julian. Could she trust Bastet not to betray him? Perhaps her stepsister secretly loved Julian. What woman would not? He was a prince of the Badari, and so handsome Sabinah could stare at him for hours.

She glanced up at the sky, watching dark clouds gather over the sea, and the sight dampened her spirits even more.

"Hurry along, young mistress, before it starts to rain."

As they headed home, Sabinah glanced up at the cook. "Do you think I will ever be pretty?"

Ma'dou looked taken aback. "How can that be important?"

"It is to me. Why do I have to be so plain?"

"Hmmph. Your stepsister may have the looks, but you are the smart one. You will do better in the long run. You just see if I am not right."

Sabinah shook her head, that was not what she wanted to hear. "Lord Julian does not even notice I am a female. If I had but one wish, it would be that he would love me."

The servant stopped in her tracks. "Young one, what a fanciful notion! Of course he will not love you! He is from a great and noble family. While your mother was of a good family, and your father was respected as a master goldsmith, you are not of high enough birth to be considered by the Tausrat family."

"But my stepmother thinks my stepsister—"

"Bah!" Ma'dou hissed. "The mistress is *certainly* not equal in rank to the House of Tausrat. Did not Bastet learn this for herself when she hoped to marry Lord Julian?"

"I had not heard that."

"You know how the servants talk, and none are more knowledgeable than those who work in the kitchen. I should not be telling you this, but perhaps it will help get these foolish notions out of your head." Ma'dou looked doubtful for a moment and then nodded to herself. "Your stepmother approached Lord Julian's grandmother, Lady Larania, a few moons past, asking if she could help arrange a match between Mistress Bastet and Lord Julian. I know not what transpired between them, but the mistress was furious for days afterward. And nothing was ever said about such a match again."

Sabinah frowned. Even if Julian's grandmother had not approved of the connection, Julian still cared for Bastet, or he would not have wanted to meet her tonight.

"Put foolishness out of your head and apply yourself to your studies. Besides," the cook said in a scolding tone, "you are much too young to be thinking such thoughts."

"Can you tell me about my own mother?"

"I will say only this—your dear mother was of a good family, who disowned her when she married a goldsmith rather than the high lord her father had chosen. Your stepmother forbids us to speak of her, so I shall say no more."

"Is my mother's family still alive?"

"Nay. There was only a grandmother left, and it is said she died two years ago."

Sabinah sighed. "So I have no one."

"It would seem not."

Her thoughts returned to Julian. There were those who would say a girl could not feel love at the tender age of fourteen, but Sabinah would argue with them. She had a deep, abiding love for Julian that would not tarnish with the passing of time, nor would her feelings for him lessen. Sabinah remained silent for the rest of the way home, trying to decide if it was wise to give Bastet Julian's message.

Whatever must she do?

CHAPTER FOUR

Apollodorus stepped from the shadow of a doorway with dread in his heart. Tapping Julian on the shoulder, he said, "Accompany me to Uriah's house. Something has happened."

"Concerning my grandmother?"

"Aye. But we dare not discuss it here."

Without question, Julian worriedly fell into step beside Apollodorus. They kept to the shadows and turned down a twisted street that led away from the marketplace. They ignored the high arched gateway that was the front entrance to the villa, choosing instead a back gate that was hidden by climbing vines, one few people knew about.

Once inside the garden, Julian glanced at the white sandstone house with its red-tiled roof that had mellowed with age. He could smell jasmine, his mother's favorite flower. He was about to speak when Apollodorus pulled him back into the shadows and made a motion for silence. It took a moment for Julian to hear what had caught Apollodorus's attention.

Faltering footsteps.

Moments passed, and the footsteps grew closer.

"I saw you enter the garden, young master. 'Tis a sad day you come to me."

Julian stepped onto the path. His old tutor was short of stature with white hair, what there was of it, and an equally white beard. His back was stooped by age, and he leaned heavily on a walking stick.

"Uriah, how are you, my friend?"

The old man studied the young boy from beneath shaggy brows. "Heartbroken, as you must be."

Julian frowned, and glanced back at Apollodorus. "What has occurred? What is wrong with my grandmother?"

The two older men exchanged troubled glances, and at last Apollodorus spoke. "Julian, we are too late. Lady Larania is dead."

Julian felt bleak despair. "When? How?"

"I do not yet know the details, but it happened sixteen days ago," the Sicilian said, lowering his head so he would not have to meet Julian's eyes. "Captain Vergilius is responsible." He turned to Uriah, inquiring, "Do you have more details?"

"This Captain Vergilius has taken over Lady Larania's holdings as his own."

Julian slumped against the rough bark of a date palm, circling the trunk with his arms. Grief and anger tore at him. "He will die by my hands. This I swear."

Julian felt Uriah's hand on his shoulder. "Loyal servants carried Lady Larania's body to be purified. I saw that your grandmother had a proper entombment."

Julian's eyes narrowed. "I shall see this Roman for myself."

"All in good time," Apollodorus cautioned him. "We shall bide here until sunset."

Julian watched lightning streak across the sky and drops of rain pelted his face. Silently, he slipped over the familiar garden walls of his grandmother's villa, with Apollodorus behind him. All the rooms were lit, and the sound of merriment fueled Julian's fury. He moved slightly out of the shadows and glanced in the window, and what he saw made him sick with rage. The room he knew so well, where he had spent much of his youth, was filled with Romans. Some wore uniforms and others were in togas. Scantily clad dancers whirled about the room while other women climbed on couches, fondling the men.

Anger tore through him like a hot desert wind, and he reached for the window latch, his other hand closing around the hilt of his knife.

A heavy hand fell on his shoulder.

"Not now, young prince," Apollodorus advised in a whisper. "The time will come—but it is not now. You must not choose to fight when the odds will not allow you to win."

"They desecrate my grandmother's memory and foul her home."

"They can no longer hurt your grandmother. And as for your sadness, nothing but the desert sands lasts forever. Remember Lady Larania as she was."

"I want to plunge my dagger into her killer's heart!"

"Patience is the virtue that wins in the end. Had you known the mighty Caesar, for whom you are named, and watched him gauge every situation, you would know this for yourself."

Julian glared at his friend. "And yet, in the end, he was slain by those he trusted. Patience did not save his life."

"And your anger will not save yours." Apollodorus nodded toward the torchlit chamber. "Note well the Roman with the scarlet toga—the one who talks loudest and boasts of his exploits."

"I see him."

"That is Captain Vergilius. He reports directly to Octavian, and no one else, which inflates his self-importance in his own mind. He, and he alone, is responsible for your grandmother's death."

"Then why should he not die tonight?"

"He has been rewarded for what he has done—this villa now belongs to him. He is a man on the rise to power. Bide your time, strike at him when he has the most to lose."

"I want to wipe the smirk off his face and drive my blade into his gut!"

"It is far wiser to know your enemy. We shall learn what he feels and thinks, whom he sees and whom he trusts."

Julian set his jaw stubbornly, reminding Apollodorus of Lord Ramtat. "That could take years."

"It will. And in that time you will grow to be a man and act less impulsively, my young hothead."

"Sometimes, Apollodorus, I do not follow your reasoning. But my father bade me obey you, and I shall do so."

The Sicilian nodded toward the wall. "We should leave now."

Reluctantly, Julian followed Apollodorus down the path and back over the wall. Dropping down on the other side, they both disappeared into the shadows.

Mounting his horse, Julian rode away, leaving his grandmother's home in the hands of her murderers.

I will return, he vowed.

Then there will be a reckoning.

Apollodorus seemed to have read his mind. "Your grandmother's death will not go unpunished."

"No," Julian said, nudging his horse forward. "It will not."

Sabinah's home, which was in one of the better parts of Alexandria, was built of white limestone. It was surrounded by a courtyard, and in the back was a garden where her stepmother grew herbs and spices for the potions she made to sell. The rain had stopped earlier, and a heavy mist shrouded the garden, but Sabinah hardly noticed as she paced down the path and back.

She was reluctant to enter the house, and even more reluctant to give Bastet Julian's message.

Her gaze settled on the jasmine hedges climbing the garden wall. New waterworks brought water to several restored fountains. The pathways had been freshly strewn with colorful pebbles from some faraway shore. The house had fallen into disrepair after her father died, but lately her stepmother seemed to have enough money to finance the needed repairs and even buy new furnishings. Trisella had also replenished her wardrobe with all the latest styles from Rome and done the same for Bastet and Sabinah.

Where had her stepmother obtained the money? Certainly not from selling her potions, or they would have had money before now.

With determined steps Sabinah turned toward the house. She would give Bastet the message, but she would not tell her the time or place of the meeting until she judged Bastet's reaction.

The thick walls of the house made it cooler inside as Sabinah paused in the entryway. Taking a deep breath, she moved through the corridor toward the small chamber where the family usually gathered in the evenings. Nearing the arched doorway, Sabinah paused when she heard Bastet's voice rise in volume.

"Think of it, Mother—me, married to an important Roman! Gallius is second in command to Captain Vergilius. Someday he will be an important man in Egypt, and perhaps even in Rome, and I have him panting after me like a lovesick fool."

Sabinah heard her stepmother laugh. "But you must not appear too eager. Hold back on your favors, a few kisses, perhaps touching, but make him want you with such passion he will beg you to be his wife. Ask him for money, jewels—he will gladly give them to you."

"You know I have already shared his bed, Mother. But as you advised, I gave him just enough so he would come back for more. He is almost ripe for the plucking. I would not be surprised if he has not already petitioned the Roman Senate for a dispensation so we can be married."

A thin stream of torchlight fell upon Trisella's face, and there was uncertainty etched on her fine features. "Are you certain? Men can be sly when they want something from a woman."

Bastet looked smug. "Last night he knelt before me with tears in his eyes, swearing I was the most beautiful woman he had ever beheld. He said he would die if I did not let him touch me."

Her mother's eyes held a ravenous expression. "Tell me, daughter, did he give you more money?"

Sabinah heard the jingle of coins as Bastet shook the leather pouch attached to her belt. "More than last time."

Trisella reached out greedily, but Bastet pulled away from her. "These coins I keep. I shall buy jewels and clothing so beautiful it will make the gods jealous."

"Well," her mother said piteously, "if you want to be selfish. Just remember who guided you in the ways to please a man."

"Do not say this to me," Bastet cried. "It is my body that has been sacrificed to the men who do not find their way to your bed. From this day on, any coin I am given belongs to me alone." Her voice became shriller. "And mark this well, when Gallius's duty is finished in Egypt, he will take me to Rome and perhaps even present me to Octavian." Bastet clapped her hands. "Think about it—I will be a great lady, and men of importance will worship at my feet."

Trisella studied her daughter for a long moment. "I never considered you might be leaving Egypt. How will I abide it if you leave me?"

Bastet shrugged. "I suppose that is the way of it when your daughter does as you bid. But you will still have Sabinah to lure Roman protectors to the house. Although I am not certain my stepsister will willingly offer herself to any man." She giggled. "And even if she did, what man would have her?"

"Sabinah is nothing to me," Trisella replied. "If it were not for her father's will, which left this house to her, I would have sent her away long ago."

"Perhaps my stepfather sensed your intentions when he wrote the will."

"I am sure he did."

"When I leave, she is all you will have." Bastet's laugh was deep and husky. "She is such a skinny, serious little thing. She will be a companion to you in your old age."

"Aiee. Sabinah will be no comfort to me. All she does is read her books. In that she is her father's daughter."

Heartbroken, Sabinah doubled over, clutching her stomach, fearing she would be sick. How blind she had been—never guessing her stepmother and stepsister had been bedded by Romans and received money for the act.

It was unthinkable.

Horrifying.

"You there," Bastet said, taking Sabinah unaware. "How dare you sneak about eavesdropping on my conversations!" She reached out and pinched Sabinah's arm, dragging her into the room. "Did you hear all you wanted to hear?"

"I was not sneaking," Sabinah protested, pulling away from her stepsister.

"And I say you were."

A sob caught in Sabinah's throat. "I am glad my father is not alive to see the degradation of this family. He was respected, we are not."

Trisella merely shrugged. "One does what one must to survive."

Bastet's eyes narrowed. "If you were not eavesdropping, why are you here?"

Sabinah decided to test her stepsister in regard to Julian. "I wanted to tell you I saw Lord Julian this morning at the marketplace."

Bastet's eyes widened in excitement. "You saw Julian? Did he ask about me?"

Sabinah sighed. Apparently she had misjudged Bastet's feelings for Julian. "He asked about the family," she said reluctantly, still not willing to tell her stepsister where Julian could be found. And she was glad she had held back when she saw Bastet's eyes narrow with cunning.

"Did Julian perchance tell you where he is hiding?"

A warning went off in Sabinah's mind. "Why would he tell me?"

Bastet drew an intolerant breath. "Foolish girl. Do you not know there is a fortune offered for his capture?"

"You would turn him over to the Romans for money?"

Bastet gripped Sabinah's arms and shook her. "Aye. And so should you." Then Bastet released her. "If you see him again, attempt to discover where he is hiding so you can tell me."

Sabinah was filled with shame when she realized how far her stepsister would go to obtain the wealth she had always desired. Sabinah would never betray Julian, nor would she allow Bastet to do so.

"No doubt Julian has returned to Alexandria because he heard of his grandmother's death," Bastet said.

Sabinah jumped back as if she had been struck. "What did you say? Lady Larania is dead!"

Her stepsister's gaze slid away from her, and her cheeks reddened with momentary shame, her gaze locking with her mother's. "I have heard rumors someone told Captain Vergilius where to locate her."

Sabinah's eyes filled with tears. "I am sorry for the loss of that dear lady. My father had great respect for her. And Julian must be so sad."

"Spare me the tears," Bastet said, fluffing her ebony hair so it fell about her face like silk. "Anyway, I do not want to think of such things today. It distresses me."

Trisella's eyes gleamed with malice. "Are we not a happy family?"

"How can you both be so unfeeling?" Sabinah accused. "We owe that family our loyalty."

Bastet watched Sabinah speculatively. "Stepsister, we owe the *Romans* our loyalty. Whose money do you think bought that gown you wear?"

"I want nothing ill-gotten touching my skin." Sabinah ran down the corridor, tearing at her robe as she went. She wanted to wash every place on her body that the garment had touched. When she reached her chamber, she ripped the rest of the material down the front and threw it on the floor.

"Get rid of that," she told her servant Isadad, who was staring at her as if she had lost her mind. "Get rid of everything in my trunk and bring me a gown that belongs to one of the servants. I will not wear anything bought with Roman money!"

Isadad, her old nurse, shook her gray head, her dark eyes filled with understanding. Every servant in the house knew how the family came by their tainted money. She was surprised Sabinah had not seen this before. "So you discovered the truth."

"Why did you not tell me?"

"I did not want to be the one to cause you pain."

"Were you aware that Lady Larania is dead?"

There was pity in Isadad's dark eyes. "Little mistress, nothing goes on in this house that is hidden from us servants. The talk in the kitchen is that the dear lady was tortured to death because she would not tell the Romans where her family could be found."

Sabinah collapsed on the floor and sobbed. Tears blinded her when she thought of Lady Larania's death.

"Little mistress, what has been done cannot be undone."

Isadad's hands had soothed Sabinah when she was ill—Isadad was the one she had always run to when she had been hurt. But nothing could help the pain that she was feeling at the moment.

Suddenly Sabinah's head came up. It was growing late, and she must warn Julian.

ᑌ CHAPTER FIVE

Heavy clouds darkened the sky, and the air smelled clean and fresh after the recent rain. The threat of another storm lingered, with lightning flashing in the distance.

Cautiously, Sabinah brushed the garden wall with her hand so she could find her way. When she reached the back gate, it groaned on rusty hinges, and she held her breath, fearing someone might hear and investigate. When she was certain no one was coming, she slipped out the gate, making her way along the outer wall.

Fearing Julian might make another attempt to contact Bastet if she did not meet him, Sabinah had decided to take her place. She must warn him of the danger. Wishing she could see better in the darkness, she leaned against the wall.

Perhaps he had not come.

She froze when she heard movement beside her, and she was pulled into strong arms. Struggling, she tried to wriggle free, but a deep voice calmed her.

"I knew you would not disappoint me, Bastet."

"Julian."

"It is I."

Sabinah knew she should explain at once that she was not Bastet, but he took her face between his hands and touched his cheek to hers. "A few weeks ago I saw you from a distance, but I dared not approach you. I saw at that time you had grown even more beautiful."

"Julian, you must not—"

His mouth swept down on hers, and he pulled her closer to his body. Sabinah felt her heart thundering, and her knees went weak. The kiss was tender, long, and drugging, and she was caught up in the wonder of it. It did not matter that Julian thought he was kissing Bastet; it only mattered that she would have this moment to remember for the rest of her life.

Tonight she would steal a little happiness for herself.

Julian broke off the kiss, but he still held her. "I have long dreamed of touching my mouth again to those beautiful lips."

His hands tightened about her waist, and he pulled her solidly against him. Sabinah felt the swell of his body and a sharp, newfound longing shook her.

"Your lips are sweeter than before," he whispered into her hair. "Just one more kiss to take away the horror of this day."

Sabinah knew she must tell him the truth, and she pulled away, placing a hand over his mouth, feeling him kiss her palm. "Julian, I am not Bastet."

He took a quick step backward. "Then who plays this trick on me?"

"It is I, Sabinah."

He sounded startled. "Little Sunshine?"

"I came to tell you—"

"By the gods, Sabinah, you are but a child. Forgive me for what I did to you. I mistook you for Bastet."

"I am not a child," she said, hurt because Julian felt the need to apologize for a moment that had been so beautiful to her. "I am fifteen summers."

"Nay, little one," he said, placing a chaste kiss on her forehead. "We both know you are the same age as my young sister, and she is but fourteen." He took another step away to distance himself from her. "Why did Bastet not come?"

"I did not tell Bastet you wanted her to meet you."

He seemed to stiffen. "Why is that?"

"I . . . my stepsister . . . Bastet is . . . she is . . . entertaining a Roman she hopes to marry."

There, she had said it!

Julian was quiet for a long moment. "She always detested Romans and told me so on several occasions."

Sabinah could not bring herself to tell him how Bastet had changed. "What I say is true, Julian. You must believe me."

"Why did you not tell me this morning?"

"I was not aware of it myself until this afternoon. Please, for your safety, do not seek out Bastet."

"You are not trying to trick me, are you?"

She reached out into the darkness until she found his hand. Taking it in both of hers, she said with feeling, "Julian, you must not come here again—it is too dangerous. I beseech you—believe me."

His hand closed around one of hers. "It is difficult to believe Bastet would betray me."

Sabinah's eyes filled with tears, and she was glad it was dark so he would not know she wept. "You do not truly know my stepsister. Do not trust her, Julian. It could mean your death."

He touched her face and felt her tears. "Do you weep for me, Sunshine?"

The pain in his voice was so deep and disturbing that she could not stem the flow of tears.

"I cry for the loss your entire family must feel. Only today did I hear about Lady Larania's death." She touched his face. "I am so sorry. She was a wondrous lady. Everyone loved her," she said, brushing away her tears.

There was gentleness in his voice. "You have a kind heart, Sunshine. I have always known this."

"You must not linger any longer, Julian. You could be discovered at any moment."

He yanked her into his arms. "If it was not so dark, I could read the truth in your eyes. Tell me why I should believe you."

"You have to—you have enemies here. You should leave at once."

He seemed reluctant to release her. "I have few friends these days, Sunshine. Therefore, I shall treasure your friendship."

They both heard footsteps in the distance.

"Please go!" she urged.

She felt his fingers leave hers, and she made a daring move, not knowing if she would ever see him again. She pressed her lips against his cheek, but he had turned his face, and their mouths met. She heard him gasp, and for the briefest moment, he pulled her to him.

Tearing his mouth from hers, he roughly shoved her away. But his tone was gentle. "Grow up, Sunshine, before you tempt a man."

"You are not yet a man," she protested, her throat contracting with emotion.

His hand ran down the side of her face. "It will be many years before I see you again. By that time some man will have stolen your heart and you will have forgotten me."

How could she bear to go years without seeing him, without knowing where he was, or if he was safe?

"I love you," she blurted out. When the words were spoken, Sabinah wished she could call them back. Unable to see his face, she imagined he would be frowning.

"You are young, little one. Your whole life is before you." With the silence that came from his Badari training, Julian slipped away soundlessly.

Sabinah leaned against the wall, wiping tears from her eyes. She had the feeling she had seen him for the last time. It was a dangerous path he trod, and there were many who would betray him for the reward.

With an aching heart, she went back inside the garden and closed the squeaky gate behind her.

Raindrops pelted Sabinah's face and lightning streaked across the sky just as her gaze fell on a small statue of Isis. With raindrops running down the face of the statue, it appeared Isis was crying.

Raucous laughter came from the house. Her stepmother was entertaining again tonight. Sabinah made her way quietly to her own bedchamber, her heart feeling bruised.

"Come back soon, Julian," she whispered.

As Julian rode into the night, his heart was heavy with grief. He dreaded the moment he must tell the family his beloved grandmother had been slain. He remembered her smile, her kindness, and the love he had for her.

"We should make camp for the night," Apollodorus suggested. "The horses are tired."

As Julian lay upon his blanket gazing at the clear desert sky, he tried not to think of his grandmother—it was too painful. He let his mind dwell on his meeting with Sabinah. "Apollodorus," he asked, "what would you do if the girl you trusted, and had been fond of, was associating with Romans?"

"I do not know. What would you do?" he asked, turning the question back to Julian.

"Sabinah told me I must not trust Bastet and warned that she would betray me."

"Then your dilemma, as I see it, is whether you trust the younger sister, or the elder."

Julian thought of the sweet-faced young girl who always reminded him of bright sunlight. She was always smiling, her dark eyes sparkling. She was earnest, her demeanor innocent. "I believe I shall trust the younger."

"And the elder?"

Although Bastet was older than Julian, he had long been infatuated by her beauty. Now that he thought about it, he remembered a trick she had had of poking her finger in her eye so it would look as if she were crying. He remembered the way she bent over so he could clearly see her breasts. Bastet had all the arts of allurement, and they seemed practiced, now that he thought about it. "I would not trust her with my life or that of my family."

"Then you have your answer."

Julian turned over on his side, pondering what had happened between him and Sabinah. She had cried for his grandmother—the tears had been genuine. She had felt pain for his loss. That had been real. The warning she had given him was also heartfelt. He closed his eyes, remembering the feel of her soft lips, and the way they had trembled beneath his. She was pure and innocent, and yet she had stirred him to passion. Her confession of love stayed with him.

But he was sixteen, and she was a mere child. He tried to dismiss her from his thoughts, but he would always remember she had come to warn him of danger.

Lost somewhere between sleep and wakefulness, Julian remembered the feel of Sabinah's sweet mouth.

CHAPTER SIX

Egyptian desert

The sunset burned against the sand, turning it golden in color. The stillness was hardly disturbed by the hoofbeats of two Badarian horses racing smoothly across the desolate expanse. Apollodorus glanced at the young prince, noticing his features were fierce with anger. Sadness weighed heavily on the young man's shoulders. He had been close to his grandmother, and her death was a devastating blow to him. There were no words to ease Julian's pain, so Apollodorus said nothing.

Silently they continued, their powerful horses kicking up sand in their wake. Twilight fell heavily over the land as Julian topped a sand dune and gazed down below. Over a hundred tents dotted the huge gardenlike oasis, but the large red leather tent in the middle was his destination. His spirited mount pulled impatiently at the reins, and Julian had no need to urge the animal forward.

Once he reached his father's tent, Julian dismounted before the horse had halted and hurried inside while Apollodorus remained outside to allow the family time to grieve in private.

Ramtat came from the curtained-off private area, and

Julian bowed his head, wishing he did not have to relate the sad news of his grandmother's death.

"Your grandmother is not with you?"

All Julian could do was shake his head.

Ramtat smiled slightly. "I suppose I will have to go after her myself."

"Father, there is great sadness." Julian quickly told his father what had happened, hardly able to bear it when he saw his father's dark eyes fill with grief. "She was dead before we even left for Alexandria," he added.

Ramtat closed his eyes for the briefest moment as sorrow hit him in the gut. When he opened them, he stared at his son. "How did it happen?"

Julian choked on his own grief. Despite his resolve to remain strong, his eyes clouded with tears. "Apollodorus discovered that the Romans tortured Grandmother in an attempt to make her reveal the family's location. She told them nothing."

Anger and grief raged inside Ramtat. "What happened to my mother's body?"

"Uriah saw her properly entombed."

Ramtat placed his hand on his son's shoulder. "The tribe must be told so they can mourn for her. She was a most beloved princess."

"I grieve that she is dead," Julian said in a voice filled with pain. "But she did die like a princess of the Badari—brave and unyielding."

"As we knew she would." Ramtat searched his son's face. "There is more you have not told me."

Julian took in a deep breath. "Someone told the Romans where to find Grandmother." Julian met his father's gaze. "Apollodorus questioned the captain of Grandmother's guard. The man spoke of overhearing several

Romans talking among themselves. It seems a reward was paid to some Egyptian woman for leading Captain Vergilius to Grandmother. The captain did not know her name. Uriah said he would make inquiries."

Ramtat slowly shook his head. "Danger walks too close to our family. My mother's death must be avenged, but now is not the time. The safety of the family must come first. We will leave Egypt with all haste."

"I do not want to leave."

"Julian, it has already been decided. This family will stay together. I will not have your mother worried about your safety. She has suffered enough, and yet I must add to her sorrow when I tell her about my mother."

"Father, I was resigned to go with you before this happened. How can we leave without first punishing the man who killed Grandmother?" Julian laid his hand on his father's arm. "He is living in Grandmother's house!"

"Julian, let it go. Say no more about the matter. Yesterday I received a message from your aunt Thalia. Her swiftest ship, the *War Hawk*, is at anchor off the shores of Neva Ma'Sud. We leave tomorrow. Octavian will never think to look for us on Bal Forea. And even if he did, the island is too mountainous for Roman troops to gain an advantage there."

Julian folded his arms over his broad chest and shook his head. "Do we leave like thieves in the night? I do not fear the Romans."

Ramtat felt pride in his son, but fear for him as well. "Speak no more of this." Ramtat placed his hand on Julian's shoulder. "It is as it must be."

His father now spoke to him as sheik of the Badari, and Julian must obey, although it was difficult to let go of his anger. "If it is within my power, I shall return one day and take up my sword to avenge Grandmother."

"It will be *my* right to avenge my mother, Julian. Do not think because I stay my hand at this time that I shall not strike that man down. The time is not now—but it will come."

By now word had reached the Badari of the death of their princess, and many keening voices were raised in grief.

Ramtat drew in a quivering breath. "I shall need a firm hand to keep my people from gathering and storming Alexandria. They will want revenge, just as we do, my son."

"Then let me lead them," Julian said with feeling. "Captain Vergilius will not be expecting us. We will have the advantage of surprise if we strike quickly!"

"That is not the way it will be. I do not want to see innocent blood spilled. As you know, many Egyptians would join our fight, and they would be slaughtered by the Romans. I will be obeyed, so calm your anger."

Julian could not understand why his father refused to storm Alexandria and take revenge on the Romans.

But his father's word was the law.

Seaport village of Neva Ma'Sud

Julian watched the crimson sails of the *War Hawk* unfurl. With wind rippling against the huge emblem of a black hawk, it gave the illusion of a bird in flight. Slowly, the ship moved away from shore. The family usually sailed from Osage when making the voyage to Bal Forea. But when his father had sent men ahead to scout the village, they'd discovered Roman spies had been there, forcing the family to choose Neva Ma'Sud, a small port that few ships frequented because the coast was hazardous. In the past, Julian had been happy to visit his aunt Thalia, who was queen of Bal Forea, but this time he felt like a coward, sneaking out of Egypt, fleeing from the Romans.

He almost choked on his anger. Why should his family be forced to leave home, and more vexing still, why had his father chosen to run instead of fight?

Apollodorus stood statue-still, his gaze on the disappearing shoreline. "There will be another day, young prince. Until then, learn the skills that will help you when you return."

Julian nodded. "I know this in my head, but my heart is uncertain."

Apollodorus nodded at the twelve fierce Badari warriors who gripped the railing—most had never been on a ship before, and it was apparent they were nervous; two of them looked white-faced and ill. "Your people are desert dwellers, yet they trust your father's word enough to place their lives under his care. Your father is a wise ruler of men. You would do well to look to him for counsel." He nodded once more at the Badari. "They know this, and so must you."

Many things were unclear to Julian. He had the hot blood of a warrior in his veins. His instincts were to fight, to avenge. It was not easy for him to flee. With a heavy sigh, he wondered how many years would pass before he could return to Egypt.

𓅿 CHAPTER SEVEN

Alexandria, 26 BC

Sabinah was angry as she waited for Isadad to put the finishing touches on her hair. Frowning at her reflection in the beaten brass mirror, she watched her servant twist a lock of hair and secure it with a silver ornament. Already she was late for her stepmother's banquet, and if she had her way, she would not attend it at all.

She caught Isadad's gaze in the mirror. "Do not hurry," she said glumly. "I am in no mood to socialize with my stepmother's guests."

"Some of the Roman officers are most handsome, are they not?"

Sabinah twisted around and stared into the dark eyes of the woman who should have known better than to make such an outrageous statement to her. "Why do you say such a thing to me? You know how I feel about Romans and especially Tribune Vergilius, who pesters me every time he sees me."

"I merely try to help you make the best of a bad situation. The mistress insists you attend her feasts as a way of thanking the Romans for what they do for this family. 'Tis a pity her guests make you miserable."

"There are still many of us in Egypt who blame Rome

for the deaths of those we loved and respected. Should I thank them for that?"

Isadad's hand fell heavily on Sabinah's shoulder. "Do not speak so. If anyone overheard, you could be accused of treason. It is whispered that many who have spoken ill of Rome disappear, never to be heard of again."

In that moment the door burst open, and Bastet stalked into the chamber, her face twisted with rage. "You insult our guests by lingering over your dressing table. Mother demands you attend her at once."

Bastet's long black hair was worn loose, falling down her back like shimmering silk. Her green gown hugged her breasts and fell past her shapely hips—there was a long slit that showed a fair amount of her legs. Sabinah recognized the sweet scent that clung to Bastet; it was one of her stepmother's concoctions that was supposed to stir a man's passion. Sabinah wrinkled her nose. The last thing she would ever want was to stir passion in a Roman. But of late, for a reason Sabinah did not comprehend, she was being showered with attention from the Romans, and Bastet was very displeased.

"I would rather entertain a cobra than spend an evening with any of your friends."

"Imbecile! The Romans are lords of the world, and you are the only one who seems to doubt it. If you continue to act as you do, you will shame this family."

"This family knows no shame," Sabinah said, watching her stepsister's reflection in the mirror.

Before Sabinah saw it coming, Bastet jerked her around and slapped her with such force the blow slammed Sabinah's head back. She toppled to the floor while Isadad gasped in distress. Bastet's dark eyes became like those of a statue: blank, and devoid of warmth.

"Have a care. One day you will irk me once too often, and you will regret it."

Sabinah rose, tilting her chin. "Do not ever do that again, or you will have to drag me to your mother's banquets!"

"Silly girl. We all know the man you favor above the rest. Julian has not been seen in years, and even when he came around, he took no notice of you." Bastet met Sabinah's eyes. "Even if Julian were to return, you must avoid him, for my sake."

"I do not know what you mean."

Bastet leaned closer, harsh laughter escaping her lips. "How can you be so unworldly? I thought you would have found out by now that it was I who told Tribune Vergilius where to find Lady Larania."

Sabinah thought she must surely have heard incorrectly. "You?"

"Aye. But you are as guilty as I am. You filled your belly with the money I received as a reward." Bastet's fingers dug into Sabinah's arm. "And know this, foolish one—if Julian dared to enter Alexandria, he would soon meet with a Roman sword. The Tausrat family have always held themselves too high, but they are lower than the desert sands now that Rome rules in Egypt. While I am admired by the Romans."

Sabinah stared at Bastet in horror. "I have known you were misguided, but never did I think you were evil. It was monstrous to betray that sweet lady!"

Bastet shrugged. "The woman once did me a harm by not thinking I was good enough for her grandson. I consider we are now even."

Sabinah choked on her anger. "If I had somewhere else to go, I would leave this house and never return."

"But you do not, do you? Whereas I shall soon be married and on my way to Rome."

Sabinah fought against the bile that rose in her throat. "It does not seem to me your Roman has marriage on his mind. Perhaps if you ask your mother, she will brew a potion to make him more amenable to the notion. How long does it take one man to decide whom he wants for a wife? You have known him four years."

Doubt crept into her stepsister's eyes, but Bastet quickly masked it. "We are the same as married."

"I hear he already has a Roman wife."

"That is merely a small matter. He will divorce her for me." Bastet had other lovers, but she preferred Centurion Gallius.

"It seems to me if the man was going to divorce his wife, he would already have done so."

Bastet waved her hand in the air, changing the subject as she always did when the conversation did not suit her. "Well, will you come with me, or shall I tell my mother you refuse her orders?"

Sabinah nodded, knowing if she refused, her stepmother would merely come after her, herself. Shaking the wrinkles out of her gown, she walked toward the door. "I will come." .

There was a smirk on her stepsister's face. Bastet looked on every situation as a challenge, and she regarded this outcome as a win. "Tribune Vergilius has shown a marked interest in you for some reason, and Mother wants you to be nice to him. Only the gods know what he sees in you."

"I find him disgusting—and now that I know you were the one who betrayed Lady Larania, I . . . feel the same way about you."

"Little I care for your good opinion. But it is time you contributed to the expenses in this house. Too long have you been allowed to take advantage of my bounty. You must soon take a lover, and Tribune Vergilius wants you."

This was a new threat, and it frightened Sabinah. The thought of the tribune touching her made Sabinah cringe. "Never! Tribune Vergilius can hardly utter a word that does not praise his own magnificence."

"Half-wit! There are many women who would give anything to be with him. When he thinks no one is looking, I see him watching me," Bastet said with a jealous gleam in her eyes. "I am sure he would choose me over you, if he did not know of my fondness for Gallius."

Bastet was becoming more self-absorbed and unreasonable as the years passed. She thought every man lusted after her, and most probably did. But once men came to know the real Bastet and her demanding personality, not to mention her unrelenting temper, they soon lost interest. For reasons Sabinah could not understand, Gallius was still enchanted by Bastet, thus giving her stepsister hope he would one day ask her to be his wife.

With considerable disdain Sabinah entered the banquet chamber, glancing apathetically about her. Distaste coiled inside her at the garish display of wealth. To be sure, the Romans had been generous. The floors that had once been chipped flagstone had been resurfaced with expensive blue and white mosaic. There was always a bounty of food on the table: wild fowl seasoned with herbs, fish spiced with garlic, stuffed pigeons with their feathers still on them. There were fruit and almonds, as well as imported walnuts. Wine overflowed from jeweled goblets worthy of a queen.

All purchased with Roman gold.

High-pitched drunken voices reverberated off the vaulted ceilings, making the noise unbearable. Women, many of whom Sabinah had never seen before, were being openly fondled by some of the men. She closed her eyes when she saw one young officer shove his hand down the front of Trisella's gown. Her stepmother laughed deep in her throat, moving so he could have better access.

Sabinah was sick with disgust. She had to get out of the chamber before she became ill.

Hurrying into the garden, she took big gulps of fresh air.

But she was not alone.

A man emerged from the shadows, and Tribune Vergilius appeared at her side. "I thought I would find you here," he remarked, stepping closer to her.

Of all the men Sabinah did not want to be alone with, Vergilius topped the list. At the moment, she could only think of him as the man who had killed Lady Larania. She feared him, and that made her angry. She groped for something to say that would discourage him but not offend.

"I like this time of day the most," she said, wishing he would go away. "I like to be alone so I can meditate."

He laughed, leaning his hip against a small replica of a stone obelisk, his sharp gaze on her face. "I believe I have just been put in my place." He moved closer. "Why do you not like me?"

"I never said I did not."

"I see no warmth in those lovely eyes when you look at me. Do you fear me?"

She raised her head, meeting his gaze. "Should I?"

He laughed. "It is I who am in danger from you."

Sabinah brushed past him. "If you will excuse me, I must see about one of our mares who picked up a thorn yesterday."

"I shall accompany you."

"Please do not bother. This mare is of the Badari breed, and she's skittish around strangers."

"Run away, little Egyptian," he said, his gaze sweeping her body. "I am a patient man, when the prize is worth winning."

Filled with disgust, she hurried toward the stable, mindful of the shadows near the end of the path.

What if he followed her?

She would be alone, and no one would hear her if she needed help.

Pausing, she listened for footsteps, but all she heard was the call of a night bird, and the wind rustling through the top of a tall tree. Satisfied she was alone, Sabinah continued down the path.

When she reached the stall where the Badari horse was stabled, she laid her face against its sleek black neck, tangling her fingers in the silken mane. Julian had given this horse to Bastet. But it was Sabinah who cared for the animal. Bastet did not like horses, and she never went near the stables.

"Where is Julian?" she whispered to the horse. "Will he return—will I ever see him again?"

She remained in the stable long enough for most of the guests to leave. Of course when everyone was gone, Centurion Gallius would accompany Bastet to her bedchamber and remain for the night.

Sabinah was ashamed of her family. It made her ill just thinking about how her stepmother allowed those men to take liberties with her body where everyone could see. Her stepmother had said it was the Roman way of entertaining. If that was so, she was even more averse to the invaders. That was what they were—no matter how hard they tried, they would never win the hearts of loyal Egyptians.

When Sabinah reentered the house, she was relieved that Tribune Vergilius had left. She crossed the room and seated herself beside her stepmother, not caring to join in the conversation, but answering only when someone asked her a direct question.

If Trisella noticed Sabinah's lack of interest, she made no mention of it. But then, her stepmother was busy charming a fat Roman who could not keep his hands off her.

Sabinah shivered with revulsion. She would certainly not allow any man to take such liberties with her. She had heard rumors that some men referred to her as cold and unfeeling. Some said her heart was made of ice. What they could not know was that her heart belonged to Julian, and it always would.

When Sabinah could safely leave the chamber without drawing attention, she hurried to her bedchamber. Tonight she had been able to escape without attracting her stepmother's notice, but it would not always be so.

Closing the door behind her, she leaned against it. How much longer must she endure the humiliation of her stepmother's and stepsister's actions?

Tossing on her bed, Sabinah could not sleep. Bastet's confession that she had told the Romans where to find

Lady Larania sickened her. When the ugliness was too heavy for her to bear, her thoughts turned to Julian, and memories of him cleansed her mind so she could at last fall asleep.

🐕 CHAPTER EIGHT

The fishing village of Osage

A small crowd of villagers gathered in a group near the shore, watching the billowing sails of a huge warship ride the waves.

"Who can it be?" a woman holding a small child on her hip inquired. "It is not Roman, is it?"

"It is like the ship we often saw in these waters some years back," her husband, a ruddy-faced fisherman, stated with assurance.

A young man stepped to the front of the crowd, shading his eyes against the sun's glare, his gaze sweeping over the billowing red sails. A smile curved his lips as he recognized the symbol of a winged hawk perched atop a crown. "I have seen this ship before. Many of you must recall it as well. Lord Ramtat and his family usually sail on that ship."

All eyes turned to the young man. "He is speaking true," a young girl agreed, frowning as a vague image teased her memory.

The young man was still smiling as if he were remembering pleasant thoughts. "Lord Ramtat's sister was once kidnapped, and I helped him find her."

"I recall the incident," his mother said, smiling. "It

caused quite a stir when Lord Ramtat, himself, came to the village in search of his sister."

"I was not here then," an old fisherman said, his rheumy eyes never leaving the red sails. "What became of the sister?"

"There were vague rumors that she became queen of some country, but I cannot say for sure," the young man said. "I still have the armband she gave me. Although some have offered to buy it from me, it is my greatest treasure."

"Perchance she's returning," the old man said. "You all saw those twelve Badari warriors enter the village two days past. We thought it strange at the time. They set up camp not far from here. If you want the truth of it, they must have come to meet someone who is on that ship!"

"Look you!" the young man exclaimed. "We shall soon know who it is. They are lowering the sails."

Julian stood on the deck of the *War Bird*, his hawk, De-oro, perched on his leather glove. The bird had been trained to attack on command. Its razor-sharp talons could rip a man to shreds, but there had never been an instance when De-oro had been ordered to harm a human. At the moment the fierce predator of the sky perched passively on its master's arm.

Julian wore a simple white robe, his only adornment a gold and leather headband and matching wristbands. As he leaned against the railing in brooding silence, impatience ate away at him. He had left Egypt as a boy and was returning as a man. His father had sent him home to seek out the sheik who was making rumblings of war among their fellow tribesmen. His gaze swept across the group of people gathered near the shoreline. In the distance he could make out a reed boat that was being rowed shoreward by fishermen who kept glancing over their shoulders in fear. He had waited long to return home and to once more walk on Egyptian soil.

Apollodorus came up beside him and stood silent for a moment. Julian had been his pupil for four years; he had trained him to the best of his ability, and others had trained him as well. Prince Ashtyn, who was married to Julian's aunt, the queen of Bal Forea, had trained Julian in spear and shield, and the arts of warfare. His aunt Adhaniá, who could outshoot any man, had helped him master the bow. Apollodorus had attempted to teach him patience, but he was not at all sure how well he had succeeded with the impulsive young prince.

Apollodorus knew Julian had been burning with the need to return home. He had been instructed by the best, and he was honed and ready for what awaited him in Egypt. The Sicilian watched him with a pensive gaze, a half smile curving his mouth. His charge was aware of himself as a warrior, but not as a man who had left many brokenhearted young women behind in Bal Forea.

While Apollodorus was tall, Julian was taller. He wore his dark hair long in the manner of the Bal Foreans. His face was finely chiseled, his green eyes bright and piercing. He had his father's strength and his mother's tenacious spirit. His voice was deep and he spoke with a sonorous tone.

"Your arrival does not go unnoticed," Apollodorus observed, nodding at the people gathered onshore, their gazes sweeping over the ship.

"Even so, there will be no Romans among those citizens, and none to tell of the landing. My father trusts these villagers, and so must I."

Apollodorus knew how difficult it had been for Ramtat to let his eldest son return to Egypt without him. But it was time one of the family rejoined the Badari to settle their disputes. There was unrest among one of the tribes, and perhaps it was more widespread. One of the sheiks was attempting to force his will on others and must be brought to account.

Apollodorus nodded at the villagers. "You must trust no one. There will be those who wear the face of friendship, but beneath their smiles lurks treachery."

"That is what my mother said to me. She did not want me to return to Egypt."

"It is only natural for a mother to have concerns, and yours more than most since she knew the danger you would face."

Julian heard the anchor splash into the water, and saw the ship's crew readying the punt boats. He glanced up at the white-hot sky, feeling the sun's heat on his face.

Home.

"The *War Bird* is a swift ship," Apollodorus said, breaking into Julian's thoughts. "The rest of the world could learn from the ship builders on Bal Forea."

"Aye." Julian fell silent, watching the small punt hit the water and bob on the waves. He placed De-oro in a cage and fastened it securely. His father had assured him there would be tribesmen waiting for him at the village, and though he saw no sign of them, that did not mean they were not there.

Both he and Apollodorus climbed down the rope ladder, settling in the small boat, and immediately, strong-armed boatmen rowed them toward shore. The six Badarian warriors who had accompanied them to Bal Forea four years ago would be in the second boat.

Julian watched the shore grow ever nearer. He still saw no horses, but the Badari were masters of blending with their surroundings. They would not show themselves until they wanted to be seen.

The punt bumped against the pier, and Julian stepped ashore. The people hung back as if frightened, and he could not blame them.

Suddenly a young man about Julian's own age broke away from the crowd and knelt before him. He wore a homespun tunic, his hair clipped close to his ears. He had huge brown eyes that at the moment held a confused expression. "Be you Lord Ramtat? You have the look of him, but different."

Julian motioned for the man to rise. "I am his son, Julian. Do you know of me?"

"Aye. You are prince of the Badari," the young man said, going back down to his knees. "I feared we would never again see any member of your family alive. You are all under a death sentence."

Julian's gaze swept the crowd. "Will any of you tell the Romans of my return? My father trusts you not to. Can I trust you as well?"

A rumble went through the crowd as the men gathered about him. Some actually touched his arm, others just smiled, welcoming him home.

"No one will hear of your return from this village. We are all Egyptians, the same as you. But three weeks ago a Roman patrol came here. They are always prowling around," the young man spat.

"Do not put yourselves in danger. If you feel threatened by them, be truthful. They will not find me, and I do not want anyone to be hurt because of me."

"We will tell them nothing," the young man said. He touched Julian's arm. "Prince, may I ask a question of you?"

"Aye."

"The young woman, Lord Ramtat's sister. Is she safe? I never heard what happened to her."

Julian grinned. He had been told the story many times of how a young lad in this village had helped his aunt. "By chance are you the one to whom my aunt gave her armband?"

"Aye. That would be me."

"Then know this—my aunt told me how you aided her escape when she was in deep danger."

"Is she . . . we heard she was a great lady . . . is that so?"

"She is a queen. But I dare not tell you the country, lest the Romans decide to press you for information. You cannot tell what you do not know."

"Let those swine come," the young man said, his mouth twisted in anger. "I hope to see the day they are driven out of Egypt."

The sudden sound of pounding horse hooves caught Julian's attention, and the crowd parted as wild Badarian tribesmen rode into the village. Julian threw off his white robe to reveal a short black kilt embellished with cloth of gold. His chest was bare but for the gold and jeweled collar that proclaimed him prince of the Badari.

Julian watched the fierce warriors dismount and walk toward him, recognizing the man in the lead as his father's general, Heikki. When they reached Julian, the Badari bowed their heads in respect.

Heikki was the first to speak. "Welcome home, my prince." His dark gaze moved to the Sicilian. "And you, honored friend, Apollodorus, welcome back to Egypt." The dark gaze settled on Julian. "You are now a man, and have much the same look as your honored father."

"He sends you his greetings."

Heikki smiled. "How fares Lady Adhaniá?"

Julian returned his smile. Heikki was a legendary warrior who was held in high esteem by the Badari. "She thinks of you with affection. When she heard I would be seeing you, she asked to be remembered to you." Julian's smile deepened. "You are part of the legend that surrounds my aunt's winning of the Golden Arrow."

Heikki grinned. "She defied all reason. And still remains undefeated."

By now the other Badari from the ship had arrived and immediately greeted old friends while horses were led forward to accommodate them all.

Heikki frowned. "I had word from your father that you are to act in his place. There is much trouble brewing and a strong hand is needed to bring peace to the Badari. I am glad you have returned."

Although he and Heikki had been speaking in Badari, Julian was sure some of the villagers understood them. "Let us leave here so these good people can go on with their daily lives," he said. "Later you can tell me the details."

The villagers had been watching with awe. They stood back respectfully as the tribesmen rode away, leaving only dust behind.

By the time they reached the desert, Julian felt exhilarated. While he had been on Bal Forea, he had known season changes and he had seen snow. During blizzards, he had been as restless as a caged lion. Now he smelled the sweet scent of the desert, and it was like a tonic to him.

He was home.

Julian straightened his shoulders and felt the power of his black stallion's long gait as they moved swiftly across the desert. They rode until late afternoon, where they came upon an encampment that had already been erected. As Julian dismounted, the Badari who had remained in the camp greeted him with enthusiasm and respect, bowing their heads.

Julian was not accustomed to such deference from the Badari, because that honor had always gone to his father. It troubled him. To have something to do with his hands, he reached for the cage and released De-oro, watching the bird take to the sky and ride the wind.

Apollodorus sensed Julian's unease. "Do not let them see your discomfort," he said in a low voice so only Julian could hear. "They are giving you the respect that is your inherited right."

Julian made no reply but went to the tent he was to occupy. Although the structure was small, it was made of dyed red goatskin, embroidered with gold threads. On entering, he saw the tribesmen had taken great pains to ensure his comfort. A tightly woven blue and red rug had been placed on the ground, and the walls of the tent were decorated with majestic hangings. One, which he remembered from his father's tent, was a woven scene of men hunting in golden chariots.

Julian removed his ornate kilt and unhooked the jeweled collar, dropping them on a cushion. When he was dressed in a plain white kilt, he felt more like himself. For a moment he paced the tent restlessly, his mind troubled. Needing to get away so he could think, Julian

left the tent and mounted his horse, riding to a distant
sand dune.

Dismounting, Julian stood silently beside his prancing
Badarian stallion. He watched the way the wind whipped
the sand into swirling patterns that resembled waves
upon the sea. The desert was in his blood; some age-old
instinct called to him. He looked down at the oasis where
they were camped, watching the date palms weave with
the motion of the wind. He then turned his gaze to the
wide arid expanse of the desert, drinking in the sights he
had missed since leaving Egypt.

The untrained eye might not see it, but the desert
pulsed with life. He saw a rabbit dig into the sand and
listened to the far-off call of a jackal. The air was like
perfume to him, and the sounds and sights were remi-
niscent of his childhood.

He knew Apollodorus had followed and now stood
behind him, although there had been no sound to give
the Sicilian away. "The sand whispers to me, Apollodorus." Julian scooped up a handful and allowed it to
trickle through his fingers. "It has the warmth of life."

"This is home to you."

Julian gazed in the distance over the flatland where
sprigs of dry grass managed to push through the hardened ground. Without the dunes as an obstruction, night
fell hard, and they were suddenly engulfed in darkness.
"It is true. The desert is in my blood."

Julian felt renewed stirrings of unease. Until now he
had pushed his troubled thoughts to the back of his
mind. His father had trusted him with this mission, and
Julian feared he was not capable of honoring that trust.
"Many times I watched my father make wise decisions,
punishing the guilty, and on occasion when the crime

required it, condemning the guilty to death. How can I step into the place of a man such as he?"

"You will know what to do when the time is right."

"Will the tribesmen accept my authority?"

"Without question."

"All those men in camp are much older than I, Apollodorus. Why should they trust my judgment?"

"Because you are their prince. For more years than any of us can count, the Badari have placed their trust in your family to guide them. It is no different with you. I am sure your father must have felt much the same as you are feeling when he replaced his grandfather."

"If the Romans should come at us in force, do I ask my people to die for me?"

"You will not have to ask."

Julian felt the wind touch his cheek. A cry came from the air, and he held out his gloved hand for De-oro to land. The hawk did not object when Julian slipped the hood onto its noble head.

"Your mother is the best animal trainer I have ever known, and I have known many. That bird would give its life to protect you."

"Aye. She would."

"And so, too, would the Badari."

Julian gazed out into the desert for a long moment. Then he turned and smiled at the Sicilian. "Have I ever told you what your friendship means to me?"

"Among friends, such things do not have to be said. It was because of you and your family that I found the courage to live when I wanted to die."

Julian glanced at him. "I have known of your pain. You loved the queen."

"We all loved her."

"But you loved her as a man."

Apollodorus met Julian's gaze. "If I did, she never knew it."

"And you never found a woman who could replace her."

"How can any woman compare with a goddess? My queen never looked at me in that way, and I could not give my heart to another."

"Still, you have known great love. And perhaps my aunt knew how you felt about her. Do not forget she always kept you near."

"I never forget that."

Suddenly Julian thought of brown eyes in a face of such sweetness and innocence, it cut him to the quick. His "Little Sunshine." She would be a woman now, probably married. "Let us seek our blankets. We must be off early."

"Do we ride for the encampment in the morning?"

"It is important that I first go to Alexandria. My mother has not heard from Uriah in many months, and she is worried about him. After I have seen that he is safe, I will settle this feud among the Badari."

"I am told the last messages your mother received from Uriah were vague, and he rambled without making sense."

Julian frowned. "It is painful to think something might have happened to the man who was my teacher."

"There is danger in entering Alexandria."

Julian turned away and mounted his horse. "We have faced danger together many times, Apollodorus. Now I must speak to Heikki."

The Badari general was waiting beside a campfire. His dark gaze followed Julian when he seated himself nearby.

"It seems right to have you home, my prince."

"It feels right that I should be here," Julian replied. "Now, tell me about the trouble."

Heikki stared into the fire. "I wish I could tell you there is nothing to worry about, but I fear if something is not done soon, the Badari will be split apart and scattered asunder."

Julian leaned forward. "Then this is worse than we thought. Do you know who the troublemaker is?"

"Sheik Moussimi. He has made no secret that he wants to stand in your father's place. He is doing everything he can to discredit Lord Ramtat and makes promises of wealth and glory to those who will follow him."

"I remember him," Julian said, knowing when a man like Heikki was worried, there was real trouble. "What else can you tell me?"

"Nothing more. But he must be stopped."

"Aye. He must. Send out riders to locate him. Tell them I can be found at my mother's villa in Lower Egypt."

The general frowned. "I fear for the future of the Badari."

Julian stood. "I will do what I can to stop this sheik."

Heikki smiled. "We trust you, as we would your father."

Nothing the fierce general could have said would have pleased Julian more. But it also troubled him. He was not his father.

Julian decided to spend his first night in Egypt sleeping in the open. He placed his sleeping mat beneath the stars. Just as he was drifting off to sleep, he felt the desert wind on his face, and he slept peacefully.

CHAPTER NINE

Short of stature, Centurion Gallius wore his black curly hair clipped short. His eyes were a deep brown, and if Sabinah did not have such a dislike for Romans, she might have thought him handsome enough. Of late, she noticed the man had begun paying her marked attention, and Bastet had noticed it as well. Since Bastet was possessive of the centurion, considering him her future husband, she was in a rage.

The night was cool, after an early evening rain. Sabinah had once again been ordered to attend one of her stepmother's banquets. She had tried to circulate through the chamber, smiling, but not stopping long enough to talk to anyone in particular. She soon realized her mistake because Centurion Gallius was moving in her direction and directing his footsteps so he would intercept her. She hurried forward, but he walked faster as well. Finding an empty space on one of the sofas, she quickly settled onto it, supposing since there were people on both sides of her, he would have no place to sit.

She was wrong. He snapped his fingers, and the man to Sabinah's right stood, hurrying away.

"If I judged by your actions, I would think you were trying to avoid me," he said, smiling.

To Sabinah's way of thinking, the man overrated his own charm. "I always try to make my actions clear," she replied, knowing she was trapped. It mattered not how often she rebuffed Gallius, he would not leave her alone. Annoyed, she turned her back on him, pretending to inspect the other guests.

"There is not a woman in this room who can match you in beauty," he said in a voice that was meant to be seductive. "Everyone agrees you outshine Bastet."

"Have you dared say this to her?" Sabinah asked coldly, turning to him. "Everyone knows my stepsister is the beauty of the family."

He laughed. "That must be a myth put about by Bastet, herself. You are by far the more fair."

He reached out to touch her hair, but she moved out of his reach. "I do not like being touched unless I invite it."

Undaunted, Gallius merely smiled. "What is your desire? Speak of it, and it is yours."

"It is my desire that you leave me alone."

"I cannot do that, my lovely one."

A shadow fell between them, and Gallius scrambled to his feet as Tribune Vergilius appeared. "Did you not hear the lady? She would like you gone," Vergilius stated in a commanding voice.

"Aye, Tribune. I was but admiring this charming lady," the centurion said, scurrying away.

"That is done. He will trouble you no further." Vergilius nodded at the cushion his subordinate had just vacated. "May I join you?"

Sabinah glanced into cold, lusterless eyes. She despised

Tribune Vergilius, and it was difficult to be civil to him. "I just remembered, I must speak to my stepmother about something."

She would have risen, but he dropped down beside her and gripped her wrist. "Remain with me for a little while. I promise not to bore you."

She recoiled from his touch and shoved his hand away. "I do not know you, Tribune."

"I can remedy that." He reached for a flagon of wine from a nearby table, and instead of sipping the honeyed nectar, he downed it with a gulp, wiping the excess from his mouth onto the back of his hand. Then he smiled as if secretly amused. "I do not know why I keep coming back to you. You are an enigma. You have the power of all beautiful women to draw attention to yourself, but you do not enjoy it."

She said nothing.

He cocked his head, catching her glance. "You are as skittish as a newly born colt. But I am dedicated to plowing through your defenses."

Vergilius was a handsome man, tall and broad shouldered, dark haired with luminous brown eyes. But nothing he could ever say would make Sabinah forget what he had done to Lady Larania. He still lived in her home and enjoyed her riches, which infuriated Sabinah. "I hope you do not expect me to respond to such a statement. I would not know how."

"What do you respond to?" Vergilius asked in frustration. "It cannot have escaped your notice that I admire you. Yet you treat me as if I am your enemy."

She turned her cool gaze on him, not caring if she made him angry. "My most fervent wish is to see all Romans gone from Egypt."

Vergilius stiffened, his gaze hard. "Attend to what I say, for your life may depend upon it. Treasonous words are not tolerated. If the wrong person heard you speak thus, you would not be beyond the reach of Roman law," he said bitingly.

She shrugged. "Before you Romans arrived, we in Egypt were allowed to speak our minds—now you tell me it is treasonous to do so. How can you possibly think you can win my approval by threatening me?"

He became annoyed. "I did not mean for you to take my words as a threat. I was merely warning you of the danger if someone other than myself had heard you. As for me, I want to know you better." He nodded toward Bastet as she flirted with one of his officers. "Your sister does not share your views on my countrymen."

"My *stepsister* has never been accused of being choosy about whom she associates with."

His dark brows met across his nose in a scowl. "Your own stepmother welcomes us into your home, but you are not so congenial. Matter of fact, I would call you hostile."

"My stepmother does not share my views and does not look upon Romans as invaders."

It startled Sabinah when Vergilius laughed.

"I am glad I amuse you, Roman."

"I cannot say why, but I find you delightful. No one has dared speak so outrageously to me, certainly not your stepsister."

"If you think I am anything like Bastet, you are mistaken. You would do well to seek other company."

Vergilius wondered why he was so intrigued by Sabinah, whose cold beauty was talked about among his fellows. He had tried every way he could think of to win her approval, but she brushed him off as if he were a pesky gnat.

His gaze moved over honey-colored skin that he so longed to touch. The torchlight lent her red hair a luster that made it shimmer as if it were on fire. When he glanced into her huge brown eyes, he felt that he was being submerged in their depths. A flirtatious curl rested against her cheek, and he wanted to press his lips against it.

Vergilius felt awkward with her, and he had never felt that way with a woman before. "I cannot seem to resist you," he said with sincerity.

Sabinah was made uncomfortable by his excessive flattery and sought to turn the conversation to other matters. "Why do you attend my stepmother's banquets?"

"We Romans find few families here in Egypt who open their homes to us as readily as your family has. I crave the company of an intelligent woman. Imagine how lonely it is for me, being unable to interact with those of my own class."

"Those who curry favor with Romans are hated and despised. My family is shunned for our association with your kind. And as for your class"—she tilted her chin upward, staring into his eyes—"I heard you were a common soldier before you became a captain and then a tribune." She blinked her eyes. "Did I hear wrong?"

His face actually reddened. "Even so, I am a tribune, and a man of wealth, and therefore worthy of respect."

"I fear, Tribune Vergilius, I am not worthy of you. Is it not true that you Romans believe all other peoples are barbarians? My poor stepsister does not understand why she cannot marry Centurion Gallius, although he has promised he would take her as his wife. She ignores the fact that it is illegal for a Roman citizen to marry a foreigner, and that our own queen's marriage to Lord Antony was not recognized in Rome."

Vergilius suddenly relaxed. "If that is all that troubles you, put your mind at rest. Egyptians are looked upon as a worthy race. And as for a dispensation, it is easy to obtain one from the Senate."

"So Bastet has nothing to worry about?"

"I was not speaking of her."

"But I was asking for her. It is my stepsister who yearns to live in Rome, not I."

"Augustus Caesar is now pharaoh of Egypt, so the laws have changed concerning marriage between Egyptians and Romans."

"Octavian proclaimed himself pharaoh, and the Senate has made him your emperor in Rome—he may call himself Caesar, but he is a mere shadow of the great Julius Caesar, who was loved by Egypt."

Vergilius's dark brows shot together, and his face became blotched with anger, his gaze boring into her. "Do not push too far, little beauty. If I wanted you, I could have you now. Remember that I choose to woo you as a gallant, but have you, I will."

Sabinah trembled with fear. She had no one to protect her against this man. "I love another, and I have sworn I will keep him in my heart until I draw my last breath."

The air was suddenly thick with malice, and it was directed at her. "Bastet has mentioned your infatuation with Julian Tausrat, who is high on Augustus's wanted list. You throw your heart away on a dead man."

She wondered how Bastet had dared speak of Julian to the man who had slain his grandmother. She rose to her feet in a flurry of silk. "Please excuse me."

Her stepmother's voice sounded shrilly behind her, and Sabinah closed her eyes in defeat. "I was watching across the room, and I see the two of you are getting along nicely."

"Indeed we are," Vergilius remarked, casting Sabinah a self-satisfied glance. "I was just about to ask your daughter to show me your stables. I have heard you have a Badari mare, and I have long wished to see one of the legendary breed."

Sabinah knew she was trapped, but still she attempted to wriggle free. "Allow Bastet to show you; the mare belongs to her."

His eyes suddenly turned cold and threatening. "I would like *you* to show me the horse. I understand Badari horses are bred by the Tausrat family." The tribune offered his arm to Sabinah. "Walk with me, and I shall tell you what I have heard of this Julian Tausrat."

Sabinah clamped her lips together, moving forward, but still refusing to place her hand on his arm. "Hurry along, then, Tribune. Let us get this done."

Sabinah could not see her stepmother's expression, but knew she would be frowning. Later Sabinah would be forced to listen to Trisella berate her for being rude to such an important Roman.

She walked fast, so Vergilius was forced to take long steps to keep up with her. When they reached the stable, a lone lantern cast shadows on the seven stalls. Only three of them were occupied, and Sabinah led Vergilius to the third. "As you see, the animal is an unusual beauty. In truth, Bastet does not ride, so I exercise the mare whenever I am able."

He was not looking at the horse but staring at her. "I

wish to know you better, even if your tongue is as sharp as the tooth of an asp."

Sabinah gripped the stall door, trying to contain her fear.

Reaching forward, the tribune gripped her chin, turning her face toward the lantern. "Are you really unaware of the effect you have on a man? By the gods, I have never seen a woman who suited me more than you. Your daring is much like my own."

She pulled away from him. "You have seen the horse. Let us return to the house."

He reached for her arm. "Wait. Linger a moment longer. I would like to talk to you."

"Then speak quickly."

He lowered his gaze to her lips and whispered near her ear, "I have lost my heart to you."

She took a stumbling step backward. "I . . . you what!"

He shook his dark head. "I know it makes no sense to you, because it makes no sense to me. With your first rebuff, I should have looked elsewhere. But once I looked into those eyes, I was lost."

Fear mingled with revulsion inside her. "I will not listen to this."

"Wait! Hear me out. I have just received a promotion. I am master of all Roman troops in Egypt. I am an important man."

"Congratulations." Her voice was flat, her gaze riveting.

"Think about it—I can do much to help your family." He looked into her eyes. "I will have no trouble receiving a dispensation from the Senate to marry whom I choose." Vergilius looked uncomfortable and glanced away as he asked, "I ask you to take me as husband."

Anger pushed fear to the back of her mind. "Are you crazed! We do not know each other well enough to wed."

"I will give you time to know me."

"I should say I am flattered by your proposal, but I am not. I could never marry a Roman." She backed farther toward the door, knowing her stepmother would force her to marry this man if she found out he had asked her. "Please take this as my last word—I do not even like you."

Fury exploded in Vergilius's brain, and he moved forward, towering over her. "You reject me because of that desert prince. Does he milk goats and wear coarse wool robes? Can he keep you in silks and adorn you with gold as you deserve?"

"I care neither for silk nor gold."

He gripped her arms and brought her closer to him. "I will have you one way or another. It is up to you to choose the circumstances."

She was oblivious to the danger of insulting him. "I shall never submit to you!"

His fingers bit into her arms painfully, and she would have called for help, but his mouth ground against hers, and she could not breathe.

Sabinah was reminded that the hands that now touched her were the same hands that had tortured Lady Larania. She tore her mouth from his. "Do not ever try that again!"

"Oh, I think I will. Who is going to stop me—your stepmother? We both know she would give you to me, even without marriage."

Struggling, Sabinah tried to free herself, but his grip only tightened. She could hear his ragged breathing and feared what he might do. Then she realized she was exciting his passion when she fought him, so she went limp in his arms, demonstrating she felt nothing for him.

He shoved her backward, causing her to slam into a stall gate and hit her shoulder. Pain shot through her arm, but she would not give him the satisfaction of knowing he had hurt her.

"You have no reason to think so highly of yourself. Your family is a joke in the barracks. Everyone laughs at Bastet most of all. Did you know most of my officers have already had her? And the others are making wagers as to which one will be the first with you."

"You dare say this to me?"

"The wager I put forth was that no one would have you, save myself."

She rubbed her bruised arm. "You overrate your charms."

"What if I told you we are close to discovering where your Lord Julian is hiding?"

Her head jerked up, and she stared at the smug look on Vergilius's face. Hot fury coursed through her, and her voice was frosty when she spoke. "I would not believe you. If you knew where he was, he would already be your prisoner."

"I tell you this for the truth." His tone was harsh. "A Persian traitor saw Julian Tausrat outside a fishing village. And I have heard rumors he was seen here in Alexandria as well. I will catch your desert dweller and when I do, he will die, along with the rest of his family."

Sabinah was terrified for Julian. "Knowing the danger, I do not think any of the family would ever return to Alexandria."

White lipped, Vergilius brushed past her and waited for her outside the stable. "If it pleases you to think so.

But know this—before long you will come begging to me for his life. Let us see at that time if you are more . . . shall we say, agreeable."

She watched him walk toward the house, feeling sick inside. What if he was telling the truth?

Could Julian possibly have come to Alexandria, knowing the danger he would be in?

Aye, he would. He had done it before.

Sabinah wrapped her arms about herself to stop her body from trembling. She had to find a way to warn him.

But how?

She remembered an occasion that had occurred many years ago when her father had taken her to visit a man who had been tutor to the Tausrat children. What was the man's name?

Uriah, the Jew!

Sabinah frowned. It had been so long ago, and she had been just a child. Could she still find the small villa where he lived?

She recalled they had turned left from the market-place. But there were so many roads that twisted and turned in every direction. Would she even recognize the house if she saw it? She remembered the place had a great arched gateway.

Perhaps if she walked the street, she would find the right villa. For all she knew, Uriah was dead—he had been an old man when her father had known him. He was the only clue she had to follow.

Sabinah hurried toward the house, reaching the door-way just as a raw wind struck, making her heart tingle with deep foreboding. She would be up before daylight in the morning and commence her search.

When she reached her chamber, Isadad yawned and

rose from the stool where she had been waiting. "Are you ready to dress for bed, little mistress?"

"Aye. But lay out a woolen gown and cloak for me to wear tomorrow."

Isadad looked taken aback. "Just where would you wear such a garment?" she inquired quickly.

"It is none of your affair." Fear for Julian made Sabinah's voice sharp. "Just do as you are told."

"Have you lost your mind?" Isadad exclaimed with the assurance of a well-loved servant who was accustomed to speaking freely with her young mistress.

"Someone I know is in trouble, and I must help him if I can."

"But—"

"I am determined. What you must do is this: if my stepmother should inquire about my whereabouts, you must tell her I have gone to the marketplace for some ribbon."

Isadad considered her briefly before she said with feeling, "Alone!"

Sabinah raised her chin, her eyes holding a stubborn look. "Alone."

The servant moved about the chamber, tidying and dusting as she always did when she was upset. "This has something to do with Lord Julian, does it not?" Isadad asked with sudden understanding.

"I do not know if he is in Alexandria, and if he is, I do not know if I can find him. He is in danger, and I have to warn him."

Isadad nodded. "Then I shall help you."

"Pray to the gods that I find him tomorrow."

"You must be careful. When I passed the main chamber earlier, I saw that tribune paying you marked attention."

"He does frighten me, Isadad," Sabinah admitted.

"That Roman desires you, and he is a ruthless man. Have a care for your safety when he is near."

"I will make certain I am never again alone with him," Sabinah said, her voice tinged with fear. "If there is a chance Julian has returned to Alexandria, Tribune Vergilius will be watching for him."

🦅 CHAPTER TEN

Julian glanced about to see if anyone was watching before he pushed aside the overgrown acacia bush that had been allowed to grow in wild profusion to hide the secret back gate to the villa. The splintery branches brushed his skin as he moved them aside to reveal the gate, which had almost rusted shut with time. He pushed against it with his shoulder, and it creaked opened a little at a time.

Finally he stood at the back of Uriah's garden, smiling faintly as warm memories reminded him of his youth. It was here his mind had been fed with knowledge and his thoughts challenged by his tutor. Julian breathed in the perfume of the garden. He knew every inch of the grounds and all the best hiding places to escape his nurse, Minuhe.

The house had actually been left to his mother by her adopted father, and she had deeded the property to Uriah for his lifetime. Julian knew he would be safe here since few people knew of Uriah's connection with the family, and those who did would never tell.

He moved through the garden, aware of exactly where to find his old tutor. In the evenings, Uriah usually wrote in the garden.

As Julian spotted Uriah, sure enough, the old man was writing in his ledger. Removing his headdress, he sat down beside his former tutor. "I forgot how pleasant it is here in the evenings."

Uriah did not take his gaze off his writing as he bobbed his head in agreement. "Some would say that is the way of it." Then he glanced up, his expression perplexed. "Do I know you?"

"Uriah, dear friend, it is I, Julian."

"Nay, nay. Julian is a young boy—you are a man."

"It is I, Uriah."

The old man studied him closely; then a smile brightened his face. "It is you! Lad, how long it has been since these old eyes have beheld your face? Where is your mother?"

"She could not come, Uriah. But she sent me. Has Apollodorus arrived?"

Uriah looked confused. "I do not quite know of whom you speak. And who are you?"

Julian felt heartsick. Sadly, he realized Uriah was growing forgetful. One moment he was lucid, and the next it was as if his mind clouded. There had been a time when Uriah had debated with the queen's most brilliant scholars. He could speak nine languages and write and converse in all of them. "Apollodorus was Queen Cleopatra's adviser. He was to meet me here," Julian explained.

Uriah shook his head. "You must not speak of the queen—she is dead, you know." He glanced down at his ledger. "Very bad, very bad."

"Uriah, I am here to help you, old friend."

Uriah smiled. "That is worth knowing. But who are you? I do not usually converse with strangers."

"I am not a stranger. I was once your student. You taught my mother and my brother and sister as well. Do you recall Lady Danaë? She is my mother."

It was as if a veil had lifted from Uriah's eyes. "My sweet Danaë. Why does she no longer come to see me?"

"My mother had to leave Egypt. Do you not remember?"

Uriah nodded sadly. "Pray the gods she will return so I can see her before I die. Did you know I was once a slave, and your mother gave me my freedom, and also this house and garden?"

"I did know."

In that moment Apollodorus appeared, as noiseless as usual. He nodded to Uriah and spoke quickly to Julian. "There is an increased number of Roman troops in the city. A woman at the marketplace told me they were looking for a desert prince. A garlic seller said much the same. It is not safe for you to remain in Alexandria longer than necessary."

"No one knows our connection with this house, or they would already have been here. I must remain long enough to discover who betrayed my grandmother to the Romans. I need one more day."

Uriah closed his ledger, shaking his white head. "Lady Larania was betrayed by one of her own people, an Egyptian." He frowned as if he was trying to remember. "I heard a rumor in the marketplace. I would know the name if I heard it again, but at the moment it escapes me." He grabbed his head and rocked back and forth. "I cannot remember important details anymore."

Julian patted the old man's hand as his sad gaze met Apollodorus's. "Rest easy, my friend. What has escaped your memory is of little matter. I shall discover who is responsible for my grandmother's death."

Uriah stood, looking one way and then the other. "There was something I must do, but I cannot remember what it is."

"You were going to lie down and rest," Julian told him. He took the frail hand in his and led the old man toward the house. "Come, I will take you to your bed-chamber."

After Julian had seen Uriah settled, he took one of the old man's robes from a peg and rejoined Apollodorus in the garden. "It is sad to see such a great mind waste away. I am fond of that old man."

"He is extremely old, Julian. By your mother's calculation he has seen over ninety summers."

"He knows who betrayed my grandmother. He may be able to help if he does remember."

Apollodorus frowned as he stared toward the house. "Let it be. He is frail, and it troubles him that he cannot grasp the smallest bit of information. There are other methods we can use to find out what we need to know."

"It will not be wise for us to be seen together. There are still those who will recognize you, Apollodorus. Since I was but a lad when I left Egypt, no one is likely to know me, especially if I wear this robe and a head cover. We should go separate ways tomorrow. If you will continue to ask questions in the marketplace, I will ride toward my grandmother's villa."

Apollodorus looked doubtful. "Your father was well known by many. Since you look like him, make sure to cover your face."

Julian picked up his headdress and draped it about his head, then straightened the striped robe he had borrowed from Uriah. "Do you think I can pass for a Jewish scholar?"

The Sicilian glanced into green eyes and shook his head. "Keep your face in shadow. You look like exactly what you are, a man of great importance attempting to hide behind a disguise."

CHAPTER ELEVEN

The sun had not yet touched the eastern sky as Sabinah made her way down the darkened streets toward the marketplace. A sudden gust of wind tore her hood back, and she gripped it, pulling it into place, not wanting to be recognized by any of the vendors who were arriving early to set up their wares.

Sabinah turned down a narrow alley that opened up to the marketplace. Torches burned from some of the stalls. Frowning, she caught the scent of rotten fish, the smell lingering from the day before. Hurrying forward, she passed a stall where the aroma of garlic clung to the air. To her right a man was plucking chickens, and up ahead a weaver was setting up her loom.

She paused for a moment in confusion; eight roadways led away from the marketplace. Turning around in a circle, she realized it would be only by chance if she was able to locate the right one.

With firm determination she made her way to the center of the marketplace and stood beside the public fountain. Her gaze swept across rooftops and down alleyways. When she sighted the goldsmith shop that had once belonged to her father, she felt a stab of sadness. If he were alive, her father could take her to Uriah. Shaking off her sorrow, she concentrated on everything she saw, hoping something would stir a memory.

The troubling aspect was how much the marketplace had changed over time. She closed her eyes, recalling that when she and her father had left his shop, they had turned to the right, but was it the first or second turn they had come to? Or for that matter, it could have been across the courtyard. When Sabinah had accompanied her father, she had been happy to be in his company and had paid little attention to anything else.

By the time she had circled the marketplace, the sun had washed the streets with a golden glow. Confused as to which way to take, Sabinah decided she would try every road and alleyway, retracing her steps if need be until she found Uriah's villa.

Several times she found her way to twisting streets that took her in the wrong direction. When the sun was high in the sky, she felt pangs of hunger, and her throat was dry. She should have eaten before she left home. But she had not thought past her need to find Uriah.

At one point Sabinah stopped to work a stone out of her sandal, wishing she had worn her soft leather boots. By the time the afternoon sun beat down on her, she was weary and discouraged. Each road she had taken had been wrong.

She leaned against a stone wall with jagged cracks all the way to the top of the structure. Dropping her face into her hands, she fought against despair. For all she knew the villa could have been torn down, or Uriah, the Jew, could be dead. She was not sure of anything. Raising her head, she glanced down the twisted street, about to turn back, when her eyes widened and her heart surged with hope.

An arched gateway.

She had found it!

With a new burst of energy, Sabinah ran toward the gate. Stopping to catch her breath, she knocked as loudly as she could.

A small opening slid apart, and a woman poked her head out and studied Sabinah with suspicion. "What can I do for you?" she asked in a belligerent tone.

"Is this the home of Uriah, the Jew?"

When the woman answered, her tone was suspicious, guarded. "What if it is? Who are you, and what do you want?"

"I must see him. It is most urgent."

"The master sees no one these days. Go along with you." The small opening closed.

In desperation Sabinah pounded on the gate with her fists. "You have to let me in. It is imperative that I speak to your master. Let me in!"

The huge gate opened a crack. "Stop making such a fuss," the woman scolded. "Do you want to call the attention of the whole of Alexandria?"

Sabinah pushed her hood back enough so the woman could see her determined expression. "I refuse to leave until I have seen Uriah," she said with feeling. "Tell him that for me."

"What is your name?" the woman asked in a disgruntled voice.

"Just say I am a friend of a friend."

The woman looked as if she might refuse but seemed to have second thoughts. "Remain where you are," she said curtly, slamming the gate shut and sliding the bolt into place.

Julian stood in the doorway watching a high breeze sway the top of the pomegranate trees. De-oro took to the sky, and his gaze moved to trace the bird's winged flight. The answers he'd sought here in Alexandria had eluded him, and he would soon need to leave for the desert. His attention became focused on Uriah's housekeeper as she hurried toward him.

"My prince, there is a woman at the gate, and she will not go away. She insists on seeing the master."

"Do you know her?"

"Nay, lord." She looked doubtful for a moment. "But she is a most obstinate young woman."

"Does she say why she is here?"

"Nay. She says it is important, though."

Julian looked toward the back of the garden, where Uriah was seated on his favorite bench. "Allow her entrance and take her directly to Uriah. Allow him to see what she wants, and then send her on her way."

Sabinah pulled her hood back in place and waited by the gate, determined not to leave until she had spoken to Uriah. Just when she thought she was going to need to knock on the gate again, footsteps approached. The bolt shot back, and the gate ground open.

"The master will see you. But you must not stay long. He is ill."

The housekeeper was a stout woman with broad arms and a stubborn twist to her thin lips. The hair that had escaped from her headdress was dark, her eyes equally dark. Sabinah suspected she might be of Badari descent.

Instead of leading Sabinah to the house as she expected, the woman followed a graveled walkway that curved around the corner. They walked through a lovely garden filled with flowers and trees of every description.

An elderly man was seated on a bench, his white head bent over a book that was opened on his lap, one gnarled hand resting on the curve of the bench. When he heard footsteps, he raised his head and stared at Sabinah. If this was the same man her father had brought her to see when she was a child, she did not recognize him. He appeared old and frail, his jowls deeply creased near his mouth, and blue veins showed through his tightly stretched skin. Dark eyes stared back at her with interest.

"Why would such a young woman seek an old man's company?" he asked, smiling. "And why do you wear that heavy cloak on such a hot day?"

"It is important that no one recognize me."

He frowned as if not understanding her words. "What can you want of me?"

"I know you are a friend to the Tausrat family. If Lord Julian is in Alexandria, I beseech you to warn him of danger."

The old man's eyes narrowed. "Who are you, young woman?"

"I do not know if you will remember me. I once came here with my father. He looked upon you as a friend."

"And your father is . . . ?"

"My father was Dulus of the house of Jannah. He has passed to the other world some time ago."

Uriah's features brightened. "The goldsmith."

Sabinah was relieved. "So you remember him."

The old man shot to his feet, his expression so fierce

it made Sabinah step back in fright, fearing he was going to strike her with the walking stick he was waving. "Now I remember. Your family are traitors!"

His eyes became wild, darting about with irregularity. Then he glanced back at her, shook his head, and hobbled toward the house, his robe flapping against his sticklike legs, his arms flailing, his voice choked. "I remember it all. The person who betrayed Lady Larania was the goldsmith's daughter!"

"Please, listen to me," she pleaded. "I am here to explain—"

"Explain it to me," an intense voice said from the end of the path. "I would be interested in what you have to say."

Sabinah could only see a vague outline of the man standing in the shadow of a date palm, and although the voice had become deeper, she knew him.

Julian!

☙ CHAPTER TWELVE

Overjoyed, Sabina felt her heart quickening.

She watched as Julian stepped out of the shadows and walked toward her. She felt fire in her blood and a longing so intense it shook her whole body.

Julian caught Uriah by his frail shoulders in a protective manner. "Calm yourself, dear friend. Take a deep breath and tell me what is troubling you."

Uriah was so distressed, tears dampened his eyes. "She must be the one—she is the goldsmith's daughter."

Julian nodded to the housekeeper. "See to his comfort. I shall question the woman."

Sabinah's gaze was anxiously fixed on Julian while he appraised her. She pressed her hand over her heart, which was fluttering like the beating of bird wings. She'd never thought to see him again, yet here he was, just a few steps away from her.

Tears stung the back of her eyes, and she was glad she wore the hooded cloak so he could not see. Her hands trembled so violently she clutched the edges of her cloak to steady them. He was no longer the boy who had captured her heart, but a man in height and stature.

There was a masculine beauty about him that struck her deep. He was tall and slender of waist, with wide shoulders. Black hair hung loosely about his face. His short tunic fell to his knees, and he wore high-top leather boots. Golden armbands circled his upper arms. At the moment he had a hawklike glare in his green eyes, and his mouth was compressed with anger.

Sabinah wanted to reach out to him, to feel his skin and know he was really there. Instead she planted her feet, hoping she could find her voice. "My heart is gladdened to see you, Julian."

As Julian glanced up at the cloaked figure of a woman, fury burned inside him. It had never occurred to him that someone from the Jannah family would betray his grandmother. And now they had found Uriah, and could possibly betray him. For all he knew she might already have directed the Romans to this house.

He fixed her with a level glare. "Who are you? Speak before my dagger finds your throat."

The cry of a hawk drew Sabinah's attention, and she quickly ducked as the bird dove at her, then instinctively threw her hands up, protecting her face.

"De-oro, desist!" Julian said, knowing the hawk had gone on the attack because of his angry tone. Pointing toward the mango tree, he spoke forcefully. "Go there and remain!"

The hawk dipped low, circled a few times, and landed on a swaying branch, its piercing golden eyes on its master.

Julian's attention focused on Sabinah.

"I have not betrayed you," she said, her throat tight.

"Uriah thinks you have."

"Nay. I never would. It has been a long time since last we met, Julian, and we have both changed in those years. It is I, Sabinah."

He stopped in front of her, yanking her hood back, scrutinizing her features. "You have changed."

"As have you."

"You heard Uriah's accusations?"

She lowered her head, overcome with humiliation. "I heard."

Julian reached forward and gripped her chin, lifting it upward. He stood for a long moment, studying each feature. At last his gaze rested on her red hair. "Why are you here?"

Sabinah felt shame as she reached out to him, placing her hand on his upper arm. "I came to warn you. Not knowing you would be here, I hoped Uriah could get my message to you."

His eyes never left her face. "What warning?"

"Have you heard of Tribune Vergilius?"

His gaze bored into hers. "I know of him."

"He is the man you must avoid. He is dedicated to your family's downfall."

"How would you know this?"

Now she felt real shame. "He told me."

"He murdered my grandmother and now lives in her house. I always knew I would discover who her betrayer was, but I never expected it would be you," he said bitterly.

"Julian, it was not I . . . it was Bastet!"

His hard expression did not change. "I recall the night you cried because of my grandmother's death. You say Bastet betrayed her. Yet I have only your word for that."

Sabinah shook her head, feeling bereft. If he thought she was guilty, he would never heed her warning. "It was not I, Julian."

He studied her face as if he could read the truth carved on her features. "Was it not?"

Sabinah reached out to him with a pleading hand. "My family has wronged you, and it is only right that I make amends in any way you choose. I will be your slave if you wish it, but even that will not undo the evil perpetrated by my stepsister."

"A pledge from a member of your family means nothing to me." Julian saw her flinch at his words, but he was in no mood to consider a traitor's feelings. "If you associate with Tribune Vergilius and he confides in you, I cannot believe anything you say. But you have a convincing little act."

She saw suspicion shadow his eyes. "I understand why you feel that way. Will you believe me when I say I do not associate with Romans of my own free will?"

He tilted her chin and studied every feature. "Nay. I will not. Your whole family *associates* with Romans. It is the talk of the marketplace."

"I know this, and it shames me. Those who knew and admired my father have nothing kind to say about us these days."

Julian turned her face, exploring her tilted nose, her full lips. Her skin was the color of melted honey, her eyes soft and brown. Her red hair swirled with each move she made, sweeping across her shoulders. "I have heard much said against your family."

Sabinah shook her head. "It matters but little what you think of me or my family. But you must heed this warning: Tribune Vergilius knows you are in Egypt, and he suspects you might be in Alexandria."

His gaze held hers. "You must be on friendly terms with the man."

"I despise him."

"Nothing you can say will make me trust you."

She searched her mind for something to convince him. Stepping closer to him, she whispered, "Perhaps this will help you believe me. I know Ptolemy Caesarion was not killed by the Romans. I also know the high priest of Isis took him safely out of Egypt."

Before she could blink, Julian whipped out his dagger and placed it at her throat. "What makes you say this?"

"I saw them the day they left the city."

She felt the tip of the blade at her throat and swallowed with difficulty. "I have told no one. I would never betray the rightful ruler of Egypt."

Julian stared at Sabinah as if deciding what to do with her. Shoving his dagger into the folds of his tunic, he jerked his head toward the house, indicating she should precede him. "Do not attempt to run or call out. Be advised, you could not make it to the gate before De-oro tore out your eyes."

"I have no intention of leaving until you understand the danger facing you," she whispered, crushed that he would want to hurt her. "It took more courage than you can imagine to come here today. Running is the last thing on my mind."

He gripped her arm and shoved her through the door, leading her down a long corridor. When he took her into a dimly lit room, she saw Apollodorus bending over a scroll. He glanced up and arched an inquiring eyebrow.

Julian shoved Sabinah toward the couch, where she landed facedown, then struggled to her knees. He nodded in her direction. "She knows Caesarion is alive."

Apollodorus gave Sabinah his full attention. "Who is this woman?"

"Uriah says she betrayed my grandmother to the Romans; she says she did not."

The Sicilian moved toward her and dipped down so he could look into her face. "What do you think you know about Ptolemy?"

All Sabinah could see was the size of the man's hands; they could crush the life out of a person with very little exertion. "I know he is not dead," she said, staring into eyes that promised death to her. She had never seen such eyes—they were alive with feeling, filled with danger.

"You only guess. You know nothing for certain," he said, watching her as a cobra watches a mouse.

"I saw him leave with the high priest, Kheleel. They sailed on a ship the day after Queen Cleopatra died."

Apollodorus stood, but his gaze never left hers. "Whom have you told about this?"

Shakily, she gained her feet. "By the gods, no one. You must believe me. I have told no one. Not even my maid, Isadad, whom I trust with my life—certainly not my stepmother or stepsister, whom I do not trust."

Apollodorus looked at Julian inquiringly.

"She is Sabinah, of the house of Jannah. Her stepsister is Bastet, whom you have heard me mention."

Apollodorus focused his attention on Sabinah. "There is much talk of your family throughout Alexandria, and none of it is good."

"I know," she admitted.

He looked at Julian. "We cannot allow her to leave."

Julian slowly nodded in agreement. "Have you told anyone about Uriah's house? If anyone should attempt to breach the walls, you will be the first to die."

Sabinah sighed. "No one knows where I am. My family knows neither of this house nor about Uriah."

Julian lowered his head thoughtfully. "What shall we do with her?"

Apollodorus studied her for a moment before he said, "If she was not being truthful, this place would already be surrounded by Roman troops."

"What are you suggesting?" Julian asked.

"Where better to hide from a viper than his own den? Vergilius will not think to look for you under his nose."

Sabinah shook her head, wishing she could make them understand. "You do not know him as I do. He will find you if he has to search every house in Alexandria."

Julian's mouth tightened angrily. "An impossible task, even for a Roman. And as to how well you know him," he remarked, "I have little doubt you know him intimately."

She bit down on her lower lip so hard she tasted blood, and still she could not stop shaking. "No, I—"

"Enough," Julian ordered harshly. "Until we decide what is to be done with you, remain in this room. Do not think you can sneak out. I am posting guards around the entire perimeter."

Sabinah felt a surge of sadness. Once Julian had called her "Sunshine." Now he despised her.

Grimly he turned away and motioned for Apollodorus to follow him. In the empty chamber Sabinah sat with her chin resting on her hand. She had gained nothing by trying to warn Julian. He had not believed a word she said.

What would he do to her?

He thought her guilty of the vilest crime. He would probably demand her death.

She heard the sound of shuffling feet and saw the shadow of a guard outside the arched doorway. She was a prisoner.

Burying her face in her hands, she was overcome with misery.

Julian silently listened to Heikki.

"Sheik Moussami fully expects to be the leader of the Badari. His two sons support him in this action, especially the elder. The younger one does not feel comfortable about going against your father."

"How many follow him?" Julian wanted to know.

"His own tribe, which number over three hundred. There are at least five other sheiks who have met with him, but I was unable to learn the outcome of those meetings."

"This is what I want you to do, Heikki. Send riders to those five sheikdoms and charge the leaders to meet me at my mother's villa on the lower Nile. Say that they must come at once and bring only enough guards to ensure their safety." Julian was thoughtful for a moment before he said, "Heikki, I want you to go to Sheik Moussami and inform him I request his presence."

Heikki bowed his head. "It shall be done at once."

"Heikki," Julian said, clasping his arm. "Thank you for your devoted service."

A smile curved the general's mouth. "I serve the

Tausrat family, as have my ancestors for hundreds of years."

After Heikki left, Julian walked alone in the garden, his thoughts troubled. He had set in motion a plan that would either bring Sheik Moussami into submission, or cause blood to flow.

CHAPTER THIRTEEN

Julian leaned against the trunk of a date palm and lowered his head. "I never imagined Bastet would be the one to lead the Romans to my grandmother." Lifting his head, he glanced at Uriah, who seemed more like his old self. "It is bitter to discover a woman I trusted was responsible for the death of my grandmother."

"As I recall you telling me," Apollodorus injected, "this younger sister warned you not to trust Bastet just before we left Alexandria four years ago."

Julian thought back to the incident that had occurred outside the Jannah garden wall. "Aye, she did. But that does not absolve her of blame in Grandmother's death."

"Let us go on the assumption that the young woman is telling the truth. What will you do?" Uriah asked.

Julian walked a little way down the path and then turned back. "She knows about Caesarion. Think what Octavian would do if he was privy to that information. He would bring the whole of Rome's might down on Bal Forea."

"And yet for five years Rome has not attacked Bal Forea," Apollodorus reminded him.

"Even so, I cannot release her since she knows about my cousin. She cannot be allowed to leave."

"Her family will make a search for her," Uriah said, bending his head to evade a buzzing mosquito. "So sad. She is such a pretty woman and so young."

"She will be my prisoner until I find out if she is speaking the truth. If we discover she is a spy for the Romans, we will decide what to do with her at that time."

Apollodorus studied the toe of his soft boot. "Julian, neither of us can go near the Jannah household asking questions and drawing attention to ourselves." He nodded at Uriah, who seemed to have fallen asleep. "Nor can he."

Julian agreed with a nod. "What if we send our own spy to the Jannah household?"

Apollodorus was thoughtful for a moment; then he slowly nodded. "It could work. No one gossips like servants."

Julian thought about his choices for a moment. "Rafta works in Uriah's kitchen. If we could find a way to get her into the Jannah house, perhaps she could discover the truth."

"It is no longer safe for you to remain here. We should move this young lady out of Alexandria," Apollodorus said flatly.

"To the desert?"

"Do you think that wise?"

"Since I will be going to my mother's villa, I will take her with me. I do not believe anyone in the Jannah family knows of its existence."

Apollodorus nodded his approval. "Inform Rafta what you want of her while I make ready for you to leave. You should take Uriah with you, while I remain behind to find out what I can. It would be a serious matter if the Romans found out about Ptolemy. Then, too, I want to learn what I can about Tribune Vergilius."

"I will leave before first light. Crossing the desert will be too difficult for Uriah, so we shall go by boat—let us hope our old friend Captain Narmeri is in port." Julian took in a deep breath. "You should look to your safety, Apollodorus. Come to me as soon as you can."

The Sicilian smiled to himself, wondering if Julian realized he was issuing orders like a general. He was a natural leader. Ramtat would be proud.

Sabinah had been placed in a small chamber with no windows and a guard at the door. After a while she was so weary she lay down on the narrow cot, turned to her side, and rested her cheek against her arm. What bothered her most was that Julian did not seem worried about the danger that faced him in Alexandria.

She had awakened early, and it had been a very tiring day. Her eyes drifted shut, and she knew nothing more.

It felt as if she had barely fallen asleep when a servant woke her, charging her to dress. The garments she was given to wear were the type worn by Badari women. Wrapping the *dalmatic* loosely about her body, she felt smothered, and it did not help when the same dour-faced servant who had let her through the gate instructed her to cover her face with a veil. After the woman was satisfied that Sabinah was properly garbed, she led her down a corridor and outside.

Torchlights blazed throughout the courtyard where there were three Badari mounted on huge black horses. Julian was standing near a restless black stallion, his gaze sweeping across her. He nodded with approval at her manner of dress.

There was a small litter, and she assumed it was for her. But Uriah was gently helped inside, and the curtains lowered.

"Do you ride?" Julian asked harshly.

She could have told him she had ridden the horse he had given Bastet, but she merely nodded. "May I ask where you are taking me?"

"You may ask nothing. All you need to know is you will be taken where you can cause no mischief."

"Then may I have a word with you?" She glanced at the Badari tribesmen who were to be their escorts. "I would like to speak to you in private."

Julian took her arm and led her a short distance away. She could feel the restlessness stirring within him, and the disapproval.

"What have you to say that could not wait?"

He was so tall Sabinah had to look up to see his face. "My stepmother may send out an alarm when I do not return. She will alert the Romans."

"I expect it of her."

"Allow me to send her a message that will keep her from involving the Romans. If she believes I have run away, she will not ask their help."

"Is this one of your tricks?" he asked skeptically.

"Nay. No trick. You can read what I write to make certain there is no hidden meaning."

Julian looked doubtful. But he took her arm and led her to the library Uriah used for his work. Manuscripts were stacked on the floor, and they had to thread their way through them to reach the desk that was piled high with scrolls. When Sabinah was seated on a padded stool, Julian shoved a roll of papyrus toward her.

"Make it convincing, and make it quick. I want to be out of Alexandria before sunup."

Her hand shook as she began to write.

> *Stepmother, I am leaving Alexandria, and I think you know why. Do not attempt to find me. Place no blame on Isadad. She is a true and faithful servant and knows nothing of my plans.*

Sabinah felt Julian at her shoulder. She handed him the scroll, and he quickly read it to himself. "Is your stepmother likely to believe this?"

"She knows I do not like the Romans she invites to our house. Perhaps she will believe I have run away."

He took her arm, pulling her upward to face him. "I have learned that a beautiful woman can lie."

She blinked. Did he think her beautiful? "The person I am being untruthful to is my stepmother. Would you rather I told her you are kidnapping me?"

Sabinah watched as he frowned in puzzlement.

"Why did you seek me here yesterday?"

"I knew of your link to Uriah, and I hoped he would be able to get word to you of danger. I did not expect you to be here."

The sun reflected the smoldering anger in his eyes, and Sabinah lifted her head high with no outward sign of sadness because he was suspicious of her.

Julian led her out of the room. When they reached the courtyard, he lifted her onto a horse and motioned a servant forward. Sabinah did not hear what he said to the man, but he handed him the scroll Sabinah had written to her stepmother.

Horse hooves clattered over stone, and the gate was thrown open. They rode single file through the narrow twisted streets, past an empty marketplace, toward the sea.

When they reached the shore, there were but a few dockworkers performing the task of loading cargo on ships. Julian lifted Sabinah from her horse, steering her toward a waiting boat, smaller than the Roman ships that rode at anchor.

"Captain Narmeri, old friend," Julian said, striding up the gangplank. "Thank you for waiting for us."

"The son of your gracious mother is always welcome on my humble boat," the man said with feeling.

It was still hours until sunup, but Sabinah could make out the captain's wide girth and his fierce features. A jagged scar cut deeply into the left side of his swarthy face, making her to want to shrink away from him when he offered her his hand to help her up the gangplank.

Uriah was brought onboard, appearing to take the strange occurrence with a shrug. The captain must have known him because he chatted with Uriah and saw that he was comfortably settled in his own quarters below deck. Sabinah knew the old man was ill and wondered how he would fare on the voyage.

Next the horses were led up the gangplank and secured in a roped-off area. The tribesmen made themselves comfortable near the horses, while Julian spoke with the captain. Julian looked in Sabinah's direction, nodding, so she knew he was discussing her.

She felt the salt breeze against her face and closed her eyes, remembering the time her father had taken the

family on a cruise down the Nile. It had been a wonderful adventure, but those days were gone.

Dead, like her father.

She was so deep in thought she had not heard Julian's
soft tread, and when he spoke, she jumped.

"You are to limit your movements to the bulkhead.
The *Blue Scarab* is not constructed to carry passengers;
however, Captain Narmeri has hung a mosquito net for
your comfort and a curtain you can pull down whenever you want privacy. It should not be too uncomfortable."

"I am not a spoiled Roman lady, Julian. I will do very
well."

He looked at her curiously.

The sun made its appearance as they sailed past the
causeway that led to Pharos Island, site of the Great
Lighthouse. "My mother first met my father when this
very boat stopped at that island to take him onboard."
Julian did not know why he felt compelled to tell her
something so personal. He could not be certain how
deeply she was involved with Rome.

Sabinah reached for something to say. "Your mother
was a tamer of wild beasts. There is a legend that she
once saved Queen Cleopatra's life when she put herself
between the queen and a cheetah that was about to attack."

"That is no legend—'tis fact."

"Your father was general of Queen Cleopatra's armies."

"That is a well-known fact," he said dully. "Come
with me, and I shall see you settled. You will have to
make do without a servant to attend you, but have no
fear for your safety. You will be well guarded."

She gave him a sideways glance. "Am I guarded for

my protection, or to keep me from jumping over the side of the boat to escape?"

Julian guided her to the bulkhead, glancing down at her. "Do not even contemplate escaping. Know that the water here is treacherous, and when we reach the Nile, a crocodile would have you for its meal before you could ever reach shore."

"How long will we be on this boat?"

Julian had never noticed the way the sunlight could play across a woman's hair and make it shimmer, or how soft a woman's skin looked beneath torchlight. He had never before gazed into a woman's eyes and felt that he was being pulled inside. "All depends on the wind. It will be several days at least." He frowned as a new thought hit him. "Are you likely to get seasick?"

"I have been on a voyage before and was not sick at that time."

Julian raised the mosquito net that had been hung in a wide circle, and she could see a stuffed mat and plump pillows.

"Perhaps you should lower the curtains and rest for a bit. You were yanked from your bed early."

"I am a bit weary," she admitted.

If he had thought to frighten her by whisking her out of Alexandria, he had been mistaken. Sabinah had strength and tenacity. "I will have water and food brought to you."

Sabinah ducked inside and untied the heavy cord that held the linen curtain in place, slowly lowering it so she could have privacy. Sitting down, she bowed her head in total misery. By now her stepmother had surely received her message. What must she be thinking? Trisella, at least, would be happy to be rid of her.

She could not imagine Julian doing her harm. But she reminded herself that he held her accountable for Lady Larania's death.

She closed her eyes and breathed heavily. She did not know what tomorrow would bring, but to be near Julian was all she had ever wanted. When she had been younger, she had spent a good deal of time thinking about him. But that had been the boy—this was the man.

Not once had he called her Sunshine.

ᚨ CHAPTER FOURTEEN

It was dark and drizzling, and Sabinah spent most of the day beneath her shelter. A raw wind struck at dusk, just as the *Blue Scarab* left the Mediterranean behind and made its way to the Nile River. The boat had not progressed far when night fell and the captain gave orders to tie up onshore because of the hazardous shallows that made it impossible to navigate in the darkness.

Sometime during the night the rain stopped, leaving it hot and humid. The boat rocked as the wind whipped up heavy waves. Sabinah yearned for daylight, when the boat would move to the middle of the river where it would be cooler.

Just before dawn the wind died down and she slept.

As the days passed, Sabinah was alone but for the tall silent Badari warrior who stood guard nearby. Not once had she seen him glance in her direction, but she knew he was aware of her every move.

She stared at the blue sky that seemed to have been washed by the rain. Puffy clouds gathered in the distance, and she watched as the *Blue Scarab* sailed past a small village. Dark-skinned children ran along the shore, waving and laughing. In the distance she saw a dusty road that curved through the village and over a hill. There were green fields past the papyrus reeds that grew along the bank. Off to her left Sabinah watched a whirlwind spinning until it played out, settling back into dust.

She felt Julian beside her and sensed his coldness toward her. "I have been wondering what those children are thinking as they go about their lives," she said, nodding toward the village that was quickly disappearing around a bend in the river.

Julian seemed to be studying the children, too, but said nothing.

"My father once explained to me," Sabinah continued, "no matter into which class people are born, their lives are familiar to them, and they are happy."

"What would your father have said about those who have ambitions to rise above the class they were born into?" he asked, lowering his gaze to hers.

Sabinah wondered what he meant. "I would not know about that. I have never aspired to reach higher than my birthright." That was not entirely true, she thought sadly. She had often thought how wondrous it would be if she could become Julian's wife.

"What about the Romans who frequent your home?" he asked harshly. "I am told some of them are of the nobility."

"I certainly do not aspire to be the wife of a Roman." She drew in an irritated breath. "I would consider that a step down."

"Tell me about Bastet," he said abruptly.

She blinked her eyes, staring at a hippopotamus that was swimming in the distance. "What do you want to know?"

"Tell me why she gave my grandmother up to the Romans."

Sabinah ached with shame. "She did it for the reward."

Sabinah felt him recoil.

"And you did not know what she had done that night you warned me away from your home?"

She pulled her headdress into place and shook her head. "I have already told you I did not know at that time. You can believe me or not."

"I have been pondering on a few things. You could easily have told the Romans where I would be that night I waited for Bastet, yet you did not. Why is that? Did *you* not care to collect the reward?"

Sabinah hung her head so he could not see the misery that must surely show in her eyes. "I would never do such a thing to you or your family, or anyone else for that matter. I am not like Bastet."

Julian cupped her face and raised it to him. "You never were."

The old familiar pain stabbed at her. Her mind ebbed to and fro like the water that swirled around the *Blue Scarab*: she ached for his touch, yet she knew he despised her. "We cannot all be beautiful," she said with a flare of anger.

Julian studied her intently, his gaze on a red curl that had escaped her headdress. "You have always looked younger than your years."

"A flaw, but at least that one I can overcome as I advance in age," she said in irritation.

Julian was silent for a moment. "My mother would say a woman's true beauty shines from inside: her thoughts, her manner, her goodness. Are these not more important traits than being fair of face?"

"Some would say so. I know some with outward beauty who are twisted on the inside."

Julian's thumb moved against her cheek and touched the edge of her generous mouth. "Which are you, I wonder?"

"I," she said earnestly, "am plain of face, but I would like to think I have never done harm to another. And I try never to speak an untruth, unless it is necessary—like when I sent the message to my stepmother."

"But you are untruthful about something else."

She frowned. "I do not know of what you speak."

"I think you do. You are not plain, as you are well aware."

Sabinah did not like where the conversation was going, so she changed its direction. "I have not seen Uriah on deck. How does he fare?"

There was a long pause before Julian spoke. "He is fragile. Ill. I do not know how he will tolerate the long voyage, yet I could not leave him behind."

"I am sorry if you thought you had to bring him because of me. You should have believed me when I told you no one knew I sought out Uriah."

Julian shifted his weight and moved away from her. "I want to tell you where we are going so you will know what to expect."

Sabinah gave him her full attention.

"This villa is located near the village of Akhetaten. Have you ever heard of this place?"

"Nay. I have not."

"The house and lands belonged to the man who raised

my mother, and he left them to her, as well as the villa in Alexandria where Uriah lives."

"I have heard your mother was adopted and that Ptolemy XII was her blood father."

They both were silent for a moment, thinking how the blood tie to the royal house was affecting the Taus-rat family.

"This villa is my family's largest holding, stretching through the desert to the Nile. Few people know of it because my mother turned it into a wild animal reserve, and she does not want the curious to disturb the animals."

"Is it safe to believe the Romans do not know of this place? If they did, they could very well be waiting for you when you arrive."

"If Vergilius was aware of my mother's villa, he would already have confiscated it, and we know he has not."

Sabinah considered his words, then a smile curved her mouth. "What is to be my fate—will you feed me to one of your big cats?"

Julian reached out and touched a strand of hair that had blown across her cheek, a smile touching his lips. "That would be a waste. I believe nothing as drastic as that will happen to you."

When he would have withdrawn his hand, she caught it in hers. "Please believe I would never betray you."

Julian searched her face. "There is too much at stake to take you at your word."

"I am a true and loyal Egyptian. I would never betray one of my own."

He glanced toward the sky and then back at her. "I would like to believe you, but I will need solid proof."

Her hand fell away from his, and she fought against burning tears. "When you decide, let me know. As I told you before, I went to Uriah's house to warn him you were in danger." She met his gaze. "I owe you a debt because of my family's wrongdoings. Make me your slave, I shall not complain. Do what you will with me."

For the first time she heard humor in his tone. "Shall I put you to scrubbing floors or working in the fields?"

Her gaze was earnest. "I will do either."

"Your fate has yet to be decided."

Sabinah watched as he turned away. He could not be blamed for being cautious. The Tausrat family had lived under a death sentence for years, and Octavian, or Augustus, as he liked to be known, would probably never rescind his orders. But it still hurt that Julian did not believe her.

Her gaze collided with the Badari guard's, and she saw mistrust in those dark eyes. Aching inside, she sought the refuge of her mat, pulling down the curtains so no one could see her.

After that day Julian no longer went near Sabinah. Her meals were served by a guard who kept his gaze averted. She noticed all the men on the boat treated her as if she were a leper; even the rough-looking boatmen avoided her. No one spoke to her, but once she did see the captain of the boat looking at her with something akin to sympathy.

It seemed hotter than usual as Sabinah pushed the mosquito net aside and stepped to the railing. On the land side of the boat, she watched Julian remove the hood from his hawk and launch it into the sky. The hawk circled, dipped, and disappeared from sight.

In the distance Sabinah could see the beginning of the desert. Sand swept across the barren land, and she found the sight exhilarating. She had always loved the desert—she supposed because she had always associated it with Julian and his wild tribesmen.

Sabinah leaned closer and rested her elbows on the railing. There was something magical and exciting in the way the sand swept up to enormous dunes. This land was ageless, as old as time itself. She wondered what mysteries of the desert Julian could share with her if only things were different.

Sabinah was startled when the captain yelled out an order and the sails were quickly lowered. The current took the boat closer to shore until it came to rest beside a large dock that jutted out over the water.

They had arrived at their destination.

On one side of the river lay the beckoning desert, and on the side where they were docked, fields of grain and grape vineyards stretched as far as the eye could see.

She spun around to find Julian staring at her.

"Are you ready to go ashore?"

She met his gaze. "Have I a choice?"

Julian said nothing as he took her elbow and led her forward, but Sabinah could feel the unrest in him, and wondered at the reason for it.

Glancing up, she saw the muscle tighten in his jaw when he stared down at her. For a long moment he looked into her eyes, then he abruptly turned and stared into the distance.

🦅 CHAPTER FIFTEEN

Uriah was placed on a litter and carefully carried down the gangplank by two boatmen, then gently hoisted into a cart. Next the horses were led ashore. The Badari warrior who had been guarding Sabinah motioned for her to follow him down the ramp, where Julian waited to place her on the same mare she had ridden before.

The weather was cool, so Sabinah removed her headdress, wanting to feel the wind in her hair. They rode past cattle with long hooked horns, grazing on the green grass close to the river. Goats and sheep were being shepherded toward an enclosure, to be sheared. Sabinah glanced at the workers that were toiling in the fields, noticing how they dropped what they were doing and rushed forward, welcoming Julian with enthusiasm.

Sabinah heard Julian inquire about one woman's children, and another's father. There was genuine happiness on the workers' faces, and the scene made her smile. Julian was obviously well loved by those who served him.

She glanced at him. "These people are not of your Badari tribe?"

"Nay. These people you see here were my mother's

slaves. When her adopted father passed from this world, she gave them their freedom."

"Yet they remain to work the land."

"Yes, they remain," he agreed.

By the time they reached the house, twilight had fallen, and Sabinah could just make out the sprawling limestone structure with its red-tiled roof. There were women in the outer courtyard milking goats, and children gleefully laughing while they chased squawking geese.

The door to the house slowly swung wide, and a tall woman came forth beaming with happiness. "Young master, you are here at last. How glad I am to welcome you home."

Servants bearing torches met them, bowing and smiling at Julian, proclaiming their happiness that one of the family had finally returned. While Julian greeted the house servants, the Badari rode toward the stables, except the two who assisted Uriah from the cart and escorted him into the house. Many of the servants looked at Sabinah with curious smiles.

On entering the house, she saw nothing ornamental about the entrance hall. The walls were white with painted scenes of the Nile River flanked by date palms and reed grass. There was a corridor that led off to her right where Sabinah imagined the bedchambers were located, and to her left she smelled the scent of garlic cooking, no doubt in the kitchen.

"Sabinah," Julian said, nodding at the woman who had greeted them, "this is our house mistress, Kadar, who will see to your needs." The woman was thin and tall, her dark eyes keen. Her gray hair was held away from her face by an ivory comb, her gown was of nubby brown linen. She bowed to Sabinah and then turned away, clapping her hands and sending the other servants scattering to resume their duties.

Julian took Sabinah's elbow, leading her forward. "I will show you to your chamber so I can explain some things to you." He took a lantern from a low table, and dancing circles of light reflected off the walls. They passed several doors, stopping before one at the end of the corridor.

"This is the bedchamber my mother occupied as a child. There is a small bathing chamber through the door to the left. I believe you will be comfortable here."

"Aye," she said, looking about her with interest. "I am sure I shall." The scenes on the walls in this chamber depicted wildcats: lions, leopards, and cheetahs.

Seeing where Sabinah's attention was directed, Julian said, "My mother's passion was training big cats. You will hear the cats from time to time, but have no fear. They are kept caged."

Sabinah examined the chamber with interest. The bed was covered with white linen, and there was netting that could be lowered, no doubt as protection against flying insects. An artfully carved ebony desk occupied a corner of the room, and a long bench stood beneath the window. A trunk was positioned at the end of the bed.

"This must have been a pleasant place to grow up."

"My mother was happy here. When I was a child, I begged her to teach me to train the big cats. But by then, she spent most of her time in Alexandria or with the Badari."

"This chamber does not feel as if it was ever vacated."

"Kadar had my mother's instructions to keep the house always in readiness. I did not know she continued to do so after we left Egypt." He shook his head, grasping Sabinah's shoulders and turning her to face him. "You do understand I must tell her you are a prisoner."

"I understand."

"Should you take it into your head to leave, let me warn you there is nowhere to go. You know there is no escape by the river. The desert is vast and dangerous. Even if you were to venture as far as the village of Akhetaten, no one there would give you aid."

"I had not planned to go anywhere."

"As soon as I find out how your family is taking your disappearance, I shall pass the word on to you."

"Am I to remain here the rest of my life, however long that is?"

Julian looked away from her. "Having you here is something I had not planned on; I have not thought past this day. For the moment, make yourself comfortable. Should you need anything, ask Kadar." He moved to the door. "I must see to Uriah's comfort, and there are important matters that require my attention."

"Am I free to explore the villa and surrounding lands?"

"Of course."

"Julian."

He glanced back at her.

"Can you tell me if your family is safe?"

He looked startled for a moment, then replied, "They are. But do not ask me where to find them."

"I have always suspected they went to Bal Forea."

Retracing his steps, Julian grabbed her so quickly she had no time to react. "Do not ever say that again. Not here, not anywhere!" he said angrily, giving her a shake.

Sabinah could feel the hard muscles of his body, and she raised her head to look up at him. "Had I told anyone of my suspicions, would not Bal Forea already have been attacked by Rome?"

For a long moment he stared down at her. Sabinah did not dare move when he lowered his head, his mouth touching hers. His arms tightened about her, and she felt the world tremble. Glorious feelings curled through her body, and she moved closer to him, sighing.

Julian dragged his mouth from hers and quickly shoved her away. "So you are not so different from your stepsister, no matter how you would deny the comparison."

Sabinah flinched as if he had struck her. Sadly, she watched him stalk toward the door and close it behind him. She touched her mouth and lowered her head. When it came to him, she had no resistance—perhaps he was right, and she was not so different from Bastet.

Had he wanted more than a kiss from her, she would not have denied him.

"Julian," she whispered, "you have nothing to fear from me. I would give my life to save yours."

Julian went directly to Uriah's bedchamber. The old man was asleep, so Julian watched him for a moment to make sure his breathing was even. He loved that dear old man and hoped he had not suffered from the arduous voyage.

Turning away, Julian left the chamber. Moments later he made his way to the pens where the big cats were kept. The enclosures were huge, with shade trees and man-made ponds for the cats to drink from. All the animals there were old, some perhaps even dying. But his mother had realized they would not survive in the wild because they had always been fed cooked meat and had no knowledge of how to hunt for food.

He reached through the fence and rubbed the ear of a toothless lioness. The animals were given the best of care, and would reside in the enclosure until the last one died; then the fences would be torn down.

He leaned his forehead against a wooden post. Sabinah's lips had been like a potion, enticing him to take more, and still more. On the voyage he had purposely kept his distance from her because she stirred within him feelings he did not want to awaken.

He frowned. When he had accused her of being like Bastet, it had wounded her deeply. In truth, there was an innocence about Sabinah, while Bastet's seductions had been calculated. In the past, Bastet had always found a reason for him to be alone with her. She would pull him behind a bush, sneak into a shed or a shadowy alcove. She had rubbed her body against his, making him ache for her. She had allowed him to touch her breasts, and even go lower, but when he was almost mindless with desire, she would pull away. He had been so young then, believing he had loved Bastet. Now the thought of her turned his stomach.

When he had left Egypt, Sabinah had been a mere child, and he had not been much older. Now she was so beautiful it hurt him to look at her.

Was she innocent?

Or did she only pretend to be?

His fists closed at his sides. This yearning he had for Sabinah went deeper than what he had felt for the faithless Bastet. His flesh was hot, his heart restless. Closing his eyes, he tried not to think how he wanted to bury himself in Sabinah's sweet body.

Angrily Julian shook his head. He would not give in to that temptation.

☙ CHAPTER SIXTEEN

Sabinah's thoughts always seemed darkest at night when doubts plagued her mind, stealing sleep. Restlessly turning onto her stomach, she gazed out the window, watching the moonlight and shadows in the courtyard. Her mind conjured up her stepmother, and dark thoughts beset her. What if her message had created a firestorm, and Trisella had ask Vergilius to help search for her? Sabinah had forgotten that her father's will specified that Trisella could only occupy the house as long as she cared for his daughter.

The night seemed endless, but at last her eyelids felt heavy, and she was drifting to sleep when she heard something that snapped her awake; although the stable was a good distance from the house, she recognized the sounds of mounted horsemen arriving at the villa. She tensed until she heard voices speaking in a language she did not understand, probably Badari.

When the first streaks of dawn filtered into the bedchamber, Sabinah was still awake. Wearily she yawned, stretching. Clasping her arms behind her head, she studied the room that had belonged to Lady Danaë. Was this the place where Julian's mother had dreamed of growing up and meeting a man she would love? She had married the most noble man in all Egypt when she had been about Sabinah's own age.

There was nothing in the room that reminded Sabinah of Julian's mother except the animals painted on the walls. She did see some deep scratch marks near the window, possibly made by one of the big cats Lady Danaë had trained.

There was a stirring at the door, and Sabinah sat up as a young servant entered with a tray of food. The girl was younger than Sabinah, and her long hair hung down her back to her waist. She was shy and kept her head lowered.

"Is the master at home?" Sabinah asked.

"I do not know, mistress. I work in the kitchen with my mother and have not seen him this day."

"What is your name?"

The young girl placed the tray of food across Sabinah's lap. "I am called Tanita, mistress."

"Tanita, have you always lived here?"

"Aye, mistress. As has my mother, and her mother before her."

"I have always lived in Alexandria. I should have liked to live here where people grow their own food, and there is no noise like we have in Alexandria."

"I have never been away from this villa. I would be frightened to leave my mother."

Sabinah glanced down at the creamy yellow cheese on her tray and could not resist taking a bite. It was so fresh it melted in her mouth. She took a sip of goat's milk that was thick with cream.

The young girl looked uneasy, as if she had never served food before. "Will there be anything else, mistress?"

Sabinah paused with a chunk of cheese halfway to her mouth. "I am content. Thank you."

"I am to tell you if there is anything you want, you have only to ask." Tanita moved silently about the chamber, tidying as she went.

Sabinah watched the young girl move toward the door, her bare feet making no sound. After she finished the cheese, she ate a small cluster of grapes and two figs. Content for the moment, she lay back against the plump cushion.

She did not know what she was expected to do with her time. Julian had said she could leave the house, but she was not familiar with the surroundings and hesitated to venture forth.

Throwing the coverlet aside, she swung her legs off the bed and slid her feet into her sandals. Going through an arched doorway, she found a marvelous bath. It had been too dark the night before for her to appreciate the mosaic pool. Though she was accustomed to Isadad tending to her needs, Sabinah managed very well to disrobe without her. She climbed down the three steps and went into the pool. There was a basket filled with sweet-smelling oils, and she worked them into her skin. Going underwater, she rinsed her hair.

At home, her bath was much smaller, and the pool was barely large enough to stand up in. She lounged peacefully in the sumptuousness of the aromatic water. At last, when her skin looked as wrinkled as an overripe plum, she climbed up the steps, wrapping herself in a thick linen cloth. Entering the bedchamber, Sabinah found the bed had been made, and a clean linen gown and a gold belt had been laid across the coverlet.

After dressing, she fastened the belt about her waist,

then slid her feet into her sandals. Finding an ivory comb, she worked the snarls out of her hair, then walked to the window and gazed out into the small courtyard.

Turning away, Sabinah paced the room and went back to the window, wondering again how she was going to pass her time. She was accustomed to being active and did not take well to idleness.

Later in the afternoon she heard the sound of more riders approaching, and after that there was a continuous stream of arrivals.

Curious, she wondered what it could all mean.

When the tribal leaders and their entourages arrived, Julian had them directed to a camp he had set up at Twelve Palm Oasis, which was but a short ride from the villa. For the moment he was unable to discern friend from foe. His father had taught him that dissension was like a canker sore, and if allowed to fester, it would affect the whole Badari people. There had been peace and prosperity among the tribes for generations, but if war erupted, it would tear them apart.

So far only four of the six sheiks Julian had sent for had arrived—Sheik Moussimi was not among them. Julian had not expected him to be, but he did expect him to have a spy among those who attended. How else would the man find out how much Julian knew about his rebellion?

Julian moved through the crowd toward the four sheiks who were gathered about a huge campfire built to ward off the cold that had come with sundown. Three of them were older and more experienced than he, men he had respected all his life. One of them, the youngest, was Julian's boyhood friend. They would test him tonight;

Julian expected no less from them. The sheiks would want to know his strengths and his weaknesses. If he wanted them to follow his lead, he must be a leader. He met each man's steady gaze, and they bowed their heads to him one by one.

Would they accept his authority? Apollodorus thought they would, but that was yet to be determined.

"My father sent me," he began, "to end the squabbling within the western tribes and to prevent a break among our people. I would ask that each of you tell me whatever you think I should know. Do not fear to voice your slightest grievance. We are all like family. We may disagree, but if we tear each other apart, we will not even be allies. None us want to see that happen. Together we are an unbeatable force—divided, we are weakened and vulnerable to our enemies."

One of the men in the crowd spoke up. "My father sent me. He could not come himself, so I stand before you in his stead."

"And you are?" Julian asked.

"Tassum, son of Sheik Moussimi. I am here to put a stop to the lies spread about my father."

Julian scrutinized the man's face, trying to remember if he had ever seen him. If he had known him in the past, he had forgotten him. The man was tall and beefy, a younger version of his father, whom Julian did remember.

Julian knew he was looking into the eyes of Moussimi's spy. "Say what you will," Julian urged him. "We all have a voice here. We are Badari."

Julian watched Tassum's eyes flicker as if he would like to argue the matter.

The man walked around Julian, his hard gaze insulting. "You will hear those who agree with you. But that is not my father's way of thinking. Too long have the Badari been held down by one family."

Tassum waited as if wanting Julian to disagree.

Julian's expression did not alter. "Continue."

Tassum frowned as if the confrontation was not going to his satisfaction. "These sheiks will speak out against my father. Know they do not speak the truth." His insolent gaze swept over the leaders.

"I have heard many things. We are here to discover the truth," Julian said in a still, calm voice.

"Your father is a traitor, Tassum, as are you," Sheik Ben-Gari interjected. "You know it, and we here know it as well."

Tassum's face reddened. "I will not remain to breathe the same air as my father's accusers. But I take mark of each man here, and my father shall know your names."

"Your father was invited—why did he not come?" Julian asked.

Tassum gave a slow, hard smile. "My father does not recognize your right to call the tribesmen together. You are not Lord Ramtat."

"And you are not yet a sheik," Julian retaliated, "yet I have allowed you to speak for your father, as I speak for mine."

Tassum stalked angrily toward his horse, leaving silence behind him.

Julian watched the man mount and ride into the night. He turned to the others. "Is there any truth in his accusations?"

"Sheik Moussimi is not a man to be trusted," Sheik Ben-Gari said, rising to his feet. "From his ambitions rise the real danger."

Ben-Gari was Julian's age, though shorter in stature

and more muscular. His face was wide, and his nose hooked at the end, but no one noticed because his smile was so engaging. He and Julian had trained together as youths and had developed a strong friendship at that time. Julian hoped he could still call him his friend.

"What kind of danger do you speak of?" Julian asked.

"The man uses fear to rule his tribe. He chose a time when your father was out of the country to challenge his authority, Lord Prince," Ben-Gari said.

His friend surprised Julian by using his formal title. When they had been young, there was no formality between them. Julian realized Ben-Gari was setting the tone of respect for the other sheiks to follow.

"Most of us have a clear notion who the troublemakers are. Sheik Moussimi has been disgruntled for years. And of late he has been talking of war, which most of us do not want."

Sheik Ajman stood, holding up his hand for attention. He was an older man with heavy eyelids that made him look sleepy, when, in fact, those dark eyes missed nothing. He was thin and short, and unlike the others, who were clean shaven, he wore a beard. Ajman looked at Julian with a steady gaze. "What Ben-Gari says is true, although many of you here have turned a blind eye to Moussimi's mischief for years. Truth be told, his ambitions go even further. He has spoken openly of breaking away from the Badari, and I am sure, since he approached me, that he has also asked the rest of you to join him."

Sheik Hodez, a white-headed man with sun-wrinkled skin and a frail appearance, nodded. "Moussimi incites people with promises of wealth if he is made leader. He craves your father's place as prince of the Badari. He says we are made weak because we serve a lord who fled from our enemies and left the rest of us defenseless."

Julian knew this was the moment to prove his strength and show he was worthy of his father. "As prince of the Badari, my father has always put the good of the tribe before anything else. Because Octavian is determined to destroy my family, the Badari would also have been in danger from Rome had we remained among you. At the time, many of you asked my father to fight Rome, but he refused to spill your blood on our family's behalf. Though I am still under a death sentence if I am discovered, I came here to settle this division among our people!"

There was a nod of heads, a look of respect.

"The one thing I expect from all of you," Julian continued, "is to look to your own safety. The Roman who has pledged to spill Tausrat blood knows I have returned and is searching for me."

"Moussimi will attempt to widen the division among our people now that you have returned," Ben-Gari stated forcefully. "We should act quickly! I saw for myself that a large number of Badari were gathering at his encampment not two weeks past."

"Then the rebellion goes deeper than I thought." Julian knew his father would have returned to Egypt had he known the extent of the insurrection. "Are there any among you who feel the same as Moussimi?"

"Nay," cried one of the older sheiks. "We are loyal."

"We serve only the Tausrat family," another chimed in. "Your family has guided us and kept us safe for generations. None here will join Moussimi."

Julian's gaze swept over the faces of his fellow Badari. "Why is Sheik Hajer not present? It is but a day's ride from his encampment."

"I have heard rumors he is considering joining Moussimi," Ben-Gari stated. "I, myself, do not believe he would join with such a man."

"Hajer is not a wise sheik and will follow whomever he sees as the strongest!" exclaimed Sheik Dawasira, rising to his feet. "Defeat Moussimi, and you will have no trouble with any of the lesser sheiks. Offer to meet him in single combat and settle this. How can he refuse without bringing shame upon himself?"

Many differences had been settled over the years by such contests. The rule was that the winner would be the first one to draw blood. "If what I have heard of this man is true, I doubt he will agree to fight me, but if he will, I will face him." Julian searched each man's eyes. "You do understand if Moussimi does not agree to meet me in combat, there will be war."

"Aye," the others agreed, one after the other.

Julian's gaze became fierce, reminding those present of his father.

"Know this—I speak with the voice of my father. If I thought it would benefit the Badari to break away from the house of Tausrat, I would allow them to leave. But we all know such a breach would only make us weaker."

Sheik Dawasira shook his head. "I do not want war—none of us do. But if it comes, we will follow you."

Julian was grateful for the support. "I shall send my challenge to Sheik Moussimi. If he takes it up, we may be able to settle this unrest without an all-out conflict."

"It is more than unrest with Moussimi. He is driven by power and greed," Ben-Gari said. "I do not believe he will agree to settle this with single combat. We should make ready to meet him in battle."

The sheiks mumbled among themselves and finally

came to an agreement. Sheik Dawasira became the voice of the others. "If you can settle the conflict, my prince, let it be."

Julian nodded in agreement. "Go to your beds for now. Tomorrow return to your encampments. Post guards and keep your women and children close. I will send word to you when I am ready to face Moussimi."

Julian was not sure he could ask these worthy men to go into battle with him should war erupt. He was still feeling his way as a leader and feared he might make a mistake. But one thing was certain—if he did not squelch Moussimi's rebellion before it escalated, war would come, and the tribes would be ripped apart.

Each sheik bowed to him before taking his leave, offering words of encouragement.

When Ben-Gari was preparing to leave, Julian asked him to remain and spoke to him quietly. "Have you someone in Sheik Moussimi's tribe that you can trust?"

"There are those I trust. Sheik Moussimi will be watched at all times."

"His son will have told him all who were here tonight. Do not do anything dangerous. Have a care for your safety."

Ben-Gari grinned, reminding Julian of the boy he had been. "Did we not face far worse dangers when we were but lads?"

Julian remembered the time the two of them had wandered away from the encampment and become hopelessly lost in the desert. By the time Julian's father had found them, they were sick from thirst and overexposure to the sun. "We learned never to go unprepared. It is a lesson I shall use if this rift cannot be healed."

The two men clasped arms.

Ben-Gari said, "I am glad you have returned. I have missed you, my friend. Did you not bring home a wife? Someone said they saw a great lady with you when you arrived."

"Nay. I have no wife." He did not want to discuss Sabinah with anyone. "What of you?"

"I have my eye on a lovely lady. She has many suitors for her hand. I do not know if she even likes me."

"I remember well your persistence. There is no doubt in my mind you will win the lady."

"I am not so certain. But I will live in misery if she chooses another."

Julian became serious. "I would ask that you leave at first light tomorrow morning. Find out what you can as quickly as you can. Meanwhile, I will send scouts to all the tribes, informing them of what we talked about tonight. We must know who is with us, and who follows Moussimi."

Julian watched Ben-Gari leave, thinking of the problem that faced him. If his father had been at the gathering tonight, would he have known how to draw the Badari together?

Julian rode back to the villa, stabling his horse. As he made his way toward the house, a shadow fell across the walkway in front of him, and Uriah appeared, searching Julian's face.

"Did your meeting go well?"

Uriah was in one of his lucid moments, and Julian wanted his advice. "There may be war, and I hate the idea of so many deaths."

"It is always so in war. But you may prevent that outcome if you anticipate your enemy's moves. Stand eye-to-eye with him, know his strengths and weaknesses, and be ready to take advantage of both. In acting thus, war may be avoided. Wise leaders throughout history have done so. You must not forget that the great Alexander's blood runs through your veins."

"What would my father do?"

Uriah smiled. "Had your father remained in Egypt, no one would have tested his strength. Show the others that you are Lord Ramtat's son, and that if they strike you, they come up against a formidable force."

Julian nodded. "I shall try."

"Nay. You shall succeed."

"I need your wisdom, Uriah."

The old man walked down the path, his hands clasped behind him as if he had not heard Julian.

"Uriah."

"Who are you?" the old man said. "Leave me alone. I must seek my bed."

Discouraged, the young desert prince closed his eyes. His father had placed power in his hands and trusted him to settle the dissension among the tribes—he must not fail.

He turned his gaze toward the west, wishing Apollodorus would arrive.

🦅 CHAPTER SEVENTEEN

It was the next morning before Sabinah had gathered enough courage to venture past the small courtyard outside her bedchamber. She expected a guard to be posted outside the wall to stop her, but there was no one there, so she ventured farther down the pathway.

The sky was clear, the land awash in sunlight, and it lifted her spirits to be away from the house where she had been a prisoner. Off to her left she could see grape arbors, and it was tempting to walk in that direction.

Hearing the roar of a lion, she smiled and turned her steps down the path that led to the huge fenced area. As she drew near, Sabinah saw how large the pens were. She counted a lion, two lionesses, and two leopards. Their surroundings, including several shade trees and ponds, had obviously been created for their comfort.

When she drew up to the lion enclosure, she pulled back when a huge male approached the fence, pressing his nose against it. Gathering her courage, she took hesitant steps toward the big cat. She could feel her hand tremble as she reached out to the animal.

Sabinah giggled when she felt its rough tongue lap

against her fingers. Feeling braver because the cat did not attempt to eat her hand, she buried her fingers in its stiff mane. The lion seemed to purr, rubbing his face against her fingers.

Sabinah felt hands span her waist, and she was lifted and jerked away from the enclosure.

Julian glared at her. "Do not think because the cats seem tame, they will not tear your hand off! You are a stranger to Tibon, and he is, after all, a wild animal."

Sabinah clasped her hands behind her back, feeling rebuked. "I love animals."

"Do not reach inside the enclosure again unless I am with you. These cats are old, and they oft have a day when they do not want any human near them."

"Why do you keep the animals in enclosures?"

"Simply because they would not know how to survive otherwise."

"You say these cats are old. I see Tibon has lost most of his teeth. Does no one here train new animals?"

"Not since my mother left."

Sabinah saw Julian glance into the distance, and her gaze followed his. There were several tents being disassembled as the sheiks prepared to leave. "What is happening there?" she asked.

"Nothing that need concern you."

Sabinah observed sadness darken Julian's eyes, and he looked weary. She wondered why. Instinctively she reached out and laid her hand against his cheek. "Something troubles you."

Her fingers were cool upon his face. Looking into her eyes, he saw concern reflected there. But not trusting her motives, he swatted her hand away as if it were a deadly spider. "I warned you before, do not try any of your tricks here. They might work on your Roman friends, but not on me."

She longed for the past when he had smiled at her and called her Sunshine. "I have no Roman friends, Julian, and I have no tricks. I stand before you guiltless."

"Your guilt is yet to be determined, but I am constantly reminded you are from that cursed family who caused my grandmother's death. If you have favor with any of the gods, now would be the time to ask for their help."

"I am too insignificant for the gods to notice. I ask help of you."

Julian stared at her long and hard. "Why should I help you?"

"I ask you to trust me. Believe what I tell you is true. Know that I would never do anything to harm you. How often must I say this to you?"

"You want my trust. Then no doubt you want me to send you back to your stepmother so you can inform Tribune Vergilius where to find me."

Sabinah raised her chin, overcome with frustration. "If I return to Alexandria, it will only be a matter of time before my stepmother forces me to wed Tribune Vergilius, and I despise him."

Julian jerked her into his arms, angry because her words had awakened a fierce jealousy inside him. "You would have me believe you despise him, and yet you say he wants you for his wife. I was right not to trust you. Have you no wish to live in glorious Rome, as part of the court of the great Augustus?" he taunted.

Sabinah pushed against him, but his hold on her only tightened. "Nay. I do not want to leave Egypt, and I will never allow that man to touch me again."

Julian studied her for a long moment as if he were weighing her words. "So he has touched you."

She looked into his green eyes, wishing she could make him understand what horrors she had experienced at Vergilius's hands. She started to say something, but he held up his hand to silence her.

"Save yourself the trouble of denying your feelings for the man." He wanted to shake her, to crush all thoughts of the Roman from her mind. "Nothing you can say will convince me to believe you."

"Must I remind you of this?" she asked, raising her head and looking into his eyes. "I have kept Ptolemy Caesarion's secret. Surely that is enough proof that you can trust me."

Julian wanted to lay his face against hers—he wanted to feel her silken body against his—he wanted to once more touch his mouth to her sweet lips. "Careful that you do not mention my cousin's name once too often, or you might hasten your punishment."

"If that is my fate, to be punished, then do it."

Julian had never met a woman like Sabinah, and he did not know what to make of her, or for that matter, what to do with her. He stared into her eyes and found himself gravitating toward her as if drawn by an invisible cord. Taking a deep breath, he dropped his arms and stepped away from her. "Return to the house and remain in your chamber until I decide what is to be done with you."

She surprised him again when she came to him, laying her head against his shoulder. "I told you long ago I loved you, and I still do."

Julian wanted to enclose her in his arms, to hold her until his body stopped quaking. Turning his head, he placed his mouth against the top of her sweet-smelling head, nuzzling the red strands. His heart skipped a beat when she nestled closer to him. When he realized what he was doing, he flung her away from him, but what he really wanted to do was hold her. "Deceiver! Never again utter such words to me."

Sabinah turned and ran toward the house, fighting tears. Nothing she could say would change Julian's mind about her.

For the next two days Sabinah did not see Julian. She had overheard one of the servants telling another that their master had ridden into the desert. Sabinah chose not to ask when he would be returning, although she wanted to know.

Sitting in a small alcove in the library with her feet tucked beneath her, she was reading a scroll she had pulled from one of the shelves. The text was a treatise on how to care for and feed wild animals. What really interested her was the mixtures of herbs and potions to treat ailments the animals might develop.

Sabinah was absorbed in what she was reading and jumped guiltily when she heard someone enter the room. She was relieved to find it was Uriah.

"So you are a reader," he said, moving toward her and taking a stool. "Let me see what has captured your interest."

She handed him the scroll, glad his mind was clear today.

"Ah. This was written by Lord Mycerinus. He was considered to be the foremost expert in wild animal training. He taught his daughter to train big cats. My sweet Danaë could train a cat to be so gentle it would eat out of her hand."

"Everyone has heard the story of how she saved Queen Cleopatra's life."

"Aye. And now she must pay because of her connection to the queen. She suffers greatly at being forced to leave Egypt."

"You were her teacher, were you not?"

He smiled as if he was thinking about treasured memories. "Most of the time, it was Danaë who taught me. She is extraordinary."

"I have always thought the whole Tausrat family extraordinary. Lord Ramtat was not only a high lord and adviser to the queen, but a prince of the desert as well."

Uriah glanced about him. "You know Danaë no longer comes to see me as she once did. Maybe she has forgotten about me."

Sabinah realized Uriah's mind was wandering. "I do not believe that is the case," she said, trying to soothe him. "Rather it must be that she is too far away to visit."

Uriah looked puzzled, and she saw the blank stare cloud his eyes. "Of whom were you speaking, and who are you?"

"I am Sabinah, Uriah," she said kindly, going down on her knees before him. "Would you like me to help you back to your room so you can lie down?"

He shook his head. "I would like it if someone would read to me. I used to read, and sometimes I still do." A tear rolled down his wrinkled cheek. "But right now, I cannot remember how."

She stood, her heart breaking for the dear old man. "Which scroll would you like to hear?"

With his hand trembling, he reached into the folds of his robe and handed her one. She thought he would be better off if he lay down, but if he wanted her to read to him, she would.

The text Sabinah read was beyond her understanding. There were many scientific words, hard to pronounce, which had no meaning to her. She stumbled over the passages, watching the old man nod his head as if he understood the difficult concepts.

Sabinah did not hear Julian, nor did she know he was standing in the doorway watching her. She came to a passage that caught her interest, and something that sounded familiar to her. She marked the place with her finger. "What does *chemy* mean? I have seen this in some of my father's scrolls."

Uriah studied the tips of his fingers for a moment as if reaching for answers. Suddenly he smiled. "That is the Greek *khymeia*, the art of melting precious metals."

"Since my father was a goldsmith, most probably I heard him mention the term at one time or another." She smiled at Uriah. "If I had been his son rather than his daughter, he would have taught me his craft." She lowered her head. "I miss him so."

"Dulus Jannah was a good and honorable man," Uriah said, nodding. "I counted him among my friends."

Sabinah reached out and touched Uriah's hand. "Thank you for saying that. With all that has happened since the queen's death, people have forgotten my father was a good man. It makes me sad that there is a stigma attached to his honorable name that not even time can erase."

"Time erases many things, my dear. It is even eating away at the corners of my mind."

"You need have no fear, Uriah. You are greatly loved and when your time comes, you will leave this life with a name of honor, whereas I will always bear the shame of my stepmother's and stepsister's misdeeds. Of all the treasures one can gain in life, I believe honor is the most important."

Uriah nodded. "You are wise to have come to that conclusion so young."

"Those were my father's thoughts. But I believe them."

The old man studied her closely. "You look nothing like Dulus Jannah."

"I am told I favor my mother in looks." She lowered her head, seeming to study the text on her lap. "But I do not remember my mother. A neighbor who knew her told me she had a kind heart. I do not know if this is so."

"You are right to doubt—we cannot always believe what we are told," Julian stated from his place at the doorway.

Sabinah glanced up to find his gaze resting on her, his eyes seeming to flame with the fire of life.

"Come forward, my boy, and join us," Uriah said. "We are discussing science, and the philosophy of family likenesses."

Julian remained where he was. "So I heard."

The old man looked suddenly puzzled. "Young man, just what did you hear?" His mind was wandering once more.

Julian's gaze remained on Sabinah—he liked the way the sunlight from the open window brought a high sheen to the red curls massed about her face. Her honey-colored skin invited a man's touch, and her full soft lips invited thoughts that he would rather not examine. Her face was turned up to his, the fringe of her long lashes fanned out against her cheeks. "By the gods," he admitted, "you are a rare beauty."

Sabinah could do no more than stare at Julian. Surely

he meant to mock her. She was no beauty, and they both knew it.

"I shall not interrupt your reading any longer. Please continue," Julian said.

Sabinah watched him leave with an ache in her heart. It was clear he could not abide being in the same room with her. When she heard him outside the window, she turned to watch him. He walked with the assurance of one highborn. His long black hair was tied back with a leather thong. She never tired of looking at him, and her heart would never turn from his.

"Read on," Uriah said eagerly, his mind returning to the present. "I like the sound of your voice."

Sabinah's thoughts were on Julian, and she had not heard Uriah.

He chuckled.

"An old man like me cannot compete with such a handsome young man. But all the same, I would like to hear you read."

She smiled slightly, lifting the scroll, and searching for the place she had left off. There was a quiver in her voice as she read, and it did not go unnoticed by Uriah.

He looked through the window at Julian, who was speaking to one of his Badari. Uriah would have to be a blind man not to see something was going on between the two young people. But there was mistrust on Julian's part, and lost hope on the lovely young woman's. Julian was highborn, and she was a goldsmith's daughter—a cruel mismatch—but young love did not care about such a difference.

Blankness hit Uriah with a suddenness that drained all present thoughts from his mind, and he rose unsteadily. "I have a strong craving for honeyed figs. I will raid the kitchen and then lie down a bit. Finish with your lessons, or your mother shall hear of it." Poor Uriah was off in another world again.

Sabinah rolled the scroll and placed it on the shelf by the window, noticing a brilliant sunset washed the land in scarlet.

Later as evening crept toward night, she walked down the corridor preceded by a young servant carrying a lantern, the smoke making a serpentine trail toward the high ceiling. When they reached her bedchamber, the young woman placed the lantern on a low table and disappeared.

Sabina eased herself down onto a cushioned stool. In this room she somehow felt close to Julian's mother, and therefore close to Julian. Here Lady Danaë had grown into a young woman.

When she had dreamed of one day meeting a man she would love, how could Lady Danaë have known she would one day marry the great Lord Ramtat?

Had there been a night for Julian's mother like this one for Sabinah when she felt lonely and wished the future would open up to her so she could see where her life would lead?

Sabinah leaned her head back, staring at the high ceiling. Lady Danaë had been highborn and must have known she would marry a man of equal station.

"Julian," she said aloud, "how long I have loved you, knowing you will never love me." The sound of her own voice echoed around the high ceiling, making her feel more alone and frustrated.

Ignoring her hunger, she stripped off her robe and climbed onto the bed. The gods had been cruel to her, leading her to love a man she could never have.

🦅 CHAPTER EIGHTEEN

Apollodorus dismounted and walked toward Julian, his expression giving nothing away.

"I am glad you arrived today. I was beginning to worry."

Apollodorus wiped sweat from his brow and stepped beneath the shade of a palm, but since it was late afternoon it afforded him little protection from the sun. "It seems hotter than usual this year. The rains are late."

"So the workers keep telling me." Julian met the Sicilian's gaze. "Have you any word?"

"It is too hot to stand out here. Let us seek a cooler place, and I shall tell you all."

When they reached the garden, Apollodorus splashed water on his face and neck before cupping his hands and drinking deeply from a fountain. "It feels better to wash some of the sand away."

"What is your news?" Julian asked impatiently.

The older man smiled, sitting down on a marble bench. "Sabinah's message was delivered to her stepmother. I am told the woman shrieked and carried on without end. Finally she questioned our messenger, and he did as he was instructed. He told her a young woman paid him a copper to take the message to her, and he did not know who the woman was or where she had gone."

"What said the stepmother?"

"According to our man, the stepsister entered the room, and after discovering what had happened to Sabinah, laughed and stated they were finally rid of the person who had done nothing but insult their Roman friends."

"And the stepmother's reaction?"

"After giving it some thought, she agreed with her daughter."

Julian took a deep breath. "Then we can assume Sabinah has been telling the truth all along."

"So it would seem. Your serving woman, Rafta, applied to the kitchen mistress and was given work. Rafta came to me last night with word of what the servants had told her. Apparently the stepmother and stepsister have no fondness for Sabinah. It seems Sabinah does insult their Roman guests every chance she gets. The head cook, who has a fondness for the youngest mistress, is worried what Tribune Vergilius might do to Sabinah. It seems the Roman has gone as far as gaining a dispensation so he can marry an Egyptian. The one he wants to marry is our little Sabinah."

"So she was truthful about that."

Apollodorus nodded.

"Did the servants say what Sabinah's answer was to Vergilius's offer?"

"She will not have him and told him so."

Julian realized he had been holding his breath, but he did not want Apollodorus to know how deep his feelings were for Sabinah.

"The young woman seems to be just what she

presented herself to be. I discreetly asked around the marketplace about the family. Few have anything good to say about the stepmother or the stepsister because of their association with the hated Romans."

"What said they about Sabinah?" Julian asked.

"I could find none who did not lavish her with praise. They spoke of her kindness to those less fortunate, and remarked upon her steadfast devotion to Egypt. Many remarked that it was a shame for such an innocent young woman to be exposed to the vices in her stepmother's house."

Julian felt ashamed of the way he had treated Sabinah when all along she had been blameless. "I misjudged her," he admitted.

Apollodorus was looking speculative. "It has occurred to me that we could use her to gain information. Think of it—she has access to the Roman commanders. No one would suspect her of being a spy."

Julian wanted to protest, but Apollodorus was right. If they returned her to Alexandria, Sabinah would be in the right place to learn how much the Romans knew about his family. But he did not want to put her in danger. And he said as much to Apollodorus. "It might be dangerous for her."

Apollodorus shrugged. "We live in dangerous times."

Julian frowned and started pacing.

Apollodorus watched him closely, suddenly understanding the young prince's disquiet. "Then again, perhaps we should explore other ways to find out what we need to know. Rafta is still working in the kitchen of the stepmother's house. And just because she has not learned anything of import yet does not mean she will not."

The last thing Julian wanted to do was send Sabinah back to that house of vipers. But what recourse had he? "There will be little chance of Rafta overhearing the Romans' conversations," he said with resignation.

"I sense a hesitation in you."

"It is strange that I cannot put my feelings for Sabinah into words. I have been with women of more beauty, and yet none of them stirred me as deeply as she has. Sabinah was in my thoughts even before I left Egypt." He met Apollodorus's dark gaze. "Why do you think that is?"

The Sicilian tried not to smile. "I have little doubt the meaning will come to you with the passage of time."

"I have treated her badly," Julian said. "She came to warn me of danger, and I made her my prisoner. I would not blame her if she refused to help me."

"It is something you will have to consider before you put the proposition before her."

"Aye." Julian turned to glance at the house. "I have had many hard choices to make since returning to Egypt." He quickly told Apollodorus what had happened at the meeting with the sheiks.

"You must face Moussimi in combat—but from what I understand the man is no longer young. He will most probably choose another to champion his cause."

"I would expect him to, and I shall accept whomever he chooses."

Sabinah sat before the window in her bedchamber, gazing at the parchment on her lap. The door was open, and she heard footsteps approaching so she put the parchment aside, glancing up in surprise to find her visitor was Julian.

"I wish to speak to you," he said, advancing into the chamber.

She stood, clasping her hands in front of her, silently waiting for him to continue.

Julian swept his hand before him. "Perhaps you would consent to accompany me to the garden—it is cooler there." He saw the puzzled expression on her face. "There is something I want to ask of you."

"As you like," she remarked. There was something different about his attitude toward her. He was treating her with respect, and she wondered what had caused the change. He wore a short pleated tunic with a gold beaded belt about his waist. His hair was covered with an Egyptian headdress that fell to his shoulders. His hawk was perched on his gloved arm, its head covered by a red leather hood. Julian looked so regal there was no mistaking his nobility.

When Sabinah stepped in front of him, Julian noticed how slender she was. Her wrists were so dainty he could snap them without half trying. The bone structure of her face was delicate. As she moved he saw the slight sway of her hips, and a lump formed in his throat. She was young and vulnerable, yet he was about to ask her to risk her life to help him.

When they reached the pond, he motioned for her to be seated while he paced before her. "I have something to say to you."

Sabinah sat silently watching him, bewildered by the change that had come over him.

Julian removed the hood from his hawk and sent it into the sky. Removing his protective glove and tossing it on the bench, he cleared his throat, turning his attention to Sabinah. "First I want to apologize for not taking your warning to heart. I have come to believe you were trying to help me."

Julian waited for a reaction from her, but she merely stared at him. "I am saying I believe you."

"I am glad you have finally discovered the truth and understand the danger you face here in Egypt."

He halted in front of her. "I ask your pardon for the way I treated you."

The smile she gave him almost took his breath away. "You had every right to mistrust me."

He sat down close to her but not touching. "How could I have forgotten how honorable you were, Sunshine?"

Sabinah was so choked up she could not speak. He had called her Sunshine, and she had thought he never would again.

Julian watched her face color before she turned away. She was young, innocent in the ways of the world, and he was about to use her for his own ends. "I have decided to take you back to your home."

"Nay," she protested. "Please let me stay with you. I will not be any trouble." Julian did not respond, he did not even look at her. "There is something you are not telling me."

He chose his words carefully. "I need information about Tribune Vergilius's movements, and I have no way to obtain it."

Sabinah's eyes widened. "I understand. You believe I can make him confide in me."

Julian turned away, wanting to hit something. "Aye," he ground out between his teeth.

She did not hesitate. "You have only to tell me what you need of me."

He had expected her to refuse, and there was a part of him that had hoped she would. "Why are you so willing to do this?"

"If I can atone for the wrong my stepsister did to your family, I do so gladly."

Julian stood, putting some distance between them. "I do not hold you responsible for Bastet's betrayal."

"I do this to repay a debt to your grandmother."

Julian fought a battle with himself. Just the thought of Sabinah being in the same room with Vergilius angered him, and yet he needed her help. "Before you so readily agree to do this, Sabinah, allow me to explain that you will be in danger if the tribune discovers you are helping me. If this does not feel right to you, I want you to refuse and nothing more need be said."

Sabinah watched him closely as he paced. "Tell me what you need to know."

"Find out, if you can do it without raising suspicion, what Vergilius knows about my family. Discover whether he believes Caesarion is still alive, and whether anyone is searching for my cousin at this time. I need to know if Vergilius plans to move against the Badari, and if so, when and where."

She nodded slowly. "I believe he will confide in me."

Julian stopped in front of her. He stared up at the sky for a moment before he could meet her gaze. "I have changed my mind. I do not want you to do this. Forget what I said."

"Julian, it is a good plan, and I am the only one who can do this for you. Allow me to help you."

He felt his heart beat faster, and he resisted the urge to take her in his arms and protect her. He was stunned by her bravery and humbled by her willingness to aid him. Never had he known anyone like her. "If you promise to be careful," he conceded.

Sabinah stood. "You need not fear for my safety. The cook is a friend, and I have a loyal maid who will help me if the need should arise."

"Apollodorus has managed to place one of my Badari women in your stepmother's kitchen—her name is Rafta. If you need help at any time, or if you feel frightened in any way, tell her, and she will get word to me or Apollodorus." His eyes narrowed. "What of your stepmother?"

"I will tell her I could not survive on my own. She will like that. I will need the clothing I wore when I left home. She will become suspicious if I return in a fine linen gown like this one."

Sabinah stood before him with an earnestness that twisted Julian's heart. "Explain to me how Tribune Vergilius treats you," he said.

She saw no reason to tell Julian that she was afraid of Vergilius. "He is sometimes overly friendly, but I manage to keep him at a distance. He has asked me to be his wife—I have refused. He is not a man who gives up easily."

Julian took her hand, measuring it to his—hers hardly covered his palm. "One day, I will ask you to forgive me for putting you in danger."

Her fingers clamped about his. "There is nothing to forgive." Sabinah was distressed as she met his gaze. "When this is over, there will be no debts between us."

The sun was setting, casting the garden in a crimson glow. He touched her cheek, gazing into her eyes.

The sensual glitter in his eyes and the seductive curve of his mouth beckoned to her. Julian was everything a man should be, and she wanted him to know how she felt.

"I honor you, Julian. I always have."

He stepped away from her, not feeling very honorable at the moment. "Perhaps you should return to your bed-chamber now," he suggested.

He seemed to be struggling with something, although she did not know what. Sabinah watched Julian's gaze become intense as he stared at her with an unfamiliar expression. There was a question in his eyes as if he were silently asking her something. Heat stirred the air about them, arcing between them. She felt warmth lick through her body and moved closer to him, unwittingly answering Julian's silent plea.

Before Julian guessed what she was doing, she stood on tiptoe, pressing her mouth against his. At first he stiffened, and then shaped his mouth to those silken lips, his arms slowly enclosing her. Her skin was smooth to the touch; her hair smelled of sweet oils.

He was dazed as his body came alive with desire. Pressing her against him, he heard her sigh. Julian pulled back, thinking to put her away from him, but the hunger between them grew stronger, and he wanted more.

Slowly he lowered his head, his passion unleashed. He heard Sabinah sob, and it fired his blood. Lifting her into his arms, he saw surrender in her eyes. With hurried steps, he carried her toward his bedchamber. He wanted more than to touch his mouth to hers. He wanted to sate the fire that raged inside him.

⟁ Chapter Nineteen

Slowly lowering his head, Julian riveted his gaze on Sabinah. He flung his headdress off, his lips settling on that tempting mouth that trembled beneath his.

Sabinah's head fell back as she surrendered to him utterly and completely. Julian lowered her back against his bed, his hand moving down her neck and leisurely pushing the gown off her shoulders, exposing her naked breasts. His hand moved slowly from her shoulder downward to touch her breasts, to caress, to lightly stroke.

Sabinah's eyes widened in wonderment, and then closed in ecstasy. "Ohhh," she moaned softly. She could hardly breathe as he leaned toward her and laid his head against her breasts. With a groan, she buried her fingers in his ebony hair while his breath teased a nipple and he flicked it with his tongue.

Sabinah dug her fingers into his back, trying to keep from crying out. His mouth was warm as it closed over the swollen nipple, and her body jerked, needing something more.

Wondrous excitement tightened inside her. "Julian," she whispered as a strange sweetness swept over her. When he raised his head, his eyes seemed to glow with green fire. The emotions building in Sabinah were so strong she could hardly endure them.

"Give yourself to me, my own Sunshine." His voice was raspy. "Will you give yourself to me, my heart?"

It took her a moment to find her voice. "I have always been yours," she admitted, feeling as if she were floating. Her only anchor was the man who kept her fixed firmly to the bed with the weight of his body.

"I think I have always known that somewhere in my mind." He brushed his mouth across hers, filled with the revelation that had just come to him. "Even in Bal Forea, thoughts of the kiss we shared lingered in my mind. You have been constantly with me although I did not realize it until this moment."

Sabinah was trying to think rationally, attempting to perceive the meaning of his words, but it was difficult when her body ached for his touch.

Julian's gaze was intense as it fell on her breasts. He watched them rise and fall with each breath she took. Gently, he kissed first one, and then the other.

"Sabinah," he said, tearing his mouth from her breasts and taking a deep breath. "If it is your wish, I will stop."

For her answer, she laced her hands through his long hair and pulled his face down to hers. "I want to be with you."

Julian's fingers trailed down her arm. "It might be that once I have taken you, this insatiable hunger that drives me day and night will be satisfied—then I may no longer want you so much it tears at my insides." He lifted his gaze to hers. "Or it might be that one lifetime will not be enough. I do not know."

His cryptic words chased away all other emotions, leaving Sabinah to contend with a deep dark fear. "Nor

do I know what the future holds. Can we not be together for this one night, Julian?"

His eyes softened as he gently touched one breast and
trailed a tan finger to the other one. "I would kill any
man who tried to lay a hand on you. I would never allow
any man to take the liberties I take with you now." He
pulled her to him, gritting his teeth to gain control over
his runaway passion. "You belong to me."

"As does your horse and your hawk," she said, smiling, not knowing what to make of his confession. There
had been times she'd thought he despised her. Now he
spoke words that went straight to her heart. He was a
complex man.

"I would not care if another man rode my horse"—his
nostrils flared—"but I would not allow that same man to
touch even one hair on your head."

Like a sword of flames, his touch moved through her
body. "Julian," she whispered.

His eyes darkened with a feral light. "Little seduc-
tress, I doubt that I will ever have my fill of you."

Sabinah could stand the wait no longer. She wanted
to feel his bare flesh against hers. She reached up and
touched his face, feeling the throbbing in his throat.
When she placed small kisses there, Julian threw back
his head.

"If you continue to do this, I will not be able to restrain myself." He took her face between his hands. "I
want you—all of you." His gaze probed hers. "Do you
trust me?"

"With all that I am," she answered, closing her eyes. "I
have always trusted you above all others. Even as a child."

A sudden vision of her as a child flashed through his
mind, and he stilled. She had been so adorable then.

Every time he had seen her, it had warmed his heart and made him smile. Now she was a woman, and his feelings for her had grown much deeper. He softly touched her cheek, and then his finger drifted to her mouth. "I doubt I am worthy of such devotion."

She swallowed twice as he pushed her gown past her hips.

His eyes feasted on every silken curve, and Sabinah could not think clearly.

"Why do you hesitate?" she asked innocently.

His lashes veiled his eyes. He touched the crown of her head, allowing his fingers to drift into the red curls. "Because I have never been on fire for a woman as I am for you. And because this is your first time, is it not?"

"I have never known a man," she admitted. "I have been waiting for you."

His eyes seemed to darken as he pushed her gown all the way off, then tossed it to the floor. "After this night, you will be bound to me, Sabinah. Let no one say you do not belong to me."

Sabinah's only covering was the long hair that fell across her breasts. She had yearned for Julian too long for modesty to bother her.

The depth of Julian's feelings was unsettling to him.

He was fire.

He was flames.

"There is an inferno burning inside me, yet I do not want to hurry this night. You are paradise," he muttered against her ear. "I want to savor each moment before I partake of your body."

He paused to look at her, feeling a flush of renewed passion so strong it left him trembling. Her eyes were heavy with passion, and in her innocence she knew precisely how to capture him. When her hand moved over his chest, he threw back his head, baring his teeth.

"Aye," he said in a voice that shook with emotion. "I need you to touch me." He untangled his body from hers and slowly stood, unhooking his belt and allowing it to fall to the floor. He ripped his tunic off and tossed it aside, his eyes on Sabinah.

She feasted on his beauty. He was muscled, his stomach flat, his shoulders wide, his chest smooth. Her gaze took a downward path from his navel. She gasped when she saw the maleness of him.

Without thinking, she slid off the bed, stepping close to him, gazing into his eyes with uncertainty. His hand closed over her silken breast, and when he watched Sabinah's tongue flick out to moisten her lips, it almost took him to his knees because his legs had gone weak.

Together they drifted onto his bed. For a long moment, he hovered above her, holding her gaze. "You know what will happen between us."

"The servants talk. I know some things."

Julian brushed her hair off her forehead and laid his face against hers. He touched his lips to her cheek, his hand taking a downward path until it rested against her thigh. "Tell me this is not a dream."

"This is no dream."

His mouth plundered hers, stirring her blood and rendering her his willing slave. Looking past the veil of dark lashes, Julian saw surrender in her eyes. Sabinah's arms slid around his waist, but he gently pushed her away so he could suckle her nipple.

The power of his unleashed desire tore through him. He explored her body, his hand moving lower. He heard her take in a quick breath when he tested her moistness.

Unable to contain his torrid passion, he slid between her legs, nudging them apart, giving her but the beginning of his length. Slowly easing forward, he tore through the barrier, and her softness closed around him. Julian's eyes drifted shut. What he was experiencing was so acute he wanted to savor the moment of their joining. His body quaked and trembled. He sought her lips, partaking of their sweetness while trying to control his movements, to still his heartbeat.

Sabinah's eyes widened in wonder as he slid farther inside her. She watched Julian bare his teeth, and she stared into those wonderful green eyes, feeling as if she had just become a part of his body. She moaned against his shoulder, allowing her instincts to take over. She arched against him, drawing him deeper, and heard him whisper roughly against her lips.

"My Sunshine, this is the moment for which we were born."

She sighed—he took a deep breath. With a moan, she felt his hot seed spill into her.

For a long moment they remained as they were, neither wanting to move. He touched his mouth to her ear. "You are magnificent."

She turned her head so she could see his eyes. "I was inexperienced."

He laughed, rolling over and bringing her on top of him. "Not any longer."

Sabinah cuddled her head against his chest, listening to the thundering of his heart. "I do not want another man to touch me."

Julian suddenly jerked her to him. "No man had better try to take you to his bed. You are mine."

Sabinah realized he had spoken of belonging and

need, but nothing of commitment. Certainly he could never offer her marriage; she had not expected it of him.

For a long while they lay with him holding her. Then she felt him swell against her, and he made love to her once more.

Afterward he turned her toward him, pushing a sweat-dampened curl from her face. "You stole my breath."

"It was—it was like nothing I could have imagined," she admitted. "I wanted to cry because it was so beautiful, and I never wanted you to stop."

Julian traced her arched brow with a finger and drew it down to her swollen lips. "You have given me . . . so much more than I expected," he admitted, pulling her head against his shoulder; he was too choked up to go on.

Her hand moved to his chest, and she felt his heart accelerate.

His laughter was warm with delight as he drew her to him.

The night was magic. He made love to her again, and they fell asleep in each other's arms.

𓅃 CHAPTER TWENTY

When Sabinah awoke there were still shadows in the room. Blinking her eyes, she tried to remember where she was. When she turned to her side, her body ached, reminding her of the night she had spent with Julian. She reached out her hand, and the place beside her was empty.

Julian was gone.

Sabinah swung her legs off the bed and watched as weak light strained through the open window. Standing, she flinched at the ache in her lower body but smiled because of the reason.

The bedchamber clearly belonged to a man. Bows and arrows competed with spears and shields for wall space. She could feel Julian's presence, and it brought tears to her eyes. Moving to the window, she saw that clouds covered the sky, and it had begun to mist. But even the weather could not dampen her spirits—last night she had been in Julian's bed, and he had made her body his own.

The door suddenly opened, and she turned expectantly, managing to hide her disappointment when she saw it was not Julian.

"Mistress, I was told to bring you this clothing. Shall I help you dress?" Tanita asked shyly.

For the first time Sabinah realized she was naked. "You may put those on the bed and leave."

The young girl bowed out of the room.

After Sabinah had washed her body, she quickly dressed and fastened the beaded belt about her midriff. She slid her feet into stiff reed sandals and picked up the homespun head covering.

Sabinah was struggling with disappointment. With a heavy heart she realized the words Julian had whispered to her in the thralls of passion meant nothing to him in the light of day. Even so, she had no regrets.

Tanita had returned, bringing food, but Sabinah did not feel like eating.

"I am to tell you, mistress, when you have eaten, Apollodorus will be waiting for you at the stables."

Apollodorus, not Julian. Sabinah could not speak past the knot in her throat, so she nodded.

Sabinah took a few swallows of milk, then nibbled on a date. Glancing at the bed where she had experienced such joy, she slipped the veil over her head and left Julian's bedchamber.

"Watch over Sabinah, Apollodorus. Meet with her as much as possible."

"You are reluctant to send her back home," Apollodorus stated with his usual astuteness.

"If I had my way, I would take her into the desert where no one would ever find her."

"I understand."

Julian glanced at him. "Do you? I do not."

"Will you see her before we go?"

Julian shook his head, his gaze going to the house. "I think it best not. Ben-Gari sent word it is imperative that I meet him at Twelve Palms, so I leave at once. As soon as possible, I shall meet you in Alexandria. I believe we can still assume Uriah's home is a safe place to stay."

"Farewell, my friend."

"And to you, Apollodorus."

Somberly the Sicilian nodded. His instinct was to accompany Julian in the event he encountered danger. The time would come when the young prince would be tested by the old sheik, Moussimi. When that happened, Apollodorus intended to be with Julian. He had met the sheik once and had disliked him on sight—his shifty eyes had held a cunning expression. Apollodorus prided himself on being able to judge people—in the past, his observations had saved Queen Cleopatra's life numerous times.

Julian was young, but he was highly intelligent. He had been trained from birth to face situations like the one before him.

"Take care of Sabinah, Apollodorus. Keep her safe for me."

Apollodorus's brow creased into a frown. There was something different about his young charge. Julian's feelings for the young woman went deep. Therein might lie future trouble; Sabinah came from the family who had betrayed Lady Larania, and so Ramtat might not look upon her with favor.

He watched Julian mount his horse and ride toward the desert. At the moment, Apollodorus must let him find his own way.

Sabinah stood in the rain on the deck of the *Blue Scarab*. Although she had pulled her headdress across her forehead, rain still pelted her face. The swells on the Nile rocked the boat, and she had to hold on to the railing to keep her footing.

She glanced up when Apollodorus joined her. "The rains will be welcome to the farmers."

He met her gaze and saw uncertainty in her eyes. "Aye. Although it comes late this year."

"Has Captain Narmeri said when we will reach Alexandria?"

"He believes it will be late tomorrow evening."

Silently Sabinah nodded, glancing out at the grayness of the day.

"Should you not take shelter beneath the tarp?" Apollodorus asked.

She smiled at him. "I do not mind the rain."

"Then do it for me. I would like to talk to you."

Sabinah considered the man who had been Queen Cleopatra's personal guard. He had always seemed unapproachable and distant. Now there was a worried expression in his eyes, and she realized he was concerned for her comfort. "Of course," she agreed.

Apollodorus felt his heart swell with tender feelings for this small young woman who had been cast into a situation not of her making. In some ways she reminded him of Queen Cleopatra, not in looks or even in temperament—it was more that when she felt strongly about a situation, Sabinah was not to be deterred from her course. She was loyal, and her feelings for Julian ran deep.

He took her elbow and guided her to the shelter. When she was seated on a cushion, he sat across from her in the small space.

Sabinah removed her damp headdress, laying it aside,

then combed her fingers through her hair in an attempt to tame the profusion of wild curls. "What did you want to speak to me about?"

"You are aware you are putting yourself in danger by returning to your stepmother's house, are you not?"

Sabinah was surprised by his concern. "I do not expect to meet with physical harm, though few can interrogate with the dedication my stepmother employs. You and I know I must guard what I say. She can never learn I was with Julian."

"Then let us put our heads together and think of a story that will satisfy your stepmother."

Sabinah gave a small nod.

"Should you have need of me, you will find me at the marketplace every afternoon. Most other times I will be at Uriah's house. Apparently your family does not know of that location."

"They would have no reason to know."

"As you say."

"Is Julian in danger?"

She deserved the truth, and he would not hold back. "He might be. Most probably."

"Then why are you not with him?"

"Because Julian wished it so. He has many loyal friends to stand at his side. You have only me."

Her eyes filled with tears, and she choked them back. Since her father's death, no one had cared what happened to her. "I thank you." She touched his hand. "I have never had a loyal friend before."

Apollodorus felt a tightness in his chest as he wondered what Sabinah's daily life was like, living with her stepsister and stepmother. "I am honored that you consider me a friend."

* * *

It was full dark when Sabinah entered her house. She was grateful to discover Trisella was away from home but sorry that she would have to face Bastet alone.

Her stepsister stormed into the small chamber where Sabinah often found sanctuary among her father's scrolls.

"So you decided to come home!" Bastet circled Sabinah, her face drawn up in anger. "You have once more disgraced this family. Look at your tangled hair, and those rags you wear. Let us hope none of our friends saw you in this condition."

Sabinah had been looking out the window, dreading this moment. "I care little what your friends think of me."

"You might have considered my mother's feelings. It would have been better for us if you had never returned at all."

Trisella chose that moment to return home. "Just where have you been?" she demanded as she entered the chamber.

"I had to get away," Sabinah said, focusing on Trisella while remembering what she and Apollodorus had decided she would say—which, in fact, was not far from the truth. "Tribune Vergilius has become too attentive to me, and I am afraid of him."

Trisella stalked across the stone floor, gripping Sabinah's arm. "Fool! The man wants to marry you. I cannot understand why he bothers with you after the way you treat him. Can you guess what he did when he learned you had gone away?" Trisella did not wait for an answer. "He was stricken to the heart." She shook Sabinah until her head snapped back. "Where did you go and who have you been with?"

Sabinah stepped away from Trisella. "At first I walked the streets." That much was true. Then she began the fabrication. "When night fell, I was afraid to come home, fearing you would force me to marry that Roman pig."

Bastet's voice had a disgruntled edge to it when she said, "I have always known you were simpleminded. Vergilius would have been better satisfied if he had sought me for his wife. I recognize a man with a shining future when I meet him."

"By the gods, I wish he had chosen you!" Sabinah declared. "I detest the man. I wish he would leave me alone."

Trisella's eyes bored into her. "I told the tribune we sent you out of Alexandria to visit relatives, which seemed to satisfy him. But he keeps asking when you will return."

When Sabinah made no reply, Trisella's eyes narrowed. "You speak of everything but where you have been hiding these many days."

Apollodorus had given her names of people he trusted and told her he would make certain they would repeat her story should anyone ask questions.

"Do you know the fishmonger and his wife?"

Trisella shook her head in disgust. "Why should I know such people? Do I look like I do the marketing? Do I look like I would be friends with such people?"

Sabinah had to keep the story straight in her mind. "They were kind to me. Gave me food and allowed me to sleep in their small shed at the back of their house."

"Which is why you smell of fish," Bastet said with disgust. "Associating with such people makes you just as revolting in my eyes."

Bastet's criticism had no effect on Sabinah, rather she

felt relieved that Bastet seemed to believe her story. It had been wise of Apollodorus to splash fish oil on her cloak. "Stepmother, will you excuse me? I am weary and need to bathe."

"Go. And do not come into my presence until you are presentable. You are a disgrace to this family. Let us hope Tribune Vergilius does not hear of your . . . adventure."

Sabinah hurried out of the room before her stepmother decided to question her further.

When she reached her bedchamber, Isadad was waiting for her. "Most precious child, where have you been?" she asked, clasping Sabinah to her. "I feared you were dead!"

Sabinah did not dare tell Isadad the truth. She told her she had been staying with the fishmonger's family. Although Isadad nodded, Sabinah could see she did not entirely believe her.

The servant wrinkled her nose. "You will want to get out of those filthy rags and into the bath."

Sabinah took a deep breath. Convincing her stepmother and stepsister to believe her lies had been easier than she had expected. Convincing Vergilius that she had changed her mind about him would be more difficult and more dangerous.

𓅃 CHAPTER TWENTY-ONE

Rome

A year had passed since Octavian had been given supreme power by the Senate. He had proclaimed himself Augustus Caesar, which to his way of thinking made him "master of the world." By becoming emperor of Rome, he had achieved a greatness that had eluded his illustrious great-uncle, Julius Caesar.

His mouth thinned in a satisfied smile. He held the power to bring down empires and strike fear in the hearts of his enemies. At the age of forty-three, he had outgrown the illnesses that had plagued his youth. He had everything he could desire except a son of his blood.

Sometimes at night when silence surrounded him, disquiet crept into his thoughts, and try as he might, he could not rid himself of the fear that his empire would crumble if he did not keep a firm grasp on every province.

Egypt.

Augustus's real worry was that if he lost Egypt, he would lose the most important territorial dominion under his rule. He felt a real fear growing inside him. Where but in Egypt could Rome find such an abundance of riches and a constant supply of food?

Augustus glanced down at his hands and watched

them tremble. He had a greater fear that he had not mentioned to anyone. Twice when he had awakened, he had found a dagger driven into his pillow. The words still swirled around in his brain, *Lift the death sentence on the Tausrat family or die.*

His body shook. How could anyone get so close to him while he slept?

Augustus was not a man to be threatened, and he had no intention of allowing anyone with Ptolemy blood to live. He had doubled the guard outside his bedchamber, satisfied that now no one could get past them.

Thus far, the Tausrat family had eluded him. How could they have disappeared without leaving a trace? Roman legions had searched for them throughout Egypt, but it was as if the sands of the desert had opened up and swallowed them. That cursed family had become a legend in Egypt, and even in Rome. It stuck in his throat that the eldest son was now a man and had the power to raise armies if he so chose.

One of Augustus's generals had convinced him to speak to an oracle. Augustus was not a man who believed in such practices, but what could it hurt to listen to the woman?

Seated on a soft sofa in his small library, he watched the soothsayer he had summoned move with an awkward gait toward him. Ka'tu's stringy white hair frizzed about her head, and her back was hunched from a birth mishap. Augustus watched her pause in the middle of the room and stare at the two stoic-faced guards who stood on either side of him.

He motioned her forward. "Approach me. Let us see if you are as clever foretelling the future as my general believes you to be."

The old woman limped toward him and dropped gratefully onto the stool that had been provided for her. She had not yet glanced at the emperor, but stared down at her own gnarled hands, which rested in her lap.

"Look at me," Augustus ordered.

Slowly she raised her head, and Augustus stared into a pair of eyes as black as a bottomless pit. He resisted the urge to shiver. "One of my officers has faith in your ability to see into the future. What do you see in mine? I put little credence in soothsayers, but it would amuse me to hear what you have to say."

Ka'tu shook her head, her white locks bobbing up and down. "I dare not."

"Do you fear me?"

"Aye," she admitted. "If I tell you something you do not want to hear, you might have me slain."

Augustus said with amusement, "If you can really read the future, you would know I have no intention of harming you. Tell me that which I seek."

Her voice was deep, almost whisper-soft. "I have learned that men of power sometimes change their minds."

She was beginning to irritate him. "My word is my honor, old woman. Tell me what you think you know."

"I can tell you if your life will be happy," she said hopefully.

Augustus gave her a dark look. "I am not so frivolous as to ask such a question. Think you I do not know a man is neither happy nor entirely unhappy for any duration?"

Ka'tu drew in a relieved breath. She would not want to be the one to tell him his death would come at the hands of his own wife, the empress Livia. Poison would be her method, and the reason would be ambition, to place her own son, Tiberius, in power. But that would not come to pass for many years, so why should she risk the emperor's anger by speaking against his wife? She had seen a dire fate ahead for this man. But she would tell him no more than he asked of her.

"Others before you have said that those who rule after me will lose their grip on Egypt. Have you seen this as well?"

She took a relieved breath. He wanted only to know about power, and she could tell him that. "Aye, Exalted One, Egypt cannot be contained, nor can any of the provinces Rome has gathered under her . . . yoke . . . er . . . protection. But none of this will happen in your lifetime."

"Will those of Ptolemy blood regain control of Egypt?"

"That is behind a gray curtain."

"You give me nothing. Tell me if I must fear the Tausrat family, especially the eldest son, Julian."

She closed her eyes and was quiet for a long moment. When she glanced back at the emperor, it was as if her irises were swirling. "In this you have two choices." She counted on her first finger: "You can pursue this family unto death, but should you do this, I see an angry people pouring out of the desert in great numbers, seeking revenge and wreaking havoc, spilling Roman blood. There is a chance these desert people will unite Egypt, and should that happen, Rome will surely lose its grip on that land, and the Ptolemy house will once more rule."

Augustus felt sweat gathering at the nape of his neck and trickling down his back. This simple woman could not know of the Tausrat family's ties to the desert Badari. He stood and began pacing, trying to gather his thoughts. "You can no more see the future than I," he accused.

"Then I am free to leave?" she asked hopefully, struggling to her feet.

"Sit down," he said, mystified by her prediction, and more than a little irritated. "You said I have two choices."

"Aye. You do."

"Well, imbecile, what is the second?"

Ka'tu did not like anyone calling her names, but she managed to hide her anger. "You can make certain you cause no harm to that bloodline. Even now the Egyptians simmer with hatred over the loss of their queen. It would only take a word from the Tausrat family to prod them into war against Rome."

The old woman's words struck fear in Augustus's heart. Whether or not she spoke of things she could foretell, he did not know. But her predictions felt like the truth.

"Be gone," he said, waving his hand dismissively.

She stood but made no attempt to leave.

"I said go!" he repeated with force. He wanted her out of his sight so he could think.

"I am but a poor woman, Mighty Augustus. To speak truth, I have but little bread to feed myself."

He picked up a bag of coins and tossed it to her, then motioned to one of the guards. "Escort her out."

After the old woman had gone, Augustus spoke to the remaining guard. "Have General Marcellus Valerius brought to me at once."

As the guard rushed to do his emperor's bidding, Empress Livia entered the chamber, making her way quickly to her husband's side. "Why do you send for General Marcellus? You know he has no liking for either of us. Do you forget he married into the Tausrat family, which makes him our enemy?"

Livia was tall for a woman. While Augustus decked

himself out resplendently, she chose to dress modestly. Her wavy hair was pulled away from her face and secured to the back of her head. She was a beautiful woman and had the habit of staring into the eyes of whomever she was conversing with at the time, making most people nervous in her company.

"True, General Marcellus is married to Lord Ramtat's sister. He will give no information about the family's whereabouts, but I am certain he knows where they are, and I wish to question him," her husband said with annoyance.

"Perhaps if you have him tortured, he will tell what he knows."

Augustus waved his hand in dismissal. "My dear," he said solicitously, giving her an indulgent smile. "Marcellus has powerful friends in the Senate, and he is a favorite with the people. He is a hero, and even I do not dare attempt to crush him. Romans especially revere his wife, though she is Egyptian. It is widespread knowledge that Lady Adhaniá risked her own life in an attempt to save Caesar. The people will never forget that."

"Take my advice and send Marcellus to one of the remote provinces so the people will forget him."

Augustus shook his head, knowing his wife's advice was usually wise, but not in this instance. She did not fully understand the loyalty Marcellus commanded in Rome. "I dare not even do that. If I sent him anywhere, it would be to Egypt. No one would criticize me for that."

Livia swept a stray curl behind her ear, determined to change her husband's mind, but ever so subtly, as usual. "Of course they would not, because it would be no punishment for him. It is well known he and his Egyptian wife maintain a large villa there. Do not forget how close Marcellus's nephew stood to the throne of Egypt."

Augustus sighed. "You are probably right; I cannot send him to Egypt. I will keep him in Rome, so he can be watched. Why am I plagued by this family?"

Livia looked at her husband in disgust. "Because you place too much importance on them." She moved across the room, waving a delicate hand. "Do as you think best, but I still advise you to send him to a faraway province—Gaul perhaps."

Augustus watched her leave, his mind going back to the oracle's warnings. If she was correct, he must not spill one drop of Tausrat blood, but perhaps he could imprison them. He shook his head. Too risky. He was angry that he had gained such power and yet still feared members of the Tausrat family.

He felt a quiver race through his body and suddenly his hands began to tremble. He, and he alone, was responsible for the deaths of Queen Cleopatra and her son. Egypt had a long memory, and the Tausrats were the highest-ranking family left in Egypt.

The mighty Augustus, ruler of the world, hoped he did not spend another sleepless night wrestling with the ghosts of the Ptolemy bloodline.

𓅃 CHAPTER TWENTY-TWO

Alexandria, Egypt

Sabinah had been home for twelve days, and nothing out of the ordinary had occurred. Trisella, for the most part, ignored her, as did Bastet. Although there had been banquets on three occasions, Sabinah had not been pressed to attend. The word was that Vergilius was away from Alexandria, and she imagined that was the reason she had been left alone.

Tonight, however, her stepmother had ordered her presence, and Sabinah supposed the tribune had returned.

The garden was softly glowing with the light of lanterns hanging from trees and others placed along the path. The banquet chamber was ablaze with light, and music filtered through the house.

Sabinah dressed in white, her only adornment a golden clasp that held her gown together on one shoulder, leaving the other bare.

When she entered the banquet chamber, her stepmother's head was bent as she listened to something a Roman officer was telling her. The man touched Trisella's breast, and he must have whispered something risqué because her stepmother gave a throaty laugh. Sabine felt a blush of humiliation climb her face.

"So you have returned."

Sabinah turned to find Vergilius right behind her. "As you see." She reminded herself that she must be nice to him if she was to help Julian. "I heard you, yourself, were away," she said, softening her voice.

Encouraged, Vergilius smiled down at her. "I was in the desert. Not a place that appeals to me."

Warning bells went off in her mind. "The desert. Why would you go there?"

He shook his head. "Nay, little beauty. You shall not coax secrets from me."

She remembered their last conversation had ended in an argument, and she needed to make amends. "Then of what shall we speak?" she asked, looking him straight in the eye.

He was intrigued. "Are you are not still angry with me?"

"Why should I be?"

He touched her bare shoulder and when she did not move away, he felt encouraged. "I am sorry we quarreled when last we met. I must find a way to make it up to you." He withdrew something from his tunic and dangled it before her. The wristband was gold with a medallion of a falcon head inlaid with lapis lazuli.

Sabinah's eyes widened. "I cannot take that. Since it has the head of a royal falcon, it must have been stolen from the tomb of a king or queen." She shivered in horror. "Is that what you were doing in the desert— breaking into a royal tomb?"

"Nay, nay," Vergilius hastened to assure her. "I bought this from a merchant, intending it for you."

"I do not believe you. There could be no other reason for you to go into the desert."

Vergilius looked stunned. "If you must know, a Macedonian boatman told me he had heard Lord Julian had been sighted in a small fishing village."

"An unlikely tale."

He sighed wearily. "You might well think so. The people in the village would tell me nothing, although I threatened their lives, and roughed a few of them up a bit."

Being nice to the tribune was not as easy as Sabinah had thought it would be. "Perhaps they did not tell you anything because they did not know anything."

"Perhaps."

"Did you do harm to those simple people just because some Macedonian boatman told you a tale?"

"Nay. They suffered no more than a few bruises." He held the wristband out to her with hope in his eyes. "Will you accept this from me?"

She folded her arms over her chest. "I will not. You may not have taken it from a sacred tomb, but someone did."

Bastet was walking past and had overheard their conversation. She grabbed the wristband and slid it onto her wrist. "If my half-wit stepsister does not want this, you can give it to me."

Vergilius held out his hand. "It was a gift for Sabinah. If she does not want it, I shall return it for something she will like."

Bastet removed the wristband and dropped it at Sabinah's feet, her face red with fury. She stalked away, her steps jerky because she was so angry.

Vergilius scooped up the wristband and turned his

attention to Sabinah. "Enchantress, while I was away I had time to think about our relationship."

"As did I." She swept her hand toward the nearest couch, aware both Trisella and Bastet were watching her. "Shall we sit? I believe my stepmother has arranged for entertainment."

"Could we not walk in the garden? I want to be alone with you."

Sabinah reached for something to say. She did not want to be alone with him. "I have not eaten since morning, and I find I am hungry."

He took her arm and led her forward. "Then let us dine."

Sabinah reached for a joint of pheasant and nibbled on the juicy meat without tasting it.

Vergilius watched her, his gaze on her lips. "I have a hunger as well, but it is not for food."

Sabinah shivered with revulsion, knowing she must turn his mind to other matters. "How is your search going for rebels against Rome?" She did not want to single Julian out lest Vergilius become suspicious.

He shrugged his wide shoulders. "I have captured a few." He leaned back on a cushion, watching her carefully. "Take for instance, General Heikki, who ranks high with the Badari, but who is now in my custody."

Vergilius reached to offer her a grape, but she refused it with the shake of her head, her mind swirling at what he had just disclosed. "You were saying?" she prodded, feeling sick inside. She remembered the dark-eyed general who rode so proudly beside his prince.

Vergilius's smile did nothing to soften his harsh features. His dark gaze reminded her of a wolf about to devour its kill.

"The Badari are a stubborn people—this man . . . Heikki will tell me nothing, although I have applied the whip. But he will talk. Before I am finished with him, he will beg me to listen to him."

Sabinah reached for a grape and slid it into her mouth, but it stuck in her throat. Reaching for a goblet of wine, she took a sip. "Do you not fear someone will try to rescue him?" she asked, hoping he would tell her where General Heikki was being held.

"I have no fear of that. He is chained in the guard-house at my villa. Not even a spider could slip past my guards."

"Your villa? Do you mean the one that belonged to Lady Larania?"

His expression hardened, and he gripped her shoulders. "That lady forfeited the property when she died," he replied in a hard tone, his fingers tightening. "As all traitors to Rome must die."

Sabinah nodded in the direction of the scantily clad dancers that had entered the chamber, whirling and swaying to the tune of a flute. She needed to get away from him. She must get word to Apollodorus about Heikki.

Looking into Vergilius's eyes, she knew he would not be easily fooled. He might even have volunteered this information in hopes she would alert Julian. As she went back over their conversation in her mind, she was sure it was a trap. But that would not stop her from telling Apollodorus. There was not a doubt in her mind that Vergilius had captured the Badari general. How else would he know Heikki's name?

Feeling his hot gaze on her, Sabinah took another sip of wine. She stared at his hand, which had suddenly landed on her thigh. There were black hairs on the knuckles, and the fingers were blunt and strong. These were the hands that had slain Lady Larania.

Feeling sick, she placed the wine goblet on the table beside her. "If you will excuse me, it is too hot in here. I am feeling unwell."

He rose beside her, noticing she was pale. "Can I take you into the garden?"

"Nay. Forgive me, I must retire." Sabinah knew as she hurried out of the room, the tribune was staring after her. Her only thought was to get word to Apollodorus before General Heikki was slain.

Trisella appeared beside the disgruntled Vergilius. "My stepdaughter is skittish. She will come around in time."

"I do not have time," he said bitingly. "I have offered her marriage, which is more than most of my countrymen would do. She should recognize the honor I pay her."

Trisella could feel the opportunity to advance in society slipping away because of her stepdaughter's stubbornness. "I wonder if Sabinah would be more amenable if I gave her a drug?"

"Of what are you speaking?" he asked, frowning.

"A drug that must be use sparingly because the main ingredient is rare and difficult to obtain. It is from the scales of a fish found deep in the sea."

"What are you saying?"

"You have my promise it cannot be tasted, and the one who drinks it will relax into a restful night's sleep if given one drop. But if I administer two drops, the victim will be rendered completely helpless."

"Are you mad, woman? Look you, I do not want Sabinah helpless when I make love to her. Rather I would have her biting and scratching."

"But think of this," Trisella said cunningly, "she will know everything you do to her, yet she will be unable to prevent it." Her eyes gleamed. "After you have had your way with her, I feel she will be more accepting of your offer of marriage. What do you think?"

Vergilius considered a long moment. "Nay. I have heard of your potions, and I have been warned against them. And further, I have committed many grievous acts in my lifetime, but I have never taken a woman who was not willing to have me in her bed."

"That is because you are handsome, and no woman would want to deny you."

"Except your stepdaughter. I want Sabinah in my bed, 'tis true, but I am opposed to your method. By the gods, woman, she is under your protection!"

Trisella slid her long shapely fingernails down his arm. "Would that I were my stepdaughter and had caught your attention. I would not say nay."

"Madam," he said, removing her hand from his arm, "as much as I admire you, you are past your prime."

Trisella took an angry step away from him. "I still stir the passions of many men."

"I have little doubt of that," he remarked graciously. "But it is Sabinah I desire."

Jealousy burned inside Trisella. "My stepdaughter is not as amenable as Bastet. Sabinah does not like the things Bastet craves."

Vergilius became impatient. "I know all about Bastet. But she is not the one I want. It is my hope to change Sabinah's mind about me. I have approached her all wrong. I should have wooed her with words."

"Why do you prefer her to Bastet? She cannot compare to my daughter, who is a rare beauty, and Bastet needs no wooing."

"What you say was once true—Bastet was and is a beauty. When Sabinah was all legs and arms and had the shape of a lad, I did not see her beauty. But have you taken a good look at Sabinah lately? She is as delicate as a flower. There is something about her that draws the eye. Nay, madam, your daughter is no longer the beauty of the family."

Trisella drew herself up in anger. "Ridiculous!"

He laughed and turned away. "Perhaps you and I see beauty in different ways."

CHAPTER
TWENTY-THREE

Sabinah crossed the corridor, heading through the garden to reach the kitchen, knowing she would be less likely to encounter any of Trisella's guests in that direction. As she hurried past the herb garden, golden light spilled into the darkness from the kitchen doorway. She slowed her steps, squared her shoulders, and went into the kitchen.

The cook, Ma'dou, stood at a scarred table, her cleaver raised to lop the head off a waterfowl. She paused in shock as she saw Sabinah standing in her kitchen.

"Mistress, is there aught you need?"

Two other servants turned their shocked gazes on the young mistress of the house. A third servant looked questioningly at her as well. There was no mistaking she was of Badari descent—she would be Rafta.

"Forgive my disturbing you," Sabinah said, her gaze first on Ma'dou, then turning slowly to the Badari. "I must have taken a wrong turn, meaning to go to the garden. The night is dark." With the slightest nod, she left quickly, fearing her strange behavior might be reported to her stepmother.

She paced the herb garden, shivering in the night air

as she waited for Rafta. Time passed and still the woman did not appear. Could Rafta have misunderstood her intentions?

Just when Sabinah was about to give up in frustration, the woman emerged from the shadows. "Forgive me, mistress. Ma'dou has eyes like the hawk—she watches my every move."

Sabinah knew how devoted to duty Ma'dou was, and when she missed this young woman, she would come looking for her. "You must get word to Apollodorus at once. General Heikki has been captured by Tribune Vergilius. Most probably he has been tortured because that is Vergilius's way."

She heard the woman gasp. "Mistress, General Heikki is a most important man to the Badari."

"I know this. Inform Apollodorus the general is being held at the guardhouse of what was once Lady Larania's villa."

The woman's eyes darted about in fear. "I will go at once, mistress."

Sabinah caught her hand. "Take this warning with you—I suspect this whole incident might have been set up as a trap. Apollodorus will know what to do."

"Mistress, what if the cook comes looking for me?"

"I shall take care of Ma'dou. Hasten! There may not be much time to save Heikki."

After Rafta disappeared, Sabinah reentered the kitchen and approached the cook. "Ma'dou, your poor helper was ill and shaking with fever, so I sent her to her room. Allow her to rest for the night. We do not yet know if she is contagious and do not want the rest of the house to become ill."

"If she be sick, I do not want her around my kitchen,"

the cook said, slicing through a plump date and dipping it in honey but giving Sabinah a guarded look as if she did not believe her.

Sabinah knew that no matter her suspicions, Ma'dou would not betray her. She left the kitchen and went straight to bed.

She lay in the dark, tense and fearful that Vergilius had set a trap and she had sent Apollodorus right into it. She wondered what could be happening at that very moment? Had Apollodorus freed General Heikki, or had he been taken prisoner as well?

It would be many hours before she knew the outcome of this night's work.

The night was dark as Apollodorus and three hand-picked Badari slid over the wide wall. He held up his hand, urging them to halt while his gaze swept across the courtyard. He spotted the two guards near the gate, smiling to himself—he would never have come through that entrance. There was another guard near the fountain—he might be a problem.

He motioned to one of his companions and whispered, "Eliminate him."

The man faded into the shadows, and there was only a soft muffled sound and a sharp crack—the Bardari had broken the neck of the man near the fountain.

Stealthily, the four of them moved toward their goal. There were three men outside the guardhouse, and most probably one or more inside. Without a sound, the Badari attacked the three Romans while Apollodorus slipped into the building. There was no one in the room except Heikki. His arms were chained to the wall, and he was unconscious.

Apollodorus, with his mighty strength, yanked the chains from the wall and freed Heikki. He bore the unconscious man's weight, and joined the others. They slipped over the fence without the guards at the gate being any the wiser.

Vergilius swore as he shoved the guard against the wall. "How is it someone came in here, took my prisoner, and yet none of you heard anything? Imbeciles! Gutless cowards!" He turned to Centurion Gallius in anger. "Fifty lashes for every man," he announced with venom. "Then two weeks of nothing but broth and bread."

In a fury Vergilius stalked away. Even as he had laid the trap for Sabinah, he had hoped she would not fall into it. Now she had committed treason, and for that she would pay!

Remembering the conversation he had had with Trisella, and how she had offered to drug Sabinah, he paused to think. Before, he would have felt guilty for taking advantage of Sabinah in such a way, but now she deserved no pity from him.

He would have her. She would not be able to refuse him anything.

Trisella laughed as she read the message from Tribune Vergilius.

Bastet glanced up inquiringly, her mouth full of grapes. "What is it, Mother?"

Trisella quickly explained to Bastet that she had suggested drugging Sabinah.

"And he has agreed!" Bastet exclaimed. She reached for a glass of wine and took a gulp. Having heard about the drug's effects, she was in horror.

"For whatever the reason, our tribune has agreed. I shall send him my answer at once. Sabinah will soon learn there are many ways to command her obedience."

Bastet frowned. "I do not like the sound of this drug. And how do I know you will not one night use it on me?"

Trisella looked at Bastet with a frown. "You, my daughter, do not need a drug to make you compliant."

Bastet stared into her mother's determined eyes. "Is there no other way?"

"Not with her," Trisella said with excitement creeping into her tone. "I shall have the potion ready tonight."

Neither of them saw the Badari woman who was on her knees near the door, scrubbing the tile floor. Nor did they see her scamper to her feet and quickly leave the chamber.

A short time later, Trisella was adding ingredients and mixing the potion. Heat from the brazier wafted across her face, and the sweet pungent smell of herbs filled the air. She reached for a bottle with shimmering blue liquid and smiled as she added two drops. The fumes alone were enough to send her mind reeling. She closed her eyes, imagining Tribune Vergilius's strong hands on her own body. He was a handsome man, and she yearned to feel his lips on hers. She swayed as passion rose inside her. She imagined him pushing her down on a bed and plunging inside her.

A moan escaped her lips, and she was panting.

Her eyes flew open, and hatred filled her mind. Trisella had married her husband, not out of any love she had for him, but because she was a slave and he was the master of the house. She had served Sabinah's mother, despising her all the while. Lately her stepdaughter had become a gentle beauty as her mother had been, and Trisella despised them both.

When the potion cooled, Trisella removed it from the brazier and poured the liquid into a vial. She held it up to the light and smiled. Sabinah would soon lose her arrogance—she would have no choice when Vergilius took her body and destroyed her pride.

Sabinah was reluctant to attend the banquet. She had heard nothing from Rafta, who was nowhere to be found. Ma'dou complained the woman had left a mountain of untended chores, and she would not have her back even if Rafta begged her.

Sabinah had no way of knowing whether Heikki had really been Vergilius's prisoner, or whether the tale had been a trick. She needed to discover what had happened, even if it meant spending the evening with Vergilius.

On entering the banquet chamber, Sabinah saw the tribune standing across the room, so she started in his direction. Her stepmother intercepted her.

"Sabinah, I know you do not wish to be here. You look pale tonight. Perhaps a cup of wine and a good night's sleep will make you feel better."

Sabinah was stunned by her stepmother's solicitude. "You do not mind if I leave the gathering?"

"I insist on it." Trisella maneuvered her down the corridor. "You get into bed, and I shall bring you wine to help you sleep."

Blinking her eyes in astonishment, Sabinah stared at her stepmother. Not even when she had been a child had Trisella shown any interest in her well-being. At the moment, however, she wanted to speak to Vergilius so she could find out what had happened to Heikki. "Usually you insist I entertain Tribune Vergilius."

"Bastet can see to his needs." They had reached Sabinah's bedchamber, and Trisella spoke to Isadad, who was straightening the bed. "You may leave. My stepdaughter is going to bed."

Isadad was stupefied, her gaze going to Sabinah questioningly. Bobbing her head, she made a quick retreat.

"I shall be back shortly, expecting to see you in bed," Trisella said, smiling as she left the chamber.

Sabinah's eyelids felt heavy, and she could only open them the merest bit. After her stepmother urged her to take a few sips of wine, Sabinah must have fallen asleep right away because she did not even remember her stepmother leaving the room.

Sabinah felt so hot. Needing to throw the bedcovers off, she discovered she could not move. She could swallow, hear, feel, but her body would not react when she tried to lift her legs.

Her whole body seemed weighted to the bed. Her blood froze in her veins, and she felt cold all over.

Fear tore at her mind.

The shadowy world of her bedchamber, normally comforting and familiar to her, now was terrifying. Sabinah was living a nightmare, yet she knew she was awake.

She tried to cry out for help, but no sound passed her lips. Attempting to raise her arms so she could pull herself out of bed, she discoved they did not respond at all.

Suddenly she heard voices, and relief washed over her. There was a flicker of light as someone approached with a lantern. Whoever it was stood just out of her view, and she could not turn her head.

She heard whispering, but did not understand the words.

Why did they not help her?

When she recognized Trisella's voice, Sabinah felt relieved. But then her blood froze when she understood her stepmother's words.

"Mark you this," Trisella said, lifting Sabinah's arm and allowing it to fall limply back onto the bed. "My stepdaughter has no control over her movements. She is yours tonight."

Whom was her stepmother talking to?

If she could have screamed, Sabinah would have. Vergilius's voice sent fear slamming into her.

"Finally she is mine. Traitor though she be—she is mine."

Sabinah felt his fingers move over her arm and down her side, and she realized she was naked! Had her stepmother removed her clothing?

"My eyes have never beheld such beauty," he said in a deep voice. "Sabinah has an audacious spirit that I want to capture."

Sabinah felt Vergilius's hand move to her breasts, and she wanted to scream, and scream, and scream.

Then she heard Trisella's laughter. "Imagine having a woman who cannot respond to your touch, but whom you can use in any way you choose, and she cannot object."

Stricken to the heart, Sabinah felt a tear seeping from her eye. Trisella had committed the most reprehensible betrayal. She had drugged her, leaving her helpless. She felt Vergilius's hot, wine-scented breath against her face, and her stomach lurched.

"Get out!" Vergilius said in a husky voice. "Leave me alone with her."

Sabinah heard her stepmother's retreating steps and wanted to call her back. There was no one to help her—no one to stop this man from ravishing her body.

His hand touched her breast, stroking gently. "Long have I wanted you. Now I will have you."

She was Vergilius's victim, and there was no one to save her.

"You are mine," he said triumphantly, touching his mouth to hers.

Sabinah felt his hand trail down her thigh, but it went no farther.

She felt his weight leave her suddenly, and he uttered a muffled sound.

"Long have I wanted my dagger at your throat. Long have I craved your death."

It was Julian!

She heard more muffled sounds and felt a covering being thrown over her body. She recognized Apollodorus as he lifted her off the bed and into his comforting arms.

"Have no fear, Sabinah, you are safe. No one will harm you now," the Sicilian murmured.

There was more scuffling, and Sabinah heard Julian speak.

"I would drive my dagger into your heart, but that would be too easy a death. I want you to experience fear such as my grandmother must have known when you tortured her. I want you to remember that Sabinah belongs only to me. Think of me lurking in every shadow. I want your sleep to be populated by nightmares of when I shall come for you. Sleep lightly, Tribune, and place guards about you, but even that will not save your life. The next time we meet, you shall die."

"You are Julian Tausrat," Vergilius said, fear in his tone.

"You had better gag him, or he will have the whole household upon us," Apollodorus suggested.

"I know you, Sicilian. You are a marked man from this night forward," Vergilius hissed in fury.

Apollodorus laughed. "I tremble in fear, Roman."

Sabinah heard Vergilius cry out in pain, and from the sounds, she imagined Julian was tying him to the bed, and none too gently.

"I assume the servants were told not to disturb you until morning," Julian said. "Your gag is tight, cutting into your skin, and the ropes will cut off circulation to your arms and legs if you make any movement. Imagine the horror of not being able to move or to speak, and not knowing what awaits you in the dark. This will be a long night for you, not exactly the way you intended it to be."

Sabinah felt no pity for Vergilius. He was merciless, and he deserved no mercy.

Julian continued to speak quietly, but there was something deadly in his tone. "I was told all of my grandmother's fingers were broken before she died. Tonight I break only two of your fingers so you will know some of the pain she suffered."

Sabinah heard the sound of bones breaking and an agonized cry that was not entirely muted by the gag.

Apollodorus had lingered so Sabinah could know her tormentor had not gone unpunished, but it was time to take her away. He could sense she was distressed by what Julian was doing, but he knew that Julian was exercising great restraint, and the villainous Roman deserved a much worse fate at his hands.

Sabinah was aware they were passing through the garden because she smelled jasmine and heard the tinkle of a fountain. She heard Julian's footsteps behind them and his voice as he spoke to someone who had just appeared.

"You must leave with us, Rafta," Julian said. "It is no longer safe for you to be here. Know that I am thankful for your service. Had you not warned us and directed us to Sabinah's bedchamber, we would not have been able to rescue her."

She heard the sound of a jingling horse's bridle, and was aware when Apollodorus lifted her into Julian's arms. Moments later they rode away into the darkness.

Julian held her close and whispered in her ear, "Beloved, what manner of drug did your stepmother give to you?"

She could not answer.

"Apollodorus, her body feels like a wilted flower left too long out of water. What did they do to her?"

"I have heard of such a drug. Worry not, there will be no lasting harm when it wears off in a few hours."

Sabinah attempted to speak, but she could not. She did not know where they were taking her, but she thought it might be Uriah's house. When Julian dismounted, she heard a gate squeak.

When they entered the house, their only guide was moonlight. She imagined they did not want to draw attention by lighting a lantern.

Julian placed her on a soft bed, gently tucking the bedcover about her.

"Sleep, Sabinah. I will not leave you this night." He took her hand in his. "I wonder if you can hear me. If you can, I ask your forgiveness for placing you in such danger. Thanks be to the gods you are with me now."

Sabinah wanted to tell him she was sorry she had failed

him. She did not know she was crying until Julian bent and kissed a tear from her cheek.

"I wanted to kill the Roman for touching you."

She had heard his threats to Vergilius. Her stepmother would find him in the morning, or perhaps poor Isadad would discover him. Vergilius would be terrified after tonight. For he would know, as she did, that Julian had meant every word he'd said.

She soon fell asleep, knowing nothing would harm her tonight. Julian was watching over her.

CHAPTER TWENTY-FOUR

Rome

General Marcellus stood before Augustus wearing his red and gold uniform, his dark gaze expressionless, his dislike for the man hidden just below the surface. "You sent for me."

The irritation on the emperor's face was easy to read. "Aye, I did. Ten days ago. You took your time."

"I was outside the city of Tivolai, Octavian, overseeing the building of the aqueduct you commissioned. Although I left at a crucial moment in the construction, I came directly here."

The emperor was furious because Marcellus continued to refer to him by the name he had abandoned when the Senate had raised him high. He bit the inside of his mouth and winced from the pain, which did nothing to help assuage his anger. Marcellus did not like him, and Augustus would no longer tolerate his disrespect. "Heed this, Master Architect—I am now known as Augustus Caesar—henceforth you will refer to me by that name."

Marcellus regarded him with thinly veiled contempt. "I ask you to pardon my forgetfulness. I have always known you as 'Octavian,' and it is difficult to call you by another name."

For reasons Augustus could not comprehend, he desired this man's respect. "Is there a reason we cannot be friends? Surely that is possible since you held my father in high esteem."

"I held your great-uncle in high esteem. I never met your father."

Augustus stood and whirled around. "You dare speak thus to me?"

Marcellus did not flinch or back down. "Is the truth banned from Rome since the Senate appointed you emperor? Great Caesar was not your birth father—that is a truth known by all."

Augustus tried to take a calming breath. The meeting was not going as he had expected. Since Marcellus was married to Lord Ramtat's sister, the Lady Adhaniá, Augustus wanted his opinion on her family. The one thing he knew about his general was that he would not lie to him. "Let us get past that and speak of the reason I sent for you."

Marcellus focused his attention on the imperial banner that was draped above Octavian, no doubt to remind people of the man's divinity. "In serving you, I serve Rome," he said woodenly.

"Put your anger aside. I did not send for you to ask where your wife's family is hidden, knowing you would not tell me anyway. I will ask you this; how powerful is your brother-in-law's desert tribe?"

Marcellus saw no reason not to answer since the Badari were in no danger from Rome. "They number in the tens of thousands—their power is beyond anything you can imagine—they owe their allegiance to only one family, the Tausrats."

Augustus's face whitened—the old oracle had spoken

true. "How is it possible that the desert can support such a large number of people? Surely there is not enough water or food."

"They are scattered not only throughout Egypt, but as far as the Sinai and the deserts of Petra, and even beyond that. When their prince calls them, they come together as one, becoming an unimaginable force. The Badari have the most impassioned warriors you will ever meet. I doubt there are many among them who would not die for Lord Ramtat, whom they refer to as 'El-Badari.' And they give that same loyalty to Ramtat's son, Prince Julian."

Augustus looked thoughtful. "So it would not be beyond reason to assume the family is hiding somewhere in the desert, protected by these desert dwellers?"

"What is your reason for summoning me to Rome?" Marcellus demanded.

Augustus was hiding a secret he had shared with no one, not even Livia. Even with the extra guards at his door, he had awoken on three different occasions to find a note pinned to his pillow with a dagger. The message was always the same, threatening his life if he did not lift the death sentence on the Tausrat family.

Someone was circumventing his guard and entering his bedchamber undetected. Whoever it was could have killed him any one of those times, but had not. It was terrifying how close death had come to him. He had to put a stop to it.

"I am not asking you to tell me where I can find the Tausrats. I want to know if any of that family has designs on the Egyptian throne."

Marcellus saw a flicker of fear in Octavian's eyes, and he saw the emperor's hand tremble. Smiling to himself, Marcellus understood the reason Octavian had sent for

him. Two of Ramtat's Badari had snuck into Rome, and
their reach was long—there was no wall that could keep
them out, no guard they could not sneak past, no bedchamber they could not enter.

"I can tell you none of them harbors such an ambition. The family wants no more than to be left alone to
live their lives as they choose."

Augustus stared into Marcellus's eyes. "Is that the
truth?"

"Rather than lie to you, I would not answer your
questions at all."

"What would happen if . . . say . . ." Augustus stroked
his chin. "If one of that family died by my orders?"

Marcellus stiffened. "Should that happen, you would
unleash a power too terrible to imagine. The Badari are
not like us—they have served the same family as far
back as their history is recorded. At this time Ramtat's
son, Julian, is the person who holds the tribes at peace.
You do this family a great wrong. If you do not want war
to erupt and spill all over Egypt, you must cease your
persecution of my wife's family."

"I have been reconsidering a decision that was made in
the heat of anger, years ago. I may have acted too hastily
when I issued the death sentence on the Tausrat family."

Marcellus was cautious, but there was something different about Octavian, a veil of fear lurking in his eyes
when he spoke of war with the desert tribe. "I am not
sure I comprehend your meaning."

Augustus met Marcellus's gaze. "If what you say about
the Bardari is true, Lord Ramtat could already have
raised an army to drive Rome from Egypt. Why did he
not do that when Queen Cleopatra died?"

"For reasons you may not understand. Ramtat did not

want to burden Egypt with another war—he wants peace for his people, both Egyptians and Badari."

"Elaborate."

Marcellus's voice deepened with emotion. "I will share this with you—Ramtat will most certainly call for war if you cause harm to another member of his family."

"How?"

"If you knew the might of the Badari, you would not ask. Do not do it, Octavian, lest you lose your grip on Egypt and see your empire crumble."

"I believe you."

"You will never know how close you came to destruction when Tribune Vergilius tortured and killed Ramtat's mother. Lady Larania was honored by Egyptians and revered by the Badari."

"The woman did not die by my orders."

"She died because she would not tell Tribune Vergilius where to locate her family, and your tribune had the authority to torture and kill her because you gave it to him. It was an atrocity. Lady Larania had no blood connection to the Egyptian queen. Her only tie was a daughter-in-law who was Queen Cleopatra's half sister. At that time, I can tell you it took all Ramtat's strength of command to hold his Badari in check. They were crying out for Roman blood—your blood. Had Ramtat not contained them, you would have found a Badari dagger at your throat one night when you were sleeping, rather than merely a note on your pillow."

Augustus paled, dropping onto a chair. "You know about that?"

"I have heard about it. I will not say how."

"Why does the person who comes into my bedchamber not kill me?"

"Because Lord Ramtat has not authorized him to do so. He is sending you a message that he can end your life any time he wants to. If Ramtat had wanted you dead, you would be dead."

Augustus knew the truth when he heard it. "I will consider what you have said. Remain here in Rome. If I decide to remove the death warrant, I will want you to deliver the message in person."

Marcellus did not trust this man. "I would accept this mission only if you put it through the Senate, and they agree to the terms."

Augustus flinched at the insult; his word alone was not good enough for Marcellus. "You dare to challenge me!"

"It is the only way Lord Ramtat will believe you. Why should he trust you when you have caused his family so much suffering?"

Augustus nodded. "I suppose looking at the situation from his point of view, I would feel much the same," he said in a bristly manner.

"One thing more. If I were Tribune Vergilius, I would hide in the deepest hole I could find. He has not long to live."

"You threaten one of my officers?"

"Nay, not I. There are many who want his death. But they have held their hands because the honor of slaying him goes to Ramtat."

"He is a trusted officer."

"He is a dead man." Marcellus stared at Octavian for a long moment. "A life for a life. I would advise you to let it go at that."

The emperor was too shocked to respond. Marcellus had just told him one of his officers would be struck down, and that he should do nothing about it. It nettled him that the master architect had won in their verbal battle. "If Tribune Vergilius is slain, you are saying I must not retaliate?"

"That is the way of it." Marcellus moved toward the door. "You know where to find me should you have need of me."

Augustus watched him leave, thinking he should never have placed a death sentence on Lord Ramtat's family. He must reverse his decision and put the matter before the Senate, who would do as he advised them. Only then would he find peace in his sleep.

He shivered, remembering the old crone's predictions and Marcellus's warnings. He could not have foreseen the dire consequences of his edict the day of Queen Cleopatra's death.

CHAPTER TWENTY-FIVE

Sabinah awoke feeling sick. Her head pounded, and her stomach felt uneasy. Blinking her eyes, she was bewildered, not knowing where she was or what had happened to her. Memories returned bit by bit, then swept over her like waves breaking on stone as she re-lived each horrible detail.

She remembered Julian had remained with her throughout the night. Turning her head slowly, she saw he was no longer there. She recognized the room as the one she had occupied in Uriah's house.

When Sabinah attempted to move her arm, it took her several tries to succeed. It took her still longer to sit up and move her legs off the edge of the bed.

Realizing she was naked, she tucked the coverlet about her and tried to stand. The room swam, and she dropped back onto the bed, tears gathering in her eyes. She remembered Trisella being so kind and solicitous to her, and realized it should have made her suspicious. Even when her stepmother had urged Sabinah to go to bed and then had brought her wine, she had not sus-pected her motives.

Sabinah dropped her head in her hands, shaking with

silent sobs. How could Trisella have sacrificed her for her own selfish desires? She would never forgive her stepmother for such an atrocity.

She jerked her head up when she heard the door open, and Julian entered.

"I see you are awake. I only left for a moment."

Sabinah wiped tears from her eyes. "When I try to move, it makes me feel ill."

He dropped down beside her, turning her face to his. "Forgive me for sending you back into that house."

"It was not your fault."

"Tell me what happened."

"M . . . my . . . stepmother drugged me!" She could not disguise the horror in her voice. "The drug put me to sleep. I awoke to hear her telling Vergilius what she had done."

"Did Vergilius . . . did he—"

"Nay. But he would have if you had not arrived when you did." A shiver quaked through her body. "I could not abide his hands on me."

Julian nodded grimly. "As you may have guessed by now, Rafta overheard your stepmother speaking to Bastet of her plans for you. Rafta came directly to us, and we went directly to you."

"I did not know you were in Alexandria."

"I had not planned to be."

Sabinah pulled the bedcovers up to her chin. "May the gods be praised you came when you did."

He smiled grimly. "I will send the housekeeper to tend to your needs. I am sure you do not feel much like talking after such a night."

She looked at him, feeling helpless. "What will I do now?"

"It is not safe here in Alexandria for you. You will come with me to the desert."

She stared at him in amazement. "You will take me with you?"

He stood. "Nothing I can do or say can make up for what happened to you. But I intend to keep you with me." He touched her hand and then moved away. "I will give you a day to rest, and then we must leave the city."

He strode toward the doorway and turned back to her. "Forgive me."

She could do no more than nod.

Julian stood for a long moment watching her, then moved out the door without another word.

Sabinah wanted to lose her sorrow in forgetfulness, to wipe out the pain of being betrayed in such a way.

Sleep.

That was what she craved.

And that was what she did.

Isadad opened the door a crack and peered around it, fearing what she would find. It was difficult to see most of the room because the lantern had burned down, and the morning sun had not yet topped the horizon. With dread in her heart, she glanced at the rumpled bed, but Sabinah was not there. Isadad opened the door wider, taking a cautious step inside.

She had been huddled outside the door all night because that Roman pig had gone into Sabinah's bedroom and had not come out. Fearing what was happening to her poor sweet mistress, she had waited until she could stand it no longer before entering the chamber.

Tiptoeing farther inside, she waited for her eyes to become accustomed to the dark. "Mistress?"

Isadad heard a muffled sound and spun around, almost jumping out of her skin when she saw the Roman tied to the bed! Even though he had been gagged, she understood his muted curses. Her gaze swept quickly around the room as she searched for Sabinah.

Where was her mistress?

Gazing back at the Roman, she could see fury in those dark eyes. She was too frightened to release him herself, so she tore out of the room. Racing down the corridor, she banged on the mistress's door. When no one answered, Isadad banged harder. "Mistress, you must come at once! Something horrible has occurred!"

While Vergilius waited for the physician to arrive to set his broken fingers, he fumed, "Someone will answer for this atrocity."

Trisella saw the fury in Vergilius's dark eyes. "I cannot think how such a thing could happen in my home."

"Madam, I might ask the same thing. How is it that the traitor, Lord Julian, has access to your daughter's room?"

Trisella's heart slammed against her chest in fright. Since the moment she'd cut the tribune free, she had feared for her life. "I have not seen Julian since his family disappeared right after Queen Cleopatra's death. You must believe me."

Vergilius held out his cup so she could pour more wine. "I hold you responsible for what happened here," he said before taking a deep swallow of wine, wincing in pain.

"But surely you must realize I am innocent of any wrongdoing. I fear for my stepdaughter, who was taken by that traitor."

He glared at her. "You did not seem overly concerned

about Sabinah when you gave her the potion. You are a heartless harlot."

Trisella's eyes widened with fright. "Surely you have not forgotten it was I who urged Bastet to show you where Lady Larania lived."

His forehead creased in thought. "You did, but even for that, I do not admire you, madam. Your stepdaughter dwelled among vipers in this house."

"Sabinah is an irresponsible child who wants her own way. Why do you not look to Bastet? She will not have to be drugged to go to your bed."

He took another long drink of wine and wiped his mouth. "Think you I have not already had Bastet, who is most willing to bed anyone who asks?" He moved his fingers and winced in pain. "It is a mystery to me how a woman such as you could have raised a rare jewel like Sabinah."

Trisella felt her anger rise above her fear. "I have opened my house to you, when other Egyptians would not even speak to you. I took in your friends—"

"And took most of them to your bed. For which you were well compensated."

In a panic, she stepped away from him. "What can I do to make this up to you?" she asked, her face reddening.

"I have had enough of your hospitality."

"I may be able to help you locate Lord Julian," Trisella said frantically. "At one time he favored Bastet. She may be able to help."

"Madam, madam," Vergilius said, swearing when pain shot through his hand. Sweat popped out on his brow, and he took another drink of wine. "All too many men have favored Bastet at one time or another."

"You insult me."

"Leave me in peace, woman. I am in pain."

The physician arrived, and Trisella took that opportunity to rush from the room. Slowing her steps, she walked out into the morning light, knowing she was in danger of losing everything she had so carefully built over the years. If Tribune Vergilius no longer came to her house, others would stop as well.

She blamed Sabinah for all that had occurred.

Trisella walked down the pathway and back, her mind whirling. She and Bastet would return to poverty without the money they received from the Romans they entertained.

She was ruined . . . ruined.

𓅃 CHAPTER
TWENTY-SIX

Sheik Ben-Gari was cautious as he approached the house of Uriah the Jew. Silently he slipped over the garden wall, making his way to the back of the house. Many times he and Julian had sat at the feet of Uriah, listening to the old man's wisdom, so he knew the dwelling well.

A Badari guard stood beyond the garden, and although Ben-Gari was being cautious, the guard heard him. "Halt!" the man called out, lowering his spear so the point rested against Ben-Gari. "Identify yourself," he demanded.

"Ssuom, you know who I am. Take me at once to the prince. I have dire news."

Julian had fallen asleep sitting beside Sabinah's bed. His keen hearing picked up the sound at the door. When he saw who it was, he motioned for silence and followed the two men into the garden.

"Prince Julian," Ben-Gari said, reaching for the water pouch at his side and taking a quick drink to wash the dust from his throat. "Moussimi has not accepted your challenge. It is unthinkable—he insults you by issuing his own challenge."

"Tell me."

"He has asked that you meet both of his sons in combat. Should you win, he will step down as sheik of the western tribe, and you can name whomever you wish as sheik in his stead."

Julian shook his head, trying to clear his thoughts. "I have the authority to replace him with whomever I choose, without the contest," he stated.

Ben-Gari looked disappointed. He knew in his heart Julian was not a coward, but others must know it as well. "It is true, you have that power," he said cautiously. "It is my thought that he expects you to decline. So he has offered to forgo the contest, if you take his youngest daughter as your wife."

"The man is a fool." Julian knew what he must do. "Send word to Moussimi that I shall meet his challenge. Twelve days hence, I shall arrive at his encampment."

Heikki had just stepped into the garden, rubbing sleep from his eyes. "One of Moussimi's sons is an expert in the bow, and the other with a spear. They believe you have not practiced your skills while you were away from Egypt."

Julian smiled at his father's general. "My good Heikki, I was not idle while on Bal Forea. Will you be comforted if I tell you my aunt, Adhaniá, instructed me in the bow?"

Heikki nodded with satisfaction. "If you are even half as good as she, you will vanquish Moussimi's son without effort."

"That still leaves the spear," Ben-Gari stated.

"My uncle, Prince Ashtyn, was my instructor with the spear and lance."

"It is cowardly that Moussimi asks you to meet both his sons. You could reject his challenge and meet only one of them in battle," Ben-Gari stated emphatically.

"I shall meet them both," Julian said with confidence. "This tyrant must be brought down. He cannot break Badari law without consequences. I will allow him to think I am caught in his trap lest I lose face with the Badari. Let us hope I can take away his victory by defeating his sons."

Heikki grabbed Julian's arm. "It is madness. Even if you are skilled and defeat the sons, Moussimi will never bend to your will."

"He will have no choice," Julian said. "You must see that the Badari demand it of him."

"You do not expect to survive," Ben-Gari said with understanding.

"If I do not, I will expect the two of you to force Moussimi to keep his word."

Sabinah's eyes were closed when she heard two servants moving quietly about the room. She was too weary to acknowledge them.

"Our prince said not to wake this lady," a young voice whispered. "I overheard the Sicilian say they must leave the city by tonight and take her with them."

"You overhear too much," an older servant rebuked. After a moment the older woman's curiosity must have gotten the better of her. "What else did you hear?"

"I heard the prince is going into combat. Alone. Against two of Sheik Moussimi's sons. It is whispered among the men that he may be forced to marry the sheik's daughter to bring peace to the Badari."

"Enough gossip," the older servant remarked.

Sabinah heard both servants leave and turned her head on the cushion. Tightening her body into a ball, she let exhaustion wash over her. She was not sure there had not been lasting effects from the drug because her arms and legs still felt so heavy. Her mind was still muddled. Did those women say Julian was going into combat against two other men?

Refusing to give in to sleep, she swung her legs off the bed and tried to stand, but her wobbly legs would not bear her weight. Frustrated by her own body's weakness, she lowered herself back onto the bed, thinking if Julian was going into battle, it would be for a good reason.

She shook her head to clear it. Did those women say that Julian was to marry the daughter of a sheik? The thought hurt too much to ponder.

It was nearing sundown when the servants returned to prepare Sabinah for the desert journey. They dressed her in buff-colored pantaloons, in the fashion worn by Persians. She was draped in a long surcoat with slits down the sides, allowing her freedom of movement. They placed a veil about her shoulders, and soft boots completed the regalia.

Though Sabinah still felt weak, she tried not to show it as the women escorted her to the back of the house.

A heavy mist hung over the land, which Sabinah thought might work to their advantage in escaping Alexandria. She was surprised to find Julian, Apollodorus, and six Badari garbed in knee-length belted tunics with long trousers. Their dark heads were covered with round leather caps embroidered in bright colors. Julian's hawk was perched on his leather glove; the bird seemed alert, as if it sensed trouble.

When Julian looked up and noticed Sabinah, he sent his hawk into the sky and walked toward her. "How are you feeling?" he inquired with concern.

Refusing to let him know how weak she felt, she met his gaze. "Very well."

"Are you up to riding?"

She was not even sure she could remain on a horse. "I always look for a reason to ride." For the first time she noticed the white Egyptian horses they would be riding, and she understood why. They would be recognized immediately if they rode the spirited Badari breed.

Julian motioned for everyone to mount. "We will be traveling through backstreets to reach the city gates. Vergilius will be expecting us to leave by sea, but he will also have men posted at the gates," Julian said, lifting Sabinah onto a swayback white horse that was no longer young. "We must remain silent until we are out of the city gates."

Sabinah pulled the veil over her head, covering her red hair. One by one the Badari rode out the arched gate. Sabinah rode beside Apollodorus, and Julian was the last to leave.

She expected them to ride swiftly, but they kept at a steady pace, as if they had all the time in the world. She glanced about to see if anyone took notice of them. No one glanced up, not even when they passed through the marketplace.

When they reached the Gate of the Sun, the Roman

guards waved them through without even searching them. The disguise had fooled them.

Sabinah turned to glance back toward Alexandria, her gaze meandering toward the causeway that led to the Great Lighthouse, which was barely visible through the swirling mist. She had no notion where she was going, or if she would ever return to her beloved Alexandria.

For a while they followed the coastline, where high blunt rocks crafted by time and the elements jutted out of the sea. Eventually they turned away from the water and headed for the desert. Once they were out of view of the city, they picked up their pace.

After riding for hours, they came to the Nile, where over a hundred Badari waited for them with fresh horses. Once Sabinah was mounted on her powerful Badari horse, she was delighted that the animal responded to her every command with the slightest urging. Despite the thick sand, the horses galloped with ease, and when she slowed to stay even with Apollodorus, the horse sidestepped in a graceful canter.

"This horse is a joy to ride," she told him.

"The breed is without flaw," he said, smiling down at her.

Later in the afternoon, when they had dismounted to walk the horses, Apollodorus handed her dried meat, which she washed down with water.

"Can you tell me where we are going?"

The tall Sicilian gave her his full attention. "It is not for me to say."

Although she tried to hide it, she heard the sadness that crept into her voice. "I already know Julian is going into battle. I do not understand why."

Apollodorus was in the process of lifting a jug of water

to his lips, and he paused. "Do not believe everything you hear."

She would not be deterred. "I also heard Julian is to marry a sheik's daughter."

He motioned for her to mount her horse. "I have not heard that."

She stared down at the tips of her dusty boots before she swung onto the saddle. Julian had not taken her in his arms since the night she had given herself to him. Discouragement pressed on her like a weight. Of course the meeting of their bodies had not meant the same to him as it had to her. He had whispered beautiful words to her that night, but he had been gone when she awoke. Isadad once told her a man will say many things when he is in the thralls of passion.

As when Sabinah had traveled with the Badari before, they reached an encampment that had already been erected by advance guards.

The sun was setting and although she had not seen Julian since the morning, he now rode up beside her. She heard the clamoring of the silver bridle, the snort of the prancing stallion.

"Do you fare well, Sabinah?"

Without looking at him, she replied, "I am but weary."

He nodded, and she could tell he was preoccupied as he galloped away.

Apollodorus seemed to understand how Sabinah felt because his voice was gentle. "Dismount and follow me. I will see you settled for the night." He escorted her to a tent that had been set apart from the others.

Too weary to think, Sabinah removed her veil and

tossed it onto a stool, then dropped down on the tiger skin robe, closing her eyes.

"May I enter?"

Her eyes flew open as she recognized Julian's voice. Sitting up, she quickly ran her fingers through her hair, but soon decided it was hopelessly tangled. "You may," she said, standing, her heart pounding.

For better or ill, he had come to her.

CHAPTER TWENTY-SEVEN

Julian threw the tent flap aside and ducked his head to clear the low entrance. He stood for a long moment, watching her. "Pity me, Sabinah. I tried to stay away from you, but I find I cannot."

She searched his eyes, frowning. "Why should I pity you?"

His eyes held a soft light in their depths. "Because a most extraordinary woman holds me captive." He gave her a long, level look before continuing. "Is that not reason enough to ask for pity?"

Her heart lurched. "I am not sure I know what you mean."

His eyes became suddenly probing and intense, making her ache and tremble. "I am utterly and completely your slave."

"Julian, I would not have it so."

He took a step toward her and before she knew it, he laid his hand on her arm. "Sabinah, you have upset my world. You disturb my sleep and haunt my thoughts." His passionate gaze burned through her body. "What should I do about that?"

"I do not know," she said, quaking inside.

He regarded her cautiously as she stood so proudly before him, not letting her true feelings show. "I know I have hurt you, but that was never my intention." His hand slid beneath her chin, forcing her to look into his eyes. Slowly he lowered his head, touching his mouth to hers. He was impatient to hold her, to feel her skin against his.

In a surge of passion he lifted her in his arms and took them both down on the soft tiger skin robe. Artfully he stripped her of her clothing, pressing his mouth to each part he uncovered.

"Forgive me for my impatience," he said, pulling back and slipping out of his own clothing. "My body aches for you."

Her gaze fused with his. "It is the same with me."

Passion stirred within him as he reached for her. "Sabinah, I need to be with you."

She nodded. "I know."

As if Julian had no will of his own, he took her in his arms and gathered her to him. His lips brushed against her hair, gliding down her neck to nuzzle the lobe of her ear. "I have been in torment since I was last with you."

Like a sword of flames, his touch ignited her body, and she swiveled her hips and arched her back, inviting him, enticing him to take what he wanted.

With a deep growl, he gathered her close, his hand stroking between her legs, making her mindless.

Sabinah grabbed a handful of his dark hair, thrusting her body against his. She was unable to speak because her heart pounded in her throat.

Julian's hot gaze moved over her nakedness. "What is it about you that makes me want to possess you so?" He cupped her face, staring into her eyes. "I can think of nothing but you tonight. Heikki was speaking to me of tribal matters, and I left him standing there with his mouth open, to come to you."

She smiled at his admission. "I am glad you did."

He gently dragged a finger across her breast. He rubbed his chin against her cheek. "How did I live before I knew you?"

Sabinah's hand slid down his back, and she arched her lower body upward, issuing him another flirtatious invitation. "Do as I do—I live only for the next time you want me."

Julian was suddenly beyond thinking. He gripped her hips and plunged into her in a rage of passion.

Sabinah touched her lips to his, her heart racing when he groaned with pleasure. Closing her eyes, she loved him to the depth of her soul. Even knowing she could never be anything in his life but the woman he came to under cover of night, she gave everything she had to him.

The passion that held them in its grip erupted, and they clung to each other trembling, their mouths touching, their fingers intertwining.

She pushed his hair out of his face and touched her lips to his strong jaw. "I know you have so much on your mind."

He rolled over and held her away from him so he could see her face while his hand moved from one breast to the other. "Being with you helps me get through this long night."

She understood he was troubled, but there was something she must know. "Will you think of me when you take a wife into—"

He covered her mouth with his, then pulled back, puzzled. "What wife?"

"It matters not at all." She took his face in her hands. "For tonight there is but the two of us."

He shook his head, bringing her body beneath his and entering her again, driving deep. With long thrusts he made her body his.

Afterward she lay in his arms as he held her possessively. With the dawning of the new day, she knew he would once again take his place at the head of the Badari, and she must ride behind. She yearned for a day when she could ride at his side, but that would be another woman's privilege. "If this is good-bye for us, Julian, think of me sometimes," she said sadly.

"My heart, how can you say that? There will never be a time when you are not in my thoughts. But to me you are like the wind, which I cannot catch or hold in my hand."

"It is as it must be."

"There are times, like now, when there is no world outside your arms."

Sabinah sighed and turned away from him. "There is a world besides this one, Julian. A world where your true life lies."

"If you speak of the Badari, you speak truth. Their well-being depends upon what happens in the next few days."

All other thoughts flew from Sabinah's mind when Julian caressed her breasts; then his hand slid down to her thighs, gently parting them. Sabinah caught her breath, biting her lips in an attempt to smother a moan as he slid inside her yet again. Neither of them could have enough of the other. Passion was a bond that held them together.

Hot desire curled through Sabinah with such force she could not have spoken if she had wanted to. There was a sweetness to the words of longing Julian whispered in her ear while he kissed her earlobe and continued to plunder her body.

Her eyes fluttered shut as she tried to slow her racing heart. Sabinah gasped when Julian thrust deeper, and she felt the hardness of him.

She twisted beneath him, her eyes wide as wild sensations curled through her. Julian plunged forward and then slowly withdrew, only to plunge forward again and again. Sabinah heard his ragged breathing, and he thrust into her with such force she could hardly keep from crying out. Her body was attuned to his, and she had no will of her own. She held on to him as her body shook and trembled in a climax more shattering than any of the others. Moments later she felt him quake, and they both went limp.

Sabinah rained kisses on his shoulder until he raised his head, and their mouths ground together.

She watched his eyes soften, and he reached out and twined one of her stray curls around his finger. "My sweet Sunshine, will you not sleep in my arms? I need you near me to keep my demons at bay." He thought of the battles he faced, and he wondered what would happen to her if he did not return. He touched her hair, allowing his hand to drift down the soft strands. "You were an innocent when I first took you."

Sabinah touched his face. "Know this, Julian. I did not turn you away." She could see his throat working as if he wanted to say something. Slowly his head descended in a kiss so sweet it took her by surprise.

When he raised his head, he had found his voice. "My need for you will only fade when I breathe my last."

Her heart swelled with love. "And I will want to be with you when I take my last breath."

He rolled to his back and reached for her, tucking her against him. "It would seem neither of us can resist this passion between us."

"I cannot resist you," she admitted, rising up on her elbow. "Yet I must soon return to Alexandria."

"You shall not." He traced his finger up her arm. "It is too dangerous for you there."

"I am not your concern."

She saw torment in his green eyes before he turned away from her and stood. "I will not allow you to leave."

Sabinah was struck by the finality of his words. "I am not a woman of the Badari tribe, whom you can command to do as you will. I am not under your guidance, and I do not ask for your help." She was on the verge of crying, but she must not.

A muscle throbbed in Julian's jaw. "You will remain here until I decide what to do about you."

"I am no longer your prisoner. You have no right to tell me what to do," she said, pride coming to her rescue.

Angrily, Julian pulled on his clothing. He jerked the tent flap open, his gaze on her. "I do not see that you have a choice in the matter."

With those as his parting words, he was gone.

The sun had just made its appearance for the day when Julian approached Apollodorus, his brow creased in a frown. "In two more days we shall arrive at Moussimi's encampment." He reached for his horses's reins. "My mind is troubled."

The Sicilian waited for Julian to continue.

"Watch over her, Apollodorus." When he had mounted, he met the Sicilian's gaze. "Should anything happen to me—if I do not return when I face Moussimi's sons, I leave her in your care."

"I shall see her safe."

🦅 CHAPTER
TWENTY~EIGHT

The island of Bal Forea

When Marcellus stepped down the gangplank, in full Roman regalia, his brother-in-law, Prince Ashtyn, was there to greet him.

Like most of the Bal Foreans, Ashtyn had shoulder-length golden hair and wore a short tunic. The small circle of gold atop his head proclaimed him to be the husband of the queen.

"The sails of your ship were spotted yesterday by a fleet of fishermen," Ashtyn said cheerfully. "Where is my sister-in-law? Does she not accompany you?"

The men clasped arms, and Marcellus spoke. "Adhaniá remained in Rome, preparing for our trip to Egypt. I have come with urgent tidings. Take me to the family at once."

Ashtyn nodded to General Darius, who had accompanied him. Leading an extra horse forward, he handed the reins to Marcellus.

Ashtyn mounted his own horse and stared up at the palace that sat atop a hill, shimmering like a red jewel in the midday sun. "Let us be on our way at once. The family is impatient to see you."

As the three men rode along stone streets that twisted upward to the palace, Marcellus noted the differences since he had first set foot on the island ten years before. At that time this was a war-torn country where the citizens were suffering and starving. Today, strings of fish were drying in the sun, rosy-cheeked children ran alongside the horses, laughing, and women stopped their chores to wave at Marcellus in welcome.

"Prosperity continues to bless this island," Marcellus remarked.

"Aye," Ashtyn answered. "The trade Queen Cleopatra opened between Egypt and Bal Forea continues to aid our people, even though she is gone."

"How is the family?"

"Everyone thrives. Yet Ramtat and Danaë chafe to return to Egypt. They have heard nothing from Julian and fear for him."

"They will soon be returning. That is why I am here."

Ashtyn looked at Marcellus searchingly but asked nothing more, knowing Marcellus would want to give Ramtat the news first. He stared up at the palace. "I am sure Thalia will insist on going to Egypt with them."

Marcellus grinned. "It will not hurt to have a sister at Ramtat's side who is also a queen."

"That will no doubt be Thalia's thinking."

Marcellus lowered his voice. "What of Caesarion?"

"He is thriving under Thalia's care. Not long ago, he began calling her 'mother,' although she is not old enough to be his mother."

"Does he ever speak of Egypt?"

"Nay. It is as if he has blocked out that part of his life. He is known here on Bal Forea as Lord Sayan—the people here believe he is Thalia's cousin who has been orphaned."

"And so he is."

"Sayan seems content with his life. Of course, he can never again step onto Egyptian soil."

"On that we all agree."

By now they had reached the palace and rode through the courtyard toward the entrance. Marcellus dismounted, and Danaë rushed into his arms. Ramtat clasped his arm and asked about his sister, Adhaniá. Then Marcellus was swarmed by nieces and nephews who threw questions at him. His gaze met Caesarion's. As the young man grew older, he had taken on the look of his father, the great Caesar. But there was a calmness in his brown eyes, and Marcellus was glad.

As Thalia went into Marcellus's arms, he gazed down at the lovely queen, and he whispered in her ear, "You have done well with your young charge."

"He is like his mother; therefore, easy to love." Thalia looked at him expectantly. "Have you news for us?" she asked.

"Aye. Let us go inside."

The horses were led away as they entered the palace. In the small chamber where everyone had gathered, tension was heavy. Marcellus turned his attention to Ramtat. "I have happy tidings. You may go home!"

Ramtat's throat tightened. "Are you saying it is safe for me to take Danaë and the children back to Egypt?"

"Octavian has given his word none will harm you."

"Do you trust him?"

"Nay. But I trust the Senate. They have ruled that all charges against the Tausrat family be dropped, and all confiscated properties returned." He reached into his toga and pulled out a document. "I have here an official apology signed by all the senators and by the emperor himself."

"We owe you for this, Marcellus," Danaë said, touching his hand. "How can we ever thank you?"

He shook his head. "Octavian's charges against you just did not hold up under close inspection." He nodded at Ramtat. "Your husband is still well respected by Rome, and the Senate was wise enough to realize it." He nodded. "Belatedly, I admit, but the deed is done."

Thalia gave a very unqueenly whoop. "I shall have a ship loaded and made ready to sail. I will be returning to Egypt with you," she stated with feeling. "I want to make certain you are all safe." She met her husband's gaze. "Do you not think that would be wise?"

He gave her the special smile he reserved for her alone. "I believe so."

Marcellus looked around the room at the family he had acquired by marrying Ramtat's sister, Adhaniá. They were a close-knit group and had taken him in as if he were a true brother. "Adhaniá and I will be joining you as well," he said, with a smile.

"I will send you to Rome on the *War Hawk*, our swiftest ship," Thalia said. "We shall enter Egyptian waters on the *War Bird*, since she makes an intimidating sight."

Sayan smiled. "Mother," he asked Thalia, "shall I be accompanying you to Egypt?"

Thalia's face whitened the merest bit. "Nay, my son," she said gently. "I will need you to remain here. The people of the island would not feel safe if we all left them. And, of course, I will be leaving the children under your care."

He gave her a resigned nod. "I understand."

That night there was a celebration as the family gathered in the great banqueting hall. Danaë was seated beside Sayan and took his hand in hers. "You do understand why you must remain here?"

His eyes, so like Caesar's, met hers. "I do, my aunt. It does not matter. Everything I loved in Egypt is gone. Everything I now love is here on Bal Forea."

She laid her head on his shoulder, fighting tears. "I am glad you have found happiness here. You are well loved in this family."

"I have my memories, but I keep them in my heart."

"My sister, your mother, would be proud of you, as am I."

He smiled sadly. "I believe she would."

A CHAPTER TWENTY-NINE

Two days passed, and in that time Sabinah only saw Julian from a distance. It was easy to see he was troubled and mentally preparing himself for battle. Although he was surrounded by warriors, he seemed so alone. She could imagine the weight he felt on his shoulders.

The sun had risen on a bloodred sky, and the dust from the cavalcade of horses sifted through the air in fine granules. Sabinah was riding beside Apollodorus when Julian suddenly appeared at her side, staying even with her but remaining silent. Casting him a sideways glance, she saw he wore a short tunic and soft knee-high boots.

Sabinah quivered as his dark gaze raked hers, reminding her how close they had been. She noticed his hands tighten on the reins and knew he was remembering as well.

Sabinah turned her head from him, but not before she saw his nostrils flare. To be near him was torture and bliss. Nothing was clear between them. Though he had said he would not allow her to leave, no words had been spoken of a future together.

At last Julian broke his silence. "I want to explain

some things to you so you will not be taken by surprise at what is happening."

She turned to face him.

"We will be meeting with tribesmen who are rebelling against my father's rule. There may be trouble. You will be kept safely away from the fray. Should it go badly for us, Apollodorus will take you to safety. Do you understand how important it is that you remain with him?"

She nodded, not really understanding why he must face this enemy. Overhead, there was the tinkling of a small bell, and Julian's hawk landed on his gloved arm. The bird turned its head toward Sabinah and stared right at her.

Julian took a deep breath. "Look to Apollodorus."

Sabinah reached out to him in desperation, then let her hand fall by her side. "Must there be a battle?"

"There must. Do not concern yourself—the Badari you see here are our best warriors. They will defend you to a man."

"I am not concerned for my safety, Julian," she said forcefully. "It is you who is going into battle, not me— you who will be in danger."

He ignored her outburst. "We will reach Moussimi's encampment by tonight." He looked as if he would have said more, but he nudged his heels into his horse's flanks, and the animal sprang forward, leaving Sabinah to ponder his fate.

She glanced up at the sky, praying to the gods to keep him safe.

They ate in their saddles and stopped only to rest the horses. Just after the noon hour, they were joined by other warriors.

Sabinah realized there could be an all-out war.

Apollodorus nodded for her to halt, allowing the tribesmen to ride far enough ahead of them so they were not bothered by the dust of flying hooves.

It was nearing dusk when they stopped for the night. This time no tents had been erected, and there were no campfires.

Apollodorus indicated that the two of them would camp a short distance from the Badari. As they sat beneath the night sky, they dined on dried meat and fruit. It was strangely quiet with only an occasional horse stomping, or one of the men coughing. Apollodorus placed their sleeping mats upon the sand and motioned for Sabinah to take the one nearest the palm tree.

"There must be over five hundred men in the encampment. Something momentous is happening. I see that the guards have been doubled."

Apollodorus agreed with a nod. "The guards are a precaution. As for the number of men, it would be closer to two thousand."

"Will you tell me what will happen tomorrow?"

"Julian hopes to avoid a tribal war. He has been challenged by Sheik Moussimi's two sons."

Her body tensed with fear. "I overheard servants speaking about it before we left Alexandria. How can he fight against two?"

"Julian is not worried, and neither should you be."

Sabinah rested her head on her folded arms and stared at the blackened sky. "Are you worried, Apollodorus?"

"Nay. I have seen Julian fight."

"Will they both come at him at the same time?"

"General Heikki will make certain that does not happen. Sleep now, Sabinah. You must be weary."

"Where is the enemy camped?" she asked.

Apollodorus sighed patiently. "There are no enemy among the Badari, Sabinah. There are only those who are misguided. The trouble is the opposing sheik is determined to rule in Lord Ramtat's place. Julian is here to stop him."

"This is why he returned to Egypt," she said with new understanding.

"Aye. This is the reason."

"Tell me about this Sheik Moussimi."

"He has broken tribal law. If he is not made to answer for his injustices, his people will be vulnerable to their enemies because the other Badari will turn away from them." Apollodorus shifted his weight and turned toward Sabinah. "Badari law is enforced by the Tausrat family. They are what hold the people together. If some of the sheiks take it into their heads to splinter off, their enemies will swoop down on them, killing the men and taking the women as slaves."

"Could that happen?"

"I assure you it is happening. The one thing that keeps the tribe strong, and what makes enemies fear the Badari, is the might of Lord Ramtat."

"And Julian?"

"He is here to enforce his father's will. He is fearless and has been taught from birth where his duties lie."

Sabinah nodded, feeling fear for Julian, but knowing he must face this challenge and win. "May the gods protect him."

"Aye. But the gods oft protect the just. Have you not known that to be true?"

She smiled at Apollodorus, realizing he was trying to ease her mind. "I have known that." She frowned. "But I have also known great leaders, like Queen Cleopatra, who have died because of a tyrant."

Apollodorus was quiet for a time, and Sabinah thought he would say nothing more, but finally he spoke. "You loved the queen?"

"I never knew her, but I was always her loyal servant, as was my father. In my heart, I still feel tied to her—is that not common among Egyptians?"

Apollodorus surprised her when he touched her face. "In some ways you remind me of her."

Sabinah brushed away a tear. "No one has ever paid me such a great compliment."

"I am aware that you have kept Ptolemy Caesarion's secret all these years. I am grateful to you for that." He fell into silence. There was much about this young woman to admire. And she did remind him of his beloved dead queen. He had not felt any emotion toward a woman in a very long time. He did not want to see this loyal young woman hurt by anyone—not even Julian.

He would make certain she was not.

"How near is Sheik Moussimi's camp?" she asked.

"If you were to climb that tall sand dune in the distance, you would see his campfires."

Sabinah turned to her side. The moon had not yet risen, and the night was as black as the inside of a tomb, and so were her spirits.

The sun had just broken across the desert, and Julian cast a worried glance at the sky. The wind was not strong, but the dust clouds gathering in the west gave him some concern. He mounted his horse—nothing could deter him from his course.

Riding away from camp, Julian was accompanied by

his two most trusted warriors—Heikki rode to his right, Ben-Gari to his left. Julian had expected to feel some fear about what awaited him, but his only emotion was indignation toward the sheik who had broken Badari law. He was ready to meet the two sons in battle and force the sheik to face Badari judgment.

Julian held up his hand and came to a halt at the top of the sand dune. Spread out before him was Moussimi's encampment.

The sheik's tribesmen were lined up at attention, their hands on their weapons. "It would seem we are expected," Heikki said with disgust. "Moussimi thinks to strike fear in your heart by showing his strength in numbers."

Moussimi's purpose might be to intimidate Julian, but such a display merely made him angry. He rode through the two rows of Badari, making eye contact with as many as possible. Some he had known from his youth, but many he did not recognize. He set his gaze on the elder son, Tassum, and he assumed the other man standing beside Sheik Moussimi was the younger son.

Dismounting, Julian saw the fury in Moussimi's small greedy eyes, and he knew why; the sheik had expected Julian to bring all his warriors into the camp, thus angering Moussimi's tribesmen. Instead, Julian faced the multitude with just two men at his side. Already he could see respect in some of the dark eyes that watched him.

Moussimi was not a tall man. He had a round face and a small cruel mouth. One pudgy hand rested on his dagger, and his voice was laced with sarcasm when he said, "So you came. I was not sure you would take up my challenge."

Julian stood a good head taller than the sheik. "Did

you not receive my message? You seem more than prepared for my arrival." He turned to the others and raised
his voice so they could hear. "Know you all that I come
in the name of my father, your lord and prince. Laws
have been broken—reckoning will be dealt swiftly to
the guilty."

A few of Moussimi's Badari stepped back from the
line they had formed, dropping their weapons on the
ground to show their loyalty. But most still held the line.

Moussimi glared at those who moved away, but he
quickly turned his attention back to Julian. "We serve
no lord who deserts us in our time of need. We owe Lord
Ramtat no loyalty."

Julian looked at the line of men. "Although my father
was forced to leave Egypt, do not our Badari still patrol
your lands, making certain you are safe? Did they not
fight battles when others tried to encroach on your territory? Look at me—I am my father's son, and I am here
at his bidding—I speak as he would if he were here."

Several others warriors moved out of line and dropped
their weapons.

Rage twisted on Moussimi's face. Clearly, events were
not going to his satisfaction. "These are my sons. I believe you know the elder, Tassum."

Julian stepped in front of the man, assessing him carefully. "Which do you wield, bow or spear?"

"I am master of the spear. Your own father awarded
me a silver dagger for my skills."

Julian met the small eyes. "If that is so, you will be a
skilled opponent." He moved to the other son. "And
you?"

"My younger." Moussimi said. "But do not let his youth
fool you—if your father was here to award the Golden

Arrow for best bowman, many agree Eanez would win the contest, just as your aunt did all those years ago."

In Eanez, Julian saw no resemblance to Moussimi. He was tall and slender, with large eyes. "If that is so, you are to be congratulated." Julian smiled at the man, who must be about his age. "If you have heard the tale of my aunt Adhaniá, who is the only woman to have won the Golden Arrow, you might like to know she was my instructor with the bow."

There was real fear in Eanez's eyes. "Everyone has heard of Lady Adhaniá's skill with the bow."

Julian turned back to the sheik. "You will honor your pledge to step down if I win the confrontation," he said pointedly.

"My word is true."

Julian would have liked to debate that, but he nodded. "Which of your sons is my first challenger?"

The elder tapped Julian on the shoulder, and the man found Heikki's sword at this throat. "You will not lay a hand on the prince. Take up your spear, and move away."

Tassum gave the Badari general an arrogant smile. "I do not have to touch him to bury my spear in his belly. You do understand this fight is to the death, do you not?" He turned his gaze to the prince, as if hoping to see fear on Julian's face—there was none.

Julian nodded, a smile twisting his lips. "You speak boldly, but how good are you with the spear? The proof is in the deed, not the telling."

𓅃 Chapter Thirty

Egyptian desert

The tribesmen made a wide circle, stretching all the way to the first sand dune. Most of Moussimi's Badari were startled when Julian's tribe rode down the dune, positioning their horses behind them.

Stepping closer, Tassum met his father's gaze and whispered so only he could hear, "I thought you said not many would come."

"I did not think so many would follow the son. But no matter. The outcome will be the same. Your arm is strong—you will win. End it quickly and go for the fast kill."

Julian retied his hair with a leather strip and turned to Sheik Moussimi. "Since the final challenge came from you, what are your rules?"

Before the father could answer, Tassum jerked up a heavy shield and ran forward. Since Julian had his back to the man, he saw only a shadow and managed to swerve so nothing but the tip of the shield struck his left shoulder. Still, the heavy impact was such that it took him to the ground.

Defiantly, Julian rolled to his feet and grabbed the spear and shield Heikki tossed to him.

"Fool," Tassum said, gathering his own spear. "There is only one rule in this contest—I win, and you die!"

Julian looked into eyes that were cold and calculating, like Moussimi's. "Tell me, are there not even the rules of sportsmanship?" he asked through clenched teeth. He remembered his father had once told him if he ever faced a larger opponent to use the man's weight against him. He was prepared to do just that.

"Just a battle to the death—your death," Tassum replied, throwing his spear, only to have it deflected by Julian's shield. Handed another spear, Tassum circled Julian. Each man looked for an opening. It only took Julian a moment to realize the big man was clumsy, so he rolled to the ground, kicking up at Tassum's knees. The crack of bone was loud, and the big man bellowed.

Now Tassum was angry, which was what Julian intended. His uncle Ashtyn had taught him that an angry opponent would always make mistakes. In a rage the big man came toward him, spear raised. Julian had underestimated the man's quickness. With a quick thrust, Tassum's spear pierced Julian's arm, sinking deep. A gasp went up through the crowd as Julian pulled out the spear and tossed it aside. Pushing aside the pain that threatened to swamp him, Julian watched carefully as Tassum prepared to charge. When he saw the man lower his shield, Julian attacked. His spear flew true, striking Tassum in the heart. The big man fell like a tree, dead before he hit the ground.

A murmur rose from Moussimi's Badari, and the sheik ran to his son, dropping to his knees, cradling him in his arms.

Julian knelt beside him, placing a comforting hand on

the sheik's arm, but the elder man shook it off. "You have not won," he snarled. "I still have another son."

"I beg of you," Julian said, "do not continue with this vendetta. Allow the blood that has been spilled here today to settle the matter."

"Coward," the sheik hissed. "You will feel the sting of my younger son's arrow in your heart!"

With a resigned sigh, Julian stood, blood running down his arm. With a sweeping glance, he saw the anguish on the faces of Moussimi's Badari—they had lost their future sheik. He also saw his own men, who were poised and ready to strike should those Badari choose to attack.

Dizzy with pain, Julian turned his full attention to the younger son. "Are there any rules to your contest?"

The young man lowered his head, but not before Julian saw the fear in his eyes. "We will be mounted on our horses, Great Prince."

Julian nodded to Heikki, who led his horse forward and handed him a quiver of arrows and a bow. Julian knew that whatever he did, he would try to spare this younger son's life.

The circled Badari spread out to allow the horses room to maneuver. Julian and Eanez stared at each other from a wide expanse. When Eanez charged forward, Julian kicked his own horse in the flanks. An arrow whizzed past his head, and another soon followed. Eanez was capable of firing with speed, but with little accuracy.

With his horse in full gallop, Julian strung his bow, positioning an arrow against the bowstring. He whirled his horse around, using his knees to guide the animal. Taking careful aim, Julian fired his arrow, catching

Eanez in the shoulder, just as he had intended. The young warrior dropped his bow and tumbled headfirst off his horse.

Julian leaped off his horse before the animal stopped and went down on his knees. Taking a single arrow from his quiver, he placed the point at Eanez's throat. He saw his opponent's throat contract, and his eyes widen with fear. "Yield or die!"

Eanez swallowed hard. "It is your right to take my life—the contest was to the death."

"I do not want your life. I want justice for your people."

Moussimi cried out to Julian while the blood of his elder son was already drying on his robe. "I had only the two sons. Will you not spare this one, Great Prince? Although he is worthless, allow him to live."

Julian stood, tossing his arrow to the ground. "This son of yours will live to give you grandchildren."

While Julian was watching the Badari so he could gauge their reaction, he did not see Moussimi creep up behind him. But every head jerked in Julian's direction. Grabbing his dagger from the folds of his robe, Moussimi buried it deep into Julian's shoulder.

With blackness closing in, Julian went to his knees and knew nothing more.

Before Heikki or any of Julian's Badari could react, Eanez jumped to his feet, grabbed up the arrow Julian had dropped, and slammed it into his own father's heart. With tears in his eyes, he addressed his father's Badari. "Since I am the only one of my father's sons living, it is my place to command you. My father brought dishonor to us all. If the prince dies, it will only be right that I forfeit my life. If the prince lives, and I pray to the gods he does, I shall await his judgment, as shall you all."

Julian's Badari moved closer to the others while Heikki lifted his fallen prince in his arms and carried him toward his horse. He spoke to his warriors. "Seal off this encampment, and let no man leave. If . . . when the prince regains consciousness, he will decide what is to be done."

🦅 Chapter Thirty-one

A strong gust of wind tore through Moussimi's encampment, the whirling sand stinging faces and blurring vision. Men tightened their grip on the horses' reins to calm the rearing animals while their women secured the tents to keep them from collapsing.

Julian's Badari made their way slowly toward their own encampment. When they arrived, Heikki handed the wounded prince into Apollodorus's uplifted arms, speaking rapidly to one of his men. "He won, but at what cost we do not yet know."

"Does he still live?" many asked, clustering around the Sicilian.

"Aye," Apollodorus said, feeling the pulse in Julian's neck.

The Sicilian quickly carried Julian toward the small tent that had been set up for Sabinah's comfort. His gaze fell on a group of huddled Badari who were, no doubt, planning to storm the enemy camp and wipe out every man, woman, and child to avenge their prince. "You must restrain those men," he told Heikki. "Julian would expect it of you."

Heikki nodded. His first concern was for the prince. "He has lost a lot of blood."

"I fear for his life," Apollodorus muttered.

Sabinah had heard the riders return. She resisted the instinct to run outside to meet Julian, but instead took in a calming breath, knowing he would expect her to wait there for him.

When Apollodorus entered the tent carrying Julian's limp body, she froze in fear.

"Julian will need you to remain calm," the Sicilian cautioned.

She clamped a hand over her mouth. "What has happened?" she asked.

Apollodorus laid Julian on the tiger skin rug and stood. "He has been severely wounded and is unconscious."

Sand struck against the tent, making it ripple—the howling wind sounded ominous. Sabinah was frantic as she glanced at Julian's pale face, dropping down beside him just as the wind struck hard through the tent opening, extinguishing the lantern.

Apollodorus tapped Sabinah's shoulder. "You must move so I can stop the bleeding."

Sabinah reached out frantically, her cry muffled by the sound of the wind. "Allow me to remain beside him."

"Then move to the other side," Apollodorus told her. "Heikki, relight the lantern."

Sabinah felt the warmth of Julian's hand—lifeblood still flowed through his body, but he was strangely still.

"The wind seems to have died down a bit. Have someone build a campfire," Apollodorus told Heikki. "I will need boiling water."

Sabinah kept her hold on Julian's hand. "You will be all right," she said soothingly. "You have come through many hardships—you are strong. Hold on, Julian—hold on to life."

"Take her away," Apollodorus told Heikki.

Sabinah glared at both men. "Nay! I shall not leave him. Do you think me some weak maiden who cringes at the sight of blood? I remain here!"

Both men exchanged glances, but said nothing further on the matter. Apollodorus worked frantically on Julian, at last stopping the flow of blood. When he was ready to apply the bandages, Sabinah helped him.

Calm settled over the land as the sandstorm that had struck so suddenly died down just as quickly. Outside the tent fierce-looking warriors waited anxiously for word of their fallen prince.

Sabinah fearfully watched the rise and fall of Julian's chest. Each struggling breath he took caused her to struggle with her own breathing. "This wound is serious, Apollodorus, but he should have regained consciousness by now."

"That is what I think as well," Heikki remarked.

At that moment Julian opened his eyes. He looked bewildered. When he made an attempt to move, he groaned in pain.

"Remain still," Apollodorus cautioned him.

Julian licked his dry lips, his gaze on Sabinah, who still held his hand. "What happened?"

"I am told," the Sicilian remarked, "you vanquished your enemies." He quickly explained to Julian what Moussimi had done, and how the younger son had slain his own father.

Struggling, Julian tried to sit up.

"You should rest," Sabinah told him.

"Nay. Help me rise. The matter is not settled. Moussimi's Badari must see that I still live—they are leaderless and must understand I bear them no ill will. They need to know I will bring them back into the fold."

"You must lie still!" Sabinah said in disbelief. "If you move about, you will surely break open your wound and start bleeding again."

Apollodorus caught Sabinah's glance and shook his head. "Julian knows what he must do."

"But—"

"Leave us," Julian told her, calling on his last bit of strength.

Sabinah rose, moving reluctantly out of the tent. With a heavy heart, she kept walking until she was a distance from the camp. Just beginning to understand the sacrifices a leader must make to control these fierce warriors, she shivered. Their prince was every bit as important to the Badari as Queen Cleopatra had been to her subjects. Julian would do what he must, even if it cost him his life.

Julian was weak, and the world seemed to spin around him, causing him to stumble. When Heikki reached for him, Julian waved him away. "I must do this on my own."

Heikki watched Julian struggle to climb onto his horse, wanting to help him, but knowing his aid would not be welcome. "You are bleeding again," he said, nodding at the back of Julian's robe.

"Then get me more padding and a clean robe."

Sabinah heard the sound of riders leaving camp, and without looking, she knew one of them was Julian. She did not need to look up to know it was Apollodorus who appeared at her side. "He is gone," she said dully.

"Aye."

"Does Julian expect trouble?"

"He is attempting to prevent it."

She turned a troubled gaze to Apollodorus. "Will he be safe?"

"You ask me that which I cannot answer. In the desert, among this wild tribe, there is always the chance of danger."

Sabinah lowered her head, needing to ask him a question that had nagged at her mind. "I had heard Julian might have to marry one of Moussimi's daughters to bring peace between the tribes."

"So you said before."

"Apollodorus," she asked, now avoiding his eyes, "does . . . Julian . . . if he were married, will he also take unto himself concubines?"

Apollodorus waited for her to look at him before he answered. "Sabinah, the princes of the Badari do not take concubines. There must never be any question about the line of succession." He smiled slightly. "I cannot imagine Julian's mother allowing another woman to lie with Ramtat."

Her eyes swam with tears. "Then there is no hope for me."

"There is always hope, Sabinah. Always."

Heikki rode beside Julian, watching him slump over his horse. But when they reached the top of the dune, Julian's shoulders straightened, and he rode down the other side as if he felt no pain.

He was stubborn and proud, this son of Lord Ramtat,

Heikki thought. Julian was very like his father—the weakness of his flesh would not keep him from his duty.

"You must remain here, Heikki. What I do must be done alone."

The general nodded. "I shall wait here for you."

Julian rode down the sand dune, hoping he could mask his pain. Sweat peppered his brow as he dismounted, but he wiped it on the sleeve of his robe, walking toward Eanez and his Badari.

Eanez went to his knees before Julian, bowing his head. "Take my life," he said with sincerity.

Julian glanced at Moussimi's Badari, who carefully watched him, awaiting his judgment. He saw acceptance in their eyes, and knew they would abide by whatever was decided here today. He had averted war.

"Rise, Eanez. I have not come to harm you, but to discover where your allegiance lies."

"My allegiance is with your family, Great Prince. I do not ask you to believe me, but my loyalty has always been to your family. My father and brother shamed me by their actions. I stand ready to pay for their crimes."

"My family does not ask that you be loyal to *us*, rather be loyal to the whole of the Badari tribe. We have all been given a sacred trust, and if any of us break it, future generations will suffer."

Eanez stood. "What would you have me do?"

Julian fought against dizziness, hoping no one noticed. "I would have you do what you were born to do. Take up the sheikdom of your tribe and see to your people's welfare."

Eanez was visibly shaken. "What my father and brother did was an abomination to me. I will always strive to be worthy of your trust."

Julian turned his gaze to the warriors who surrounded him, recognizing the hope in their eyes. "Do you accept Eanez as your sheik?"

A unanimous shout rippled through the crowd of men.

"It is done. Sheik Eanez, guide your people well. If there are still dissenters in their numbers, punish them."

Without another word, Julian mounted his horse and rode away. When he reached the other side of the sand dune, he slumped forward, and Heikki was there to assist him as he slid off his horse into unconsciousness.

"You did well, my prince."

Chapter Thirty-two

Julian swam in and out of consciousness, sometimes burning up, then racked with chills that made his teeth chatter.

"There is something more here than the knife wound," Apollodorus said, touching Julian's forehead. "The wound on his arm is not serious. The one on his shoulder is more troubling, but should not be causing such fever." Suddenly the big man's eyes darkened as understanding came to him. He took his knife and sliced through the shoulder bandages. The wound was black and had red streaks. "By the gods, Heikki, Moussimi's dagger was dipped in poison!"

The Badari general dropped to his knees beside Julian. "Have you the knowledge to help him?"

"Not I." His brow creased in thoughtfulness. "It is possible I know who might. Sabinah's stepmother dabbled in potions," he said, remembering how the woman had given Sabinah the drug that rendered her helpless. "I was told the woman passed some of her knowledge to Sabinah. Bring her to me at once."

Each time Sabinah had approached the tent where Julian lay, his guards had denied her entrance. She was frantic to know his condition. When Heikki heard her voice, he opened the tent flap and motioned her inside.

She paused for only a moment to allow her gaze to become accustomed to the darkened interior. She hurried to Julian and went to her knees beside him. Her heart lurched when she saw his pallor. Lifting the bandage, she stared at the inflamed wound. "He has been poisoned," she said, her frantic gaze going to Apollodorus.

"Can you help him?"

She closed her eyes, trying to remember her stepmother's teachings on poisons. "I will need to know what kind of poison was used. Can you find out for me?"

Heikki turned toward the tent opening. "Eanez may know what his father used."

While she waited for Heikki to return, she sprang into action. "Apollodorus, I will need several ingredients—although I do not know if they are available here in the desert."

"Tell me."

"Venom of an asp."

His eyes widened. "Cure poison with poison? How do we know it is not what Sheik Moussimi used on his dagger?"

"It is doubtful. When diluted and mixed with other ingredients, it can work to draw poison from a wound. Have someone get me a pot in which I can boil the elixir—instruct them to keep the fire hot."

"What else will you need?" he asked.

"Blight from an acacia tree." She closed her eyes, trying to think. "Milk from a female goat that is about to give birth. It would be prudent to ask at the encampment if they have a woman practiced in herbs. If so, she might have some of the ingredients I need." She touched

Julian's face. "If only we had known about the poison sooner. Let us hope it has not had time to enter his blood."

Without questioning her instructions, Apollodorus left the tent.

Sabinah took Julian's limp hand in hers. "You shall not die—do you heed me?" She brushed his long hair out of his face, aching inside. It was difficult to see such a strong man so helpless. No doubt the poison had been hastened through his body when he'd insisted on leaving the encampment.

"Hold on to me," she said, touching her mouth to his. "I will be your mainstay."

"Thanks to the gods we have all the ingredients," Sabinah said, adding more wood to the campfire. She stirred the liquid and then asked Heikki to scoop up sand so she could make a paste. When it was done to her satisfaction, she nodded to him to carry it into the tent.

Heikki did as Sabinah instructed. "It was good that Eanez knew what his father had used on his dagger, but difficult to understand how such a delicate flower as the desert rose could be used to poison a man."

"Let us hurry," she said.

Kneeling beside Julian, Sabinah met Heikki's inquiring glance. "The mixture must be applied while still hot. It will not only draw out the poison but also cauterize the wound." Sabinah worked quickly, causing Julian to moan. She met Apollodorus's gaze. "Let us hope I used the right amount of each ingredient. I know of nothing else I can do."

Julian's Badari had been joined by Sheik Eanez's warriors, and they waited in silence for word of Julian's condition. The fierce desert dwellers paid homage to a brave man who had fallen for the good of the tribe. They would talk of this time for generations to come and sing of Julian's bravery.

Daylight slipped into night, and still Julian did not stir. In the late hours of the next morning Sabinah gently washed the packed mud away from the wound, fearing she would find it still blackened and swollen.

With a joyful smile, she lifted her face to Apollodorus. "The worst is over, although he will feel weak for some time." Tears swam in her eyes. "He will live."

Sabinah felt all the strength leave her body, and she sank down on the fur mat beside Julian, her head hitting hard against a stool.

Apollodorus scooped her up in his arms and, against her protest, carried her to another tent, where he gently laid her down on a fur rug. "You will rest now."

Sabinah felt her body relax. Her eyes closed, and she fell into an exhausted sleep.

Apollodorus stood over Sabinah for a long moment, thinking what an extraordinary young woman she was, and he realized she had won his heart.

Julian awoke, tried to move, and pain swamped him. "What is happening?" he asked Heikki, who had been keeping watch on him.

"You have survived the poison from Moussimi's dagger." Heikki quickly explained what had happened and how Sabinah had saved him.

"There is much I must do. Help me rise," Julian said, ashamed to admit how weak he felt.

The Badari general grinned. "You have not eaten in three days. It is no wonder you are weak. I shall go to Sabinah to find out what food you are allowed."

Julian arched his brow. "Am I bound by her orders?"

Heikki paused at the tent opening. "She saved your life and stood over you like a dog guarding a bone. I would not want to be the one to go against her orders."

Julian smiled, relaxing. His shoulder ached but not as it had before. He had always known his Little Sunshine would do him good. Julian heard Sabinah enter and saw the concern in her eyes.

She went down on her knees and touched his forehead. "You have no fever." She peeled back the bandage and smiled at him. "That scar will always be a reminder of how near you came to death."

His lips curled into a smile. "A lesson well learned." He reached out to her, but she did not give him her hand. "I understand I have you to thank for my life."

She frowned, becoming serious. "I had the knowledge because my stepmother instructed me on poisons. I never thought I would be called on to use that knowledge."

Julian's gaze crept from her lips to her eyes. "Come hold my hand, Little Sunshine."

His use of the pet name warmed her, and she felt a blush work its way across her face. "I am told you are hungry."

His gaze settled back on her mouth. "Ravished."

"Today you may have goat milk and a bit of mutton broth."

"That will not do," he said, trying to rise, but she pushed him back. "I crave roasted meat and wine."

Sabinah was thoughtful for a moment. "Very well, you may have one glass of wine, but no meat."

"You order me about?" he accused, smiling.

"Grumbler," she countered, frowning.

He took her hand and raised it to his lips. "I will do as you say, but only until tomorrow."

Sabinah withdrew her hand. "Perhaps tomorrow you will allow me to leave."

Julian looked taken aback. "Leave? Where would you go? Nay, you will not leave."

Sabinah stood. "You must rest. When you are feeling stronger, we will discuss my departure. I cannot remain with your Badari for the rest of my life."

Julian watched her depart just as Apollodorus entered. "She wants to leave me. I cannot allow that."

The Sicilian stared down at Julian, a touch of anger in his tone. "What will you offer her that would entice her to remain?"

Julian was quiet for a long moment. When he spoke, his tone was decisive. "Tomorrow I will make her my wife."

For the first time in the young prince's life, Apollodorus was angry with him. "You cannot make promises to her that you may not be able to keep. Sabinah is not of your social standing and your family may not approve of her."

"I love her. I will make my parents understand."

"What makes you think Sabinah will have you?"

For the first time, Julian looked doubtful. "I do not know for sure. I hope she will."

"Treat her well. She is exceptional," Apollodorus stated with force.

Julian studied his old friend for a long moment. "Is it possible you have feelings for Sabinah yourself?"

"I am old enough to be her father. Yet if I were

younger, I would not so easily allow you to take her from me."

Julian was completely stunned. "You love her."

"As does everyone who sees her true worth."

CHAPTER THIRTY-THREE

Sabinah had just risen for the day and had washed her face and run her fingers through her hair to remove the worst of the tangles.

There was the sound of footsteps outside the tent. "May I enter?"

"Julian!" She rushed to the opening and glared at him. "You should not be about. You have not had time to heal."

He wondered why he had never noticed the enchanting way Sabinah's eyes glittered when she was angry or how stubbornly she could set her chin. "If you continue to berate me, I may lapse back into a fever."

She nodded, crossing her arms. "That could very well happen if you do not take care."

Julian brushed past her, and she turned to face him. "I needed to talk to you," he said.

Her anger melted away. "You could have sent someone for me, and I would have come to you."

Julian pulled her to him, knowing he could not go another day without binding her to him. "I understand you put the poison of an asp on my skin." He drew her closer, nibbling at her ear. "Perhaps if I bit you . . ."

She melted against him. He could not possibly know how much she had feared for his life. "Julian."

He released her, stepping away. "I have something to ask you."

Sabinah swept her hands up in a hopeless gesture. "Why would you ask anything of me? You do not follow my advice."

"I have been thinking about taking a wife."

Sabinah felt as if he had just delivered her a death-blow. "I have been expecting it."

Julian arched a dark brow. "You have?"

"I overheard two of Uriah's servants discussing your possible marriage before we left Alexandria."

He frowned, deep in thought. "They could not have had that knowledge, since the only person I told was Apollodorus, and that was only yesterday."

Left with a sense of hopelessness, Sabinah began folding the fur rug to have something to do with her hands. "They said you might wed Sheik Moussimi's daughter to unite the tribes."

Julian smiled slowly as he understood her confusion. "There is only one woman I want as my wife, and I do not even know Moussimi's daughter."

"Oh."

"Sabinah, since you saved my life, will you not walk by my side until death takes us?"

She met his gaze, her breath trapped in her throat. "Julian, we both know I am not of noble birth."

He watched tears gather in her eyes. "You will be noble when you become a member of the Tausrat family." He stepped closer, afraid she might refuse him. "Say you will be my wife."

Sabinah was suddenly angry, thinking she knew why

he was asking her to marry him. "You do not owe me anything."

She watched his green eyes deepen with passion. "I want you," he whispered. "I need you."

Time passed, and she could do no more than stare at him. "You do not have to marry me to share my bed."

"I want more of you than just your body."

Her heart seemed to take wings, and happiness washed over her. Whatever the reason, he wanted to wed her and she would not refuse. "I do not know what to say to you."

"Say 'aye.'"

Sabinah heard herself saying, "Aye."

His smile was infectious, and she smiled back at him. "It must be soon—now—today."

To be Julian's wife, to have him hold her and make love to her was all Sabinah had ever wanted. How could she bear so much happiness?

Julian held out his hand. "Come." He led her out of the tent and called to everyone present. "Come forward and share my joy. Come forward and witness our marriage."

Apollodorus took Sabinah out of Julian's arms and hugged her to him. "You are going to be happy. Nothing can harm you now."

Sabinah pressed her face against the Sicilian's rough robe. "I love you, Apollodorus."

He held her away from him and smiled sadly. "As a father?"

"As my very best friend."

Julian took Sabinah's hand and turned her to face the men who had gathered around, smiling and happy at the joyous occasion. "Witness here this day that I, Julian of the house of Tausrat, take unto myself Sabinah of the house of Jannah, to be my wife."

Sabinah stared into his green eyes, which seemed to have captured the light of the setting sun. "I, Sabinah of the house of Jannah, accept Julian of the house of Tausrat as my husband."

A roar of approval rose through the wild Badari while Julian pulled Sabinah against him. "It is done, sworn before witnesses. You are mine now."

"I have always been yours," she whispered.

He pulled her into his tent, his mouth finding hers. "I now know why I have always felt overwhelming joy when you were near me. Do you think the gods created you for me?"

"I have always thought that."

His brows came together in a frown. "Do you understand why there cannot be a proper celebration of our marriage?"

She shook her head, wanting only to be with him.

"Sabinah, I must leave the area at once and allow Sheik Eanez to assume control over his tribe. Should I linger, it might weaken his authority." He looked at her longingly. "The tents must be struck at once, and we will ride to my family's encampment."

Sabinah smiled, trembling at the thought that this wonderful man was now her husband. "I shall celebrate in my heart."

He laid his face against hers, holding her body close. She could feel his heart beating, and she could feel the evidence that he wanted to be with her.

Releasing her, Julian gave a regretful smile, for already there was the sound of the camp being struck. "Later, Sabinah," he promised.

It was dark as they began their journey, but in no time the sky was alight with thousands of stars to guide them, and the swift Badarian horses knew the way home. Silently they made their way over high sand dunes and across long stretches of desert. They stopped at a small oasis where other Badari met them with fresh horses, and their journey continued.

Sabinah was weary, but she would not speak of it. At last she rode beside Julian as his wife.

A full moon guided the weary travelers, and Julian noticed Sabinah was slumping in the saddle, so he reached out, pulling her onto his horse and across his lap.

"This is where you belong now," he said, touching his mouth to her ear and sending shivers of delight through her body. "Sleep if you can."

Sabinah did not think she would sleep because she was too happy. Julian's arms closed around her, and she eventually closed her eyes.

It was much later when they stopped at a Badari outpost to change horses for a second time. She blinked and slid off the horse.

Bending down beside a cool pond, she dipped her hands in water and took a drink. "Come," Julian said, holding his hand out to her and lifting her onto his horse. Sabinah snuggled against the warmth of his body.

The sun was tinting the eastern sky when they reached the main Badari encampment. A cheer went up as people poured out of their tents to greet their returning prince. With joyous laughter, they congratulated Julian on his marriage. Women and children came up to Sabinah, smiling and welcoming her to the tribe.

Julian held his hand up for silence. "We who have just arrived are weary. Allow us to rest, and then we shall have a feast to honor my bride." He took Sabinah's hand and led her into the huge red leather tent that was reserved for his family. Guiding her to the inner room, he lifted her in his arms and placed her on the bed.

"You will have to forgive me," he said, dropping down beside her without even removing his boots. "It seems I am not as recovered as I thought."

Sabinah took Julian in her arms. He had been gravely wounded and had ridden all night. "Sleep, my love," she said, stroking his hair. "We have all the time in the world."

Sabinah stirred, feeling a finger tracing her mouth. Her eyes opened, and her first sight was sparkling green eyes. She was flooded with so much happiness she could scarcely breathe. For reasons she could not understand, Julian had wanted her for his wife.

"I have been watching you sleep," he said in a soft voice. "I have never seen anyone so beautiful."

Her arms slid around his neck. "How is your wound?"

"Continuing to heal." He grinned, rubbing his cheek against her face. "You see, this little temptress who knows potions cured me." He pulled back and looked into her eyes. "I have another ache that needs a cure. Will you help me with that, Little Temptress?"

She laughed aloud, wondering if it was possible to be any happier than she was at that moment. Slowly he removed her clothing, and then his own, and Sabinah discovered it was possible to know much more happiness.

Possessively, Julian took her body, and they rode the crest of passion until they were both exhausted, and then they slept, their legs tangled, their bodies straining for closer contact.

It was two days before the newlyweds came out of seclusion. When they appeared before the tribe, the Badari quickly gathered, preparing a feast that lasted another two days.

Sabinah was delighted by how readily the Badari accepted her amongst them. Gifts were laid at her feet, and young children clamored for a place at her side. These were a fierce people to their enemies, but to her, as the wife of their prince, they showed gentleness and respect.

For the first time in Sabinah's life, she felt that she belonged. At night when Julian took her into his arms, she knew great joy.

There was not a breath of air stirring as Sabinah stepped out of the brass tub. Twisting her hair into a knot and securing it with an ivory comb, she quickly dressed. She had just slid her feet into her sandals when Julian entered.

He smiled, taking her hand. "It matters not what I am doing during the day. I find my mind wandering back to you. Heikki has accused me of being less than useless."

Sabinah laughed. "How can he speak so to you?"

Julian pulled her into his embrace. "He can because he is correct."

Sabinah's arms slid around his waist as her brow creased into a frown. "Julian, I have been thinking about Uriah. I fear for his health—he was very frail when we left. Should we not go to him?"

"I have received word from the villa that he is about the same as when we last saw him. I believe that dear old man holds on to life until he can see my mother once again."

Sabinah rested her head on his shoulder while he held her tightly. "There is something else I am worried about," she admitted.

Julian tilted her chin up so he could see her eyes. "Tell me so I can make it right."

Doubt ate at her mind. "Will your family approve of your choice of wife when they discover what my stepsister did?"

"When my father sees how happy you have made me, he will love you as I do."

"And your mother?"

Before Julian could answer, they heard the sound of many riders entering the encampment. He took her hand and led her outside, and they both watched in shock as Lord Ramtat dismounted, then reached up and lifted Julian's mother off her horse.

Sabinah stepped back as Lady Danaë flew into her son's arms. "You are safe!" she cried. "We were told you were sorely wounded."

Julian smiled down at her. "I am well. Why are you here? Is it not dangerous?"

Lord Ramtat clasped his son's arm. "Let us go into the tent, and I shall tell you all that has occurred."

"Where are my brother and sister?"

"We thought it best to leave them behind on Bal Forea until everything is settled."

Julian nodded, not really understanding. "But is it safe for you and Mother to be here?"

Ramtat smiled. "The death sentence had been struck down."

Julian could hardly believe it. "How? When?"

"I suspect your uncle Marcellus had something to do with changing Octavian's mind, although he will not admit it."

Sabinah watched the happy reunion, taking a step backward. She froze when Lady Danaë's gaze fell upon her. She had never been so near to Julian's mother, and she was struck by her beauty. To be in the presence of Queen Cleopatra's half sister was daunting, especially because Sabinah did not know if Lady Danaë would accept her as Julian's wife.

Striding in Sabinah's direction, Danaë smiled at her. "Can this be my son's new wife? You are Sabinah, are you not?"

Sabinah bent to her knees, lowering her head. "Aye, lady."

Danaë took her new daughter-in-law's arm and helped her rise. Looking her over carefully, she hugged Sabinah to her with tears in her eyes. "Then you are my daughter. We have been told how you saved my son's life more than once."

Ramtat appeared at her side. "So I have a new red-headed daughter. Think of what our grandchildren will look like," he said gently. "Welcome to the family, Sabinah."

The Badari let out a boisterous yell. There would be more celebrating—their lord prince had come home!

That night as they feasted, Julian explained to his father and mother all that had occurred since he'd arrived back in Egypt.

"I knew you would have the strength to bring the tribes together," Ramtat said matter-of-factly. "No one could have done better."

Danaë explained to them that Marcellus and Adhaniá, along with Thalia and Ashtyn, were waiting for them in Alexandria.

Julian's gaze locked with his father's. "When do we leave to join them?"

"In the morning." Ramtat turned to his wife. "I thought you and Sabinah could remain here so you can become better acquainted."

Sabinah was still in awe of her powerful father-in-law, but she did not want to be left behind, so she stated with feeling, "I shall certainly not remain behind. I want to be there when Tribune Vergilius discovers his dreams have turned to ashes."

"As do I," Danaë said, standing and linking her arm through Sabinah's. "You are not leaving without us!"

Ramtat's expression hardened for the briefest moment as he looked from one woman to the other. He finally shrugged and smiled at his son. "What kind of bloodthirsty women have we chosen to wed?"

"Aye," Julian agreed. "What kind indeed?"

A CHAPTER
THIRTY-FOUR

Bastet yawned, stretching her arms over her head. There was movement in the bed beside her, and she smiled, remembering her night with Vergilius. She had used all her sexual knowledge to please him; and she had succeeded, she was sure of it. Her one hope was to make him want her and not her pathetic stepsister. During a passionate moment in their lovemaking, Vergilius had called out Sabinah's name, angering Bastet. She was more determined than ever to make him want her so much he would cry out *her* name.

She slid quietly out of bed so she would not disturb Vergilius, and hurried to the bath. She wanted to make herself presentable before he awoke.

Bastet stood on the first step of the pool when she heard the sound of footsteps, marching in unison. Grabbing up her discarded robe, she dashed back to her bed-chamber just in time to see six Roman soldiers enter. One of the men wore the uniform of a general!

What did they want?

Vergilius awoke, shaking his head to clear his thoughts. When he saw General Marcellus, he quickly wrapped the coverlet about himself, attempting to keep it in place while snapping to attention.

He slapped his hand across his chest. "General Marcellus. I am honored . . . but why—"

"You are under arrest, Tribune Vergilius." Marcellus snapped his fingers, and one of the soldiers stepped forward and began to read from a scroll.

"You are to be transported back to Rome, where you will be tried for the murder of Lady Larania of the house of Tausrat."

Vergilius's jaw went slack. "There was no impropriety in the traitor's death," he said, his knees going weak.

"Furthermore," the young soldier continued, "you confiscated property belonging to the Tausrat family. You are also charged with attempting to seduce the wife of Lord Julian Tausrat."

Vergilius looked confused. "Sir, I do not even know Lord Julian's wife."

Bastet, who was standing in the shadow of the door, stepped farther back into the shadows, fearing the Romans would arrest her for being associated with Vergilius.

"Lord Julian and all his family are condemned traitors," the tribune said, still trying to make sense of General Marcellus's accusations.

"The death sentence on the Tausrat family has been lifted," Marcellus said. "Dress yourself as befitting a soldier of Rome." Marcellus turned on his heel. "Take him prisoner," he told the soldiers who had accompanied him.

With fear driving his actions, Vergilius ran for the door that led into the garden. When he was halfway down the curved walk, a man stepped in front of him, blocking his way.

Lord Ramtat!

Vergilius trembled, falling to his knees. "Please understand—I was merely tending to duty. I implore you, do not kill me!"

Ramtat tossed the man a dagger. "For what you did to my mother, you shall die. But I give you the chance to defend yourself."

"Nay," Vergilius said, raising his hands pleadingly. "I have been arrested. I am under Roman jurisdiction."

"You are just where we expected you to be," Ramtat said, his eyes narrowing. "Knowing the coward you are, we expected you to flee. I am here to stop you."

Vergilius suddenly understood. "General Marcellus is married to your sister. The two of you planned this."

Ramtat nodded at the dagger. "Defend yourself."

Vergilius's hand inched toward the dagger. If he could grab it in time, and if his aim was true, he could eliminate Lord Ramtat and escape.

Ramtat allowed Vergilius to claim the weapon. Then he unsheathed his own dagger and threw it. The blade struck true, piercing Vergilius's heart. Ramtat did not even wait to watch the man fall. He had promised himself he would one day avenge his mother's death.

This was that day.

Now he would reclaim Tausrat Villa.

Sabinah clasped Julian's hand, needing his nearness, as she made her way to the open doorway. "I had hoped never to set foot in this house again."

"You must if you are ever to rid yourself of ghosts from the past. I will be with you. No one will harm you."

Trisella had been watching out the window and met them at the door, her hand at her throat. Bastet stood behind her. Sabinah shook her head as she looked at the two women who had cut her to the heart. "I believe you know my husband, Lord Julian," she said quietly.

"Uh . . . ah . . . I do. Although it has been many years since I have seen him." Her stepmother's face turned even paler. "You say he is your husband?"

"Aye, Mother," Bastet said, finally finding her voice. "Our little Sabinah has hooked the biggest fish of them all." Her gaze fell on Julian and she shrugged. "There was a time when you favored me."

Julain merely looked at her with disgust.

Sabinah held up her hand. "I just wanted the two of you to know you are no longer a part of my life. Do not try to contact me. Ever!"

"But what will become of us?" Trisella cried, realizing how bleak her future had become after Vergilius's dead body had been discovered in her garden, and all Romans had been forbidden to frequent her home. "You know about your father's will, Sabinah. If you leave us, the house will go to you. That is why you did this, is it not?"

Sabinah gazed into her stepmother's eyes and saw real fear. "I will allow the two of you to keep the house—I do not want it."

"But I need new clothing—the kitchen is all but empty. The servants have run off."

Sabinah felt bile rise in her throat but took a deep breath when Julian squeezed her hand reassuringly. "Not all of them have run away. Ma'dou and Isadad are with me."

"I will not take the house, not as charity from you." Trisella glared at Sabinah. "Never!"

Bastet stepped forward. "Aye, you will, Mother. We

both will." She looked at Sabinah quizzically. "Why would you help us?"

Sabinah raised her head. "Because there was a time when my father loved you both. I believe it is the right thing to do."

Julian, who had remained silent all this time, took Sabinah's hand. "It is finished," he told her.

She walked out into the sun, her heart feeling lighter. Julian had been right—it was good she had closed that door to the past.

She looked into green eyes that held the promise of the future. He lifted her onto her horse, and they rode away. Sabinah was not even tempted to look back.

Her future was before her.

CHAPTER THIRTY FIVE

Tausrat Villa

The banquet hall was filled with chatter as the family gathered to celebrate. Uriah was seated beside Danaë, smiling and touching her hand to make certain she was there.

Adhaniá was explaining to Marcellus how Julian had united the Badari, while Queen Thalia was reminding her husband, Ashtyn, that they had first met in the gardens of this villa.

Julian gave Sabinah a bite of his fish, watching her eyes widen.

"This is delicious. What kind of fish is it?"

Julian met his aunt Thalia's gaze. "It was delivered by a young man who told the cook it was a gift for my aunt. It seems he lives in the fishing village she once passed through on her way to Bal Forea."

Thalia smiled, nodding. "I remember him."

Ramtat took Danaë's hand and led her out of the room. They slowly made their way to the garden, where he drew her into his arms. "We have come a long way together, wife."

"And we have farther to go," she said, nestling against

him. "I miss the children. I cannot wait until they join us."

He stared up at the night sky. "Do you think she is watching us?"

Danaë did not even need to ask whom he was referring to. "I would like to think so. It would ease my mind if I thought Cleopatra knows her son is safe and happy."

"Our son is happy, too. He cannot take his eyes off that lovely young girl he married."

"Hmm. I have seen this for myself."

"Next week we travel to the desert. The Badari will soon be gathering for the games."

Danaë sighed, feeling content. "Everything changes, and everything remains the same, my beloved."

Ramtat gathered her close. "Our son will be ready to step into my place when the time comes. He has proven that."

She heard Julian's deep laughter from inside the house. "But not for a time."

Ramtat smiled. "Not for a time."

EPILOGUE

The Badari encampment

Julian rode to the top of the sand dune and waited for Sabinah to catch up with him. Together they watched the sun rise over the desert. He dismounted and lifted her from her horse, holding her close. "Are you happy, Sunshine?"

"I have but one other wish to make my life complete."

He touched his mouth to the top of her head. "What can that be?"

She took his hand, placing it on her stomach. "The safe birth of this son or daughter that grows beneath my heart."

His eyes softened, and he laughed aloud. "Then neither of us can ask for more."

Standing outside the red leather tent, Apollodorus heard the sound of laughter—he could easily distinguish Sabinah's voice from the others. Her life was full, she was loved, and never again would she have reason to fear.

He closed his eyes, allowing himself the pleasure of hearing her laughter for a moment longer. Then he walked leisurely toward his horse and mounted. He had completed his duty to Queen Cleopatra.

Lately, Apollodorus had felt an urge to return to Sicily. He had three brothers—perhaps one of them was still alive.

He breathed in the desert air, thinking he had loved two exceptional women, one a queen, the other merely a goldsmith's daughter. But in their different ways, they had stirred something within that he would carry with him, no matter how long he lived nor how far he traveled.

Heikki stepped out of his tent, and Apollodorus raised his hand. "Tell them I have gone home," he said as he rode past.

JANE CANDIA COLEMAN
Award-winning Author of *Tumbleweed*

He was a self-made king who couldn't survive without

THE SILVER QUEEN

RAGS TO RICHES

Augusta Tabor may have been the first woman in the Colorado silver-mining camps, but she never dreamed of making the big strike. She labored hard to support her family, while her husband went out prospecting for months at a time and gave away their store credit to just about anyone who asked. And then one of his schemes finally worked out. Suddenly they were the richest folk in Colorado Territory and Haw Tabor was elected lieutenant governor. But untold wealth and power led them to a scandal that shocked the country—a scandal that would push Augusta's strength to its limits....

Jane Candia Coleman is a six-time Pulitzer Prize nominee, three-time winner of the Western Heritage Award, and two-time winner of the Spur Award. *The Silver Queen*, based on the actual memoirs of Augusta Tabor, was a finalist for the Willa Award, named in honor of *O Pioneers!* author Willa Cather.

ISBN 13: 978-0-8439-6105-8

Fallen

"If you haven't read the Wind books, I suggest you do
so; you won't be disappointed." —Fresh Fiction

Cindy Holby

Fallen…

He was the product of illegitimacy, son of a noble house
with no claim to its title or riches. For John Murray, the
only hope of a decent life was his career as a British officer.

Fallen…

Had she lost her heart when he rescued her from ruf-
fians, or when she first looked into that face like a golden
angel's? No matter when it began, Isobel knew there was
no hope of a happy ending for a rebel Scottish lass and a
red-coated Sassenach.

Fallen…

Betrayed by the girl he loved, disgraced before his commander, wounded in battle and left for dead, John thought
he'd hit rock bottom. But the sweet touch of a lover he'd
never thought to see again taught him that no matter how
far a man falls, with the right woman at his side, he can
always stand tall.

ISBN 13: 978-0-8439-6026-6

Alissa Johnson

"A joyous book from a bright star."
—Kathe Robin, *Romantic Times BOOKreviews*
on *As Luck Would Have It*

Tempting Fate

The feud between them has scandalized the ton for years.

Whittaker Cole, Earl of Thurston, is every debutante's dream come true. Handsome, rich, and a prime catch on the Marriage Mart, Whit is also reputed to be one of the most unflappable gentlemen in all England. Nothing ever puts him in a temper. Until...

He comes within twenty feet of Miss Mirabelle Browning and loses all control. The women in his household believe divine providence sent Mira to live on the estate adjoining theirs. After the hellion breaks his nose, Whit decides that the divine has nothing to do with it. Until...

He kisses her. After all, it was either that, or wring her neck. But when sparks fly, he's forced to admit that there might be something to this destiny thing after all. If he can just convince Mirabelle to give fate—and love—a chance.

ISBN 13: 978-0-8439-6156-0

☐ **YES!**

Sign me up for the Historical Romance Book Club and send my FREE BOOKS! If I choose to stay in the club, I will pay only $8.50* each month, a savings of $6.48!

NAME: _____

ADDRESS: _____

TELEPHONE: _____

EMAIL: _____

☐ I want to pay by credit card.

☐ **VISA**   ☐ **MasterCard.**   ☐ **DISCOVER**

ACCOUNT #: _____

EXPIRATION DATE: _____

SIGNATURE: _____

Mail this page along with $2.00 shipping and handling to:
Historical Romance Book Club
PO Box 6640
Wayne, PA 19087
Or fax (must include credit card information) to:
610-995-9274
You can also sign up online at **www.dorchesterpub.com**.
*Plus $2.00 for shipping. Offer open to residents of the U.S. and Canada only.
Canadian residents please call 1-800-481-9191 for pricing information.
If under 18, a parent or guardian must sign. Terms, prices and conditions subject to change. Subscription subject to acceptance. Dorchester Publishing reserves the right to reject any order or cancel any subscription.